Never A Lawman

Break Heart Brides
BOOK ONE

Rachel Bird

BEASTIE PRESS U.S.A.

Never A Lawman
(Break Heart Brides Book 1)

Rachel Bird

Copyright 2018 Rachel Bird
Published by Beastie Press

Cover design by eyemaidthis

Published in the United States by Beastie Press 2018

ISBN: 9781791577650

Love can ruin the perfect getaway...

When Belle LeClair's US Marshal husband dies, she flees Boston and her wealthy, overbearing mother-in-law—who has already chosen Belle's next husband! Belle won't rule out marrying again, but any prospective partner better not have a job that will get him killed.

Sheriff Brady Fontana's fiancée was murdered on her way to join him in Break Heart, Colorado. Since then, guilt and regret have made him impervious to love. But when he rescues a family of would-be homesteaders attacked by the notorious Deckom gang, one of the sisters shines a light on his cold, locked-down heart.

The last thing Brady deserves is happiness, and he fights his unwelcome feelings for Belle. Which is fine with her, since she'll never let herself care for another lawman—even one as wonderful as Brady.

Table of Contents

Chapter 1

Boston, May 1877

Belle LeClair was in Boston when she received word that her husband, US Marshal Wade LeClair, had been murdered, shot in the back by the last remaining member of an outlaw gang he'd pursued all the way to the Dakota Territory.

They had been newlyweds, eager to begin their life together just as soon as Wade returned from his special assignment. But he'd come home in a casket, a good and brave man destroyed in the time it took a coward to fire a six-gun. If only Wade hadn't been a lawman!

It had been a week since she'd learned of

his murder and three days since his preserved body had arrived, shipped home by train. Two days ago, they'd buried him. She'd sleepwalked through it all, numb to the world, and now she had to figure out what she was going to do, something she was terrible at.

Belle tended to suffer in silence until she snapped—and then she'd act on a whim and find herself stuck with the consequences, like when she'd agreed to marry Wade LeClair only hours after meeting him.

Now she was trapped in this great, grand house on Bowdoin Street with Sophronia Mandeville LeClair, her relentless and frightfully wealthy mother-in-law.

Who was very good at making decisions.

"I don't want you to worry about your position, Christabel." Mrs. LeClair had finished her breakfast and waved off the maid who tried to refill her teacup. "We'll see you're taken care of."

Belle must have misheard. She'd been expecting quite the opposite—that she'd be thrown out of the house as soon as public opinion would allow.

"In fact, I've been thinking," Mrs. LeClair went on. "As you know, my dear, Wesley is unmarried."

Belle froze. None of this made any sense.

One, the woman had never liked her. Belle Steele, a nobody from Minnesota with no money and no connections, had been nowhere near good enough for Mrs. LeClair's favorite son.

Two, she already had an heiress in mind for her other son, Wesley—Miss Evangeline St. James of New York City, whom Belle had befriended at a Christmas party last December, the one thing she'd done right in her mother-in-law's eyes. *So you can be useful as well as ornamental!*

"I see I've shocked you," the old lady said. "I suppose I'm being selfish. You're a living memento of my Wade, even if you aren't going to have his child."

This was a sore point. Belle and Wade had been married a total of eight months, but they'd only lived together as man and wife four days before he'd taken that cursed assignment. No. There wasn't going to be a baby.

"It would be a consolation to keep you as part of the family."

Belle couldn't believe it, but Mrs. LeClair was sincere. She'd be relentless in this, as in all things. Once an idea was fixed in the woman's head, no matter how morbid, it stayed fixed.

Mrs. LeClair always knew she was right.

"I'm not sure—"

"You'll have to wait a decent interval of mourning, of course," she went on blithely, as if Belle had already agreed to the idea. "But as Wesley is my son, there can be nothing improper in his accompanying you to church or visiting this house. In fact why don't we call on him this afternoon? You can wear your long veil."

"Oh no, Mother-in-law. I couldn't."

Mrs. LeClair fixed on Belle with her beady stare, then relented and smiled. "No, you're right. You don't want to appear too eager."

While her mother-in-law was out for the day, the afternoon post brought a letter from Belle's mother in Minnesota—and a glimmer of hope, if Belle could muster the courage to act.

***

It was well past midnight when Belle woke to the sound of inconsolable crying somewhere downstairs and ventured from her room to investigate. The dim light of the lamp she carried didn't dispel all the shadows in the hallway—or the feeling she was being observed from some dark corner.

In this house she always felt watched, followed, never left alone.

She followed the sobs downstairs to Wade's study. She should have known. She paused outside the room that had been locked to her all the time she'd lived here. Another heart-wrenching wail—Mrs. LeClair was in there again.

Belle pressed her palm to the door. The woman would be crying over treasured artifacts of Wade's life. Things she'd never share. Mrs. LeClair was merciless in her need to control her world.

But then she'd lost her firstborn child. It was impossible not to feel some pity. If only she'd allow Belle to comfort her. If only they could comfort each other! But the one consolation the old lady demanded was something Belle couldn't give. The thought of marrying Wade's brother was repugnant.

Aside from the obvious objection, the Wesley LeClair was an unappealing, pale imitation of his older brother, terrified of his mother and indifferent to his occupation. He held no opinions of his own—at least, none he'd ever expressed in Belle's presence.

"Oh Wade!" The cries intensified. "My wonderful boy!"

Was it all for effect? Did she know Belle

was standing outside the door? She was so strong. Righteous and unyielding as marble.

In Mrs. LeClair's presence, Belle had learned to second-guess her own desires and opinions. She was losing the memory of who Belle Steele was before she became Belle LeClair. With each passing day, a bit of her true self fell away, to be reconstructed and reorganized by Mrs. LeClair. Soon Belle would be an entirely different person, one of her mother-in-law's design.

"Wade!" Another morose cry.

If Belle had any sense, she'd ignore this drama and go back to her room. *The letter, Belle. Think of the letter.* But her heart went out to the distraught mother behind that door. She should at least offer a kind word. She put her hand on the knob—which refused to turn.

Still locked! Even now.

Something clicked in Belle's brain, and she scoffed at her naivete. What had she expected? Mrs. LeClair would always lock her out, even while trying to lock her into a life under her rule. With a burst of anger, she rushed back upstairs, her mind clear. Suddenly, the way forward was obvious— whatever the consequences.

As she reached her bedroom, a nearby movement startled her. Her maid Finola stood not three feet away in the shadows, obscured by the deepest black she wore from head to toe. Mrs. LeClair hadn't paid for the maid's clothes, of course. Finola's mourning was her own, from a past loss.

"Finola, you scared me! I nearly dropped the lamp."

"Is everything all right, madam?" Finola Burke had to be the coldest lady's maid in the history of cold lady's maids.

"Your mistress is downstairs. She's upset."

Finola was officially Belle's maid, but in practice she was Mrs. LeClair's spy, there to ensure Belle never went anywhere, did anything, or voiced any opinion without it being reported back.

Finola sniffed. Her disdain for Belle was greater even than Mrs. LeClair's, especially once they'd despaired of Belle's being pregnant. *She's a pretty enough ornament, but useless.* Belle had overheard a conversation between the two. *She couldn't even give me a grandchild!*

Producing Wade's child might have redeemed her. Would have compensated for the shame of being a poor sexton's daughter from Minnesota.

"Can I get you anything, madam?"

It was an obligatory question. Finola didn't really want an answer. This time Belle didn't care.

"Yes, you can." Her heart pounded. If she was to escape, she had to set it in motion now. "I'd like tea brought up to my room. I can't sleep. I'll read for a while."

"Of course, madam." Finola sniffed again, clearly put out.

Belle turned up her lamp and got into bed. She set aside the book she'd been reading and instead reread her mother's letter.

My darling Christabel,

> *It is with some trepidation I write to tell you that Mr. Steele has chosen to remove us from the bosom of all our friends and relations and set upon a new path. He is done with fighting locusts and a sexton's low pay and will lay claim to a homestead in the new state of Colorado. To finance the endeavor, he has sold all our earthly possessions, including this house where our children were born.*

> *We leave Minnesota forever on Saturday next. I will write you again when I know our new address.*

Your loving mother—

The bedroom door opened and Belle shoved the letter into the back of the book. She pretended to be engrossed in *The Odyssey* and didn't look up until Finola set the tray on the bed.

"Very nice." There was a steaming pot, a teacup, milk and sugar—though Finola knew Belle preferred honey—and a plate of the shortbread cookies Belle had made that morning after breakfast. "I expect I'll sleep late. I'll set the tea things out in the hall when I've finished so you won't disturb me collecting them."

And that was the boldest thing Belle had ever said to Finola Burke.

As soon as the maid was gone, she wrapped all but one of the cookies in a handkerchief and tucked them into her handbag for later. *I'm going to do it. I'm going to do it.* Then she took half a cup of tea to her desk and penned a note to Mrs. LeClair.

My dear Mother-in-law,

> *I would have told you last night of my plans but did not wish to disturb you in your grief.*

> *I have been invited to visit my*

friend, Miss Evangeline St. James, in
New York for a time, and I've decided
to accept her kindness. I shall consult
her as to your suggestion regarding
Wesley.

Take care of yourself,

Christabel Steele LeClair

Oh dear. The signature was too formal. Well, it was too late. Nothing to do about it now. Belle couldn't concentrate well enough to write it over. Everything in the letter was a lie, sort of. Evangeline *had* invited Belle to come to her, but Belle hadn't accepted. And she had no intention of marrying Wesley.

It was cowardly to do it this way, run off like a thief in the night. But it was the coward's way or no way at all, for she simply had not the power to stand up to her mother-in-law in person.

She added three generous drops of laudanum to the teapot. The doctor had given vials of the stuff to her and Mrs. LeClair as a balm against their grief. Belle didn't believe Wade's mother had taken any—the woman wouldn't give up her precious agony—but once in despair Belle had tried a dose.

She'd liked it—too well. For a brief time the world had become a very pleasant, if false, place indeed. She'd never taken any more for fear she wouldn't wish to stop. The real world was unpleasant and heart-breaking, but better to face that reality and make peace with it than be forever lost in a phantasmagorical, but false, illusion.

She set the tray outside her door, not surprised to hear the deft swoosh of Finola's skirts from somewhere down the hall.

Belle didn't close her eyes all night, afraid she'd fall asleep and lose her chance. She packed a traveling satchel with a nightgown, change of stockings and underthings, her toothbrush and the little bottle of toothpaste made from Dottie's secret recipe—dear Lord! What was she doing, abandoning civilization?

She added Wade's photograph and of course his letters.

Several times she patted her skirt pocket to be sure the watch he'd given her was still there. *To count the hours until our reunion.*

The mantel clock chimed a quarter past four. It was now or never.

She peeked outside her room. All clear, the tray gone. She crept downstairs feeling her heart would pound its way out of her body through her ears and throat, down to the basement kitchen, the one place in this house where Belle had been happy.

The alcove caught her eye. It was where Cook kept her journals of accounts—and cash for the household's petty expenses.

Belle reached under her bonnet and took a pin from her curls. She found the cashbox, and her hand trembled as she worked the lock, thinking of her brother in heaven. *Mark, if you're looking down, tell St. Peter you taught me this skill.*

The lock clicked open, and she removed twenty dollars. She'd return it as soon as she could, even if she had to sell her jeweled mourning brooch, but right now she needed the cash money.

A loud snore scared an involuntary squeak out of her. She spun around to see Finola, passed out, her cheek smashed against the servants' table and a bit of drool at the corner of her open mouth.

Belle swallowed a laugh. Finola had taken the bait. The teapot and an empty cup sat near her head. Belle had always suspected the maid of finishing what was left on her trays—and even understood it. Mrs. LeClair didn't feed her staff overly well.

Tucking the money into her handbag, Belle crept out of the alcove and past Finola. All that remained was to get outside through the servants' entrance and take the back stairs up to the street. She'd find a cab to the station, or walk if she had to, then board the first train heading for Minnesota.

She pushed open the door, and a cold whoosh of predawn air stole into the warm house. She shouldn't have been so nervous. This had been easy!

"What are you doing?"

Belle whirled around to find Dottie staring at her, wide-eyed. She must have come in to see to the morning fires. She was Cook's niece but twice the cook her aunt would ever be.

They stared at each other for a good minute. Dottie, like the other servants, wore a black armband. All the staff had adored young Mr. LeClair and would show their respect. Belle blinked away a tear.

"Madam?" In dismay, Dottie looked from Belle's satchel back to her face.

She had taught Belle so much. Cooking and baking, but also how to run a kitchen, to estimate and order supplies, and plan for special events. *One day soon you'll be mistress of your own house. You'll be prepared when that day comes.*

Belle had promised to take Dottie to run the kitchen at her new establishment. And now Belle was abandoning her.

"I'm sorry," she said. "I can't stay here."

"I didn't see a thing." Dottie squared her shoulders. "But when you're able, Madam Belle, do let me know you're all right."

"I won't forget." Belle hugged her. "You have been my one friend in this house. I'll remember everything you've taught me."

She checked again to make sure she had Wade's watch. Then she left the house on Bowdoin Street forever.

Chapter 2

White Feather River, Colorado
a week later

You're late."

Belle raised an eyebrow at her sister.

"Only a few minutes." Cheerful as ever, Charity took her own sweet time, balancing easily on two strapped-together logs as she meandered to the back of the raft where Belle was stationed at the rudder.

A few minutes ago, they'd lost the sun behind a mountain. Here the river flowed faster, and a cold breeze chafed Belle's cheeks. She snapped Wade's watch shut with a deft *click*. The timepiece had become a soothing crutch; its steady *tick, tick, tick, tick,*

tick made the world seem less chaotic and random.

She shook her head at her sister. "You're a grown woman, and still you take Naomi's things without asking."

"Ma has the keys to the trunks." Charity shrugged and pulled their older sister's favorite shawl close, then took hold of the rudder. "Naomi won't mind."

Each of the family's two rafts had a large chest bolted down in the center. Naomi's housed their special personal treasures. The chest on Belle's raft contained their actual treasure—gold and silver coins sewn into hems and secret pockets in their second set of clothes, which made them too heavy and dangerous to wear while traveling over the water.

Belle usually escaped Charity's habit of borrowing other people's clothes willy-nilly, since she was shorter and had a smaller waist. Poor Naomi. Those two were so close in size that, when their hair was covered, you couldn't tell them apart from the back.

Ugh! Belle was acting just like Mrs. LeClair, judgmental. Leaving home had aged her. But in some ways, the change had been good. Treated like a proper adult in Boston, she'd come to see herself as one. Someone's wife. No longer someone's child. Her sisters seemed so much younger to her now, more innocent. Charity was nearly twenty-one, but she gave the impression of being no more than sixteen or seventeen.

My family has been much sheltered from the world.

Belle chided herself. Nothing should bother her today, certainly nothing so unchangeable as Charity's bad habits. She loved her imperfect sister and everything that came with her.

She loved all her sisters! Naomi, Charity, Faith, and Hannah.

And her little brother, Luke.

And Ma and Pa.

It was heaven to be with them all again. Even hurtling along a frightening river on two open, makeshift rafts in an unknown country, she felt at home. She was with her family. This time her snap decision—to run away from Mrs. LeClair—had worked out for the best. Soon, maybe around the next bend or the one after, they'd arrive at Clementine, where the land office was located. Another step closer to her new life.

By now, Mrs. LeClair must know Belle hadn't gone to New York, but it was too late for her to do anything about it. Belle had gotten away. She was free!

"Ma doesn't look well." Charity looked over the water at their other raft about ten yards away. The Steeles had divided up, four to a raft. Ma was with Naomi, Faith, and Luke, while Belle and Charity were with Pa and Hannah.

"No. She doesn't at all."

Their mother was standing near Naomi, who was manning the raft's rudder. Ma's shoulders were hunched, and suddenly she grasped Naomi's forearm as if to draw on her strength.

"Ma!" Belle cupped her hands around her mouth. "Mother, you should lie down! Faith, help her!"

In one movement, Faith jumped to her feet. As nimble as Charity, the nineteen-year-old easily negotiated the bobbing raft and guided Ma inside the lean-to beside the trunk, where there was a makeshift bed.

Faith was the tallest of the sisters and all angles, awkward and gangly, but it was a mistake to believe first impressions with her. When need arose, she was as graceful as a cat. She could ride astride as if she'd been born on horseback. And she was the best shot of anyone in their town, male or female.

Yesterday when the men were building

these rafts, for a lark she'd walked across a single log balanced on two sawhorses, then challenged the McKinnon brothers to do the same. With each turn, she added a little trick, a jump, a spin, or a skip.

Chet McKinnon had fallen on his first try. When everybody laughed, he hadn't liked it, but he tried to be a good sport about it. Faith finally bested the lot when she crossed the beam backward and Daniel McKinnon couldn't match her.

The raft dipped, and Belle lost her balance. Suddenly all she could see was dark water rushing toward her face.

"I've got you!" Charity grabbed hold of the back of her dress and pulled her away from the raft's edge.

"Thank you." Belle threw her arms around her sister and scolded herself for not paying better attention.

"I hate this." Charity gritted out under her breath. She glanced at Pa, sitting with Hannah at the front of the raft. "What was he thinking, traveling on water after what happened to Matthew and Mark? Ma looks so haggard. She must be thinking of them every minute."

Belle couldn't help thinking Ma's eleventh pregnancy had more to do with it, but Charity had a point. Their brothers had drowned several years back. Ma must be thinking of them. When Matthew and Mark died, Charity had taken it the hardest of anybody—well, besides Ma. And then she'd learned how to swim. At the time, Belle had thought it an overreaction. Now she wished that all those years ago she'd joined in the lessons.

Up ahead, a third raft carried the McKinnons. These were friends from Minnesota who in fact had given Pa the idea to move to Colorado and claim land under the Homestead Act.

But Mr. McKinnon had never said anything about taking the river until yesterday after they departed the train at Greeley. It was 1877, goodness' sake! Who traveled by raft anymore?

Maybe I've grown too soft to be a homesteader.

There it was. Something she should have thought of *before* running away. Maybe Belle had lived too long in Mrs. LeClair's fine house, become too fond of carriages and trains to New York and bookstores well stocked with the latest novels and only a street or two away.

"Great thunder!" Charity cried out as

their raft veered a little too close to Naomi's. She quickly corrected their course. "Sorry! I was distracted, thinking about Ma."

"I was too."

"I never want children." Charity's cheeks flushed, as if she hadn't meant to say that aloud. She tilted her head. "Do you wish you'd had one?"

"Of course. Well. Sometimes."

Of the five Steele sisters, Belle was the only one who'd yet tied the knot. She didn't like talking about her odd marriage, but respect for other people's privacy wasn't Charity's strong suit.

"On the other hand, if I'd had a child, I never could have gotten away from Mrs. LeClair."

With Wade there hadn't been time to get pregnant. Their marriage had been conducted mostly through the mail, memorialized in *billets-doux* exchanged after his departure. His final letter, written at the beginning of April—only seven weeks ago!—had included a photograph taken in the notorious town of Deadwood in the Dakota Territory. It showed him posing in manly fashion in front of a place called the Cricket Saloon.

A week later, word of his death had followed.

A child would have been a far superior keepsake, but Belle treasured what she had: Wade's letters, the photograph, her wedding ring, and his pocket watch.

She might never marry again. Never have a child. She felt older than her years. Tragedy aged a person. Just look at Ma. In addition to the two sons who'd grown to adulthood before they drowned, two of her other children had died of illness before the age of five.

"You might marry again." As if Charity had read her thoughts. "You're young yet, and they say women are in high demand in Colorado. You could marry a man with a goldmine."

"If I do marry again, it won't be to someone rich."

Charity laughed. "Right."

"Trust me, rich people are different. They treat everyone around them like... like they don't have hearts and dreams of their own. Mrs. LeClair acts as if the other human beings in this world were put here for the sole purpose of seeing to her whims and well-being."

"But Mr. LeClair didn't treat you that way."

"I don't think he would have. How can I

know? We were together only four days before he left for the Dakota Territory. Still, I saw how the rich men in Mrs. LeClair's circle treated their wives, especially those who came to the marriage with less money and worse connections. No." Belle shuddered. "Rest assured, if I do marry again, it'll be to a nice, safe farmer, whose biggest risk will be working himself to an early grave. And I'll *never* give my heart to another man of the law. They can be cut down at any time for no reason at all."

"You don't ask for much." Charity sighed dreamily. "I figured you'd have a beau in Boston right away. Your letters were always so full of news about balls and society affairs." Charity's eyes went large. "I don't mean to say you were a flirt! It's just you're so pretty, Belle. I expected some banker or judge or railroad millionaire would have claimed you as soon as word got out that... you know."

"Mrs. LeClair wouldn't let that happen. Mourning is practically a religion in her crowd. She said it wouldn't be proper to leave the house except to go to church on Sundays, and then I was to be hidden under a black veil that came down past my waist. She had my future planned. While in mourning I was to receive no callers, speak to none but family or my most intimate friends. She let me know my only escape would be to marry again."

"Good luck under such conditions. They'd make it rather impossible to find another husband."

"Oh, she had that worked out too. She wanted me to marry her other son. As my husband's brother, Wesley would be allowed to spend time with me, you see."

"Ew, that just sounds... wrong." Charity wrinkled her nose. "Isn't there something against it in the Bible?"

"I'll have to ask Faith."

"No wonder you came home! I would have high-tailed it out of there too. But still, how odd it must be to go into full mourning after knowing Mr. LeClair so short a time."

Belle didn't expect anybody to understand. True, she and Wade had met a mere two weeks before they wed and had parted only days after that. But through their letters they'd become profoundly close. She couldn't remember the sound of his voice or the feel of his kisses, but she remembered his friendship and the sweet promise of his return.

She missed him. Or the idea of him, anyway.

The current was picking up. They'd

drifted away from Naomi and the center of the river. Belle lent her weight to the rudder to help maneuver.

"I'm so glad you came with us." Charity squeezed her arm. "*Do* you think you'll marry again one day?"

Belle felt her cheeks warm, and she stole a glance ahead at the McKinnon raft.

"Great thunder on the mountain! Has Chet McKinnon made you an offer?"

RACHEL BIRD

Chapter 3

"Hold your tongue." Belle looked to see if Pa had heard. She didn't want to talk about it. Didn't want to think about it. Not yet.

"How dare he presume! I mean you *are* still in black." Charity frowned, and then her eyes went wide. "He must be in love with you."

"I doubt that very much." Belle scoffed. "I think he just wants someone to help work his homestead."

Charity *could* be right, but though Belle had known Chet all her life, she'd never thought of him as anything but a family friend.

Yesterday, instructing her on the finer points of rafting, he'd been quite attentive.

He showed her how to use the rudder to steer, cautioned her to stay away from the raft edges, to keep as dry as possible.

Then he'd suggested she make her own claim to land. He told her that as a widow over twenty-one and a citizen, she qualified to homestead a hundred and sixty acres, just like any man. *We could find plots next to each other. And then*—he'd smiled oh so winningly—*if one day we joined them together, we'd have over three hundred acres.*

But as Charity had pointed out, Belle was still in black. Rather than being flattered, Chet McKinnon's attentions had made her uncomfortable—and his reference to joining homesteads together was certainly impertinent.

And there was something else. "Mrs. McKinnon reminds me of Mrs. LeClair," she told Charity. "I've had my fill of overbearing mothers-in-law."

She was tired of people telling her what to do!

In Chet's favor, he intended to establish his own place, separate from his parents.

"River's getting choppy, girls." Pa came back from the front of the raft. "Why don't you let me take over until things settle."

"Thanks, Pa." Charity handed over the

rudder, and Belle followed her to the center of the raft.

The river snaked around another bend, and a group of crude shacks came into view, huddled around a large house near the riverbank. The words TRADING POST were painted on a broad canvas hanging from the porch of the largest structure, and a young woman sat on a boulder at the water's edge, sunning herself.

"Great thunder." Charity gaped, wide-eyed. "Is that a... a tart?"

The girl was half-naked, dressed in a simple shift, the straps fallen down and baring her shoulders. *As if displaying her wares.* She waved at the McKinnons' raft, then leaned forward seductively and called out to the men who stared hungrily, including Chet.

Belle was both scandalized and fascinated.

The largest woman she'd ever seen emerged from the main building and joined the girl on the rock—now that they were closer, it was obvious she *was* a girl, no more than Hannah's age. It turned Belle's stomach.

The woman was maybe in her late forties. She had to be six feet tall, her formerly muscular flesh going to fat. A once-fine emerald-green evening dress hung on her body like a defiant declaration of former glory. Her graying brown hair, piled angrily atop her head, rebelled against instruction, and loose strands stirred in the breeze.

"Come along now, boys," the big woman called out lustily. "This could be your last chance! We have everything you need."

The McKinnons resisted the sirens on the rock, and the rafts drifted on. As the Trading Post disappeared from sight, the old woman's taunting cackle made Belle shudder. Colorado might now be a state, but it was still part of the Wild West.

What had the woman meant by their last chance?

"Pa," Belle said, "do you think Mr. McKinnon took the wrong fork back a piece? It seems we should have reached Clementine by now."

The water was moving yet faster, and Belle thought she heard the rushing of rapids—or worse, a waterfall—ahead. They should never have taken the river. If there was no train, surely there must have been a stagecoach to their destination.

To be fair, Pa worried about having enough cash to purchase all they'd need to begin their new life. Surveys and patent fees, plus seed, tools, and horses, not to mention materials to build a house and likely a million other things they hadn't thought of. The train tickets they'd already bought had been dear enough with eight in the family.

Belle had helped. Yesterday in Greeley she'd spent the last of the twenty dollars borrowed from the kitchen cashbox on sandwiches and lemonade for their dinner.

If only these treacherous waters didn't flow so quickly. Mr. McKinnon had promised a steady, easy trip, smoother than the train.

The raft dipped again.

"Oh!" Hannah cried out as she lost her balance and fell hard to her knees. Belle rushed to help her, and a sound like an explosion came from up ahead. A man's surprised cry carried over the water.

Belle looked up to see two of the McKinnon men—she couldn't tell who—thrown into the water. Mrs. McKinnon screamed and fell in after them. With another wrench of splitting wood, several logs ripped loose from their raft.

"Watch out!" Pa hollered.

A fat log rushed at Naomi's raft, but there was nothing she could do. It bashed against the raft, and all aboard fell to their knees. Naomi held fast to the rudder and pulled herself to her feet, screaming at Ma to get back inside the lean-to.

The evil log now rushed toward Belle's raft, then narrowly missed it.

"We've drifted into rapids!" she cried out. The river roared and it seemed Naomi was hollering, but Belle couldn't make out the words. The McKinnons' raft was nowhere to be seen. Had they all gone under?

"Belle! Hannah!" Charity cried. "Get your clothes off!" She'd already removed her own boots. She tossed them inside the lean-to, along with Naomi's shawl, and started pulling her dress over her head.

Belle and Hannah shared a mystified look. "What in heaven's name—"

"Take off your boots!" Charity screamed. "And everything else. Strip down to your knickers."

"Have you gone mad?"

"Do it!" Charity stood there in her stockings and unmentionables. The raft clattered over a cluster of rocks, and they went to their knees again. She gripped Belle's arms with both her hands. "When this thing comes apart and we all end up in the water, do you want to drown because your clothes are so heavy they drag you under?"

Driving home her meaning, the outermost logs on either side of the raft broke loose.

Hannah nodded. Face resolute, she started unhooking her boots.

"Charity!" Pa called out. "Come take the rudder."

"Do what I said, Belle." Charity went to help Pa.

There was no time to think. Belle pulled Hannah's dress over her head, then started in on her own clothes. Charity was right—Belle's skirt was already heavy with water splashing over the raft and up between the unsealed logs.

Another log detached and pulled away while Pa tried to pry loose the chest.

"Pa, what are you doing?"

"All the money we have in the world is in here!"

"Naomi's coming," Charity called out. "Belle, get Hannah over to the other raft. Ours isn't going to hold."

Everything was happening too fast, but Charity's steadiness helped Belle keep hold of her own wits. She remembered Wade's watch and dug the precious object out of a pocket in the wet heap that had been her skirt. She stuffed the timepiece down the front of her camisole, snug between the stays of her half corset.

The raft raked over a cluster of boulders unseen below the surface, and another log was torn away. Nevertheless, Charity and Naomi managed to bring the two rafts together.

"Jump to me!" Faith held out her arms.

Hannah was only fourteen but already as tall as Belle. As she jumped, Belle lifted her by the waist and pushed. She made it to the edge of the other raft where Faith threw her arms around her and pulled her onto it. They were going to be terribly banged up, but Hannah was safe.

"Now you, Belle!" Charity still had hold of the rudder. She'd have to let go sometime, but her efforts were the only thing keeping them barely steady.

"What about you and Pa?" Belle stood there in her knickers and camisole, ice-cold water spilling over the raft and covering her bare feet.

"You go." Charity looked from Belle to Pa and back to Belle. "I can swim, if it comes to it."

Pa was still caught up in freeing the chest.

"Let it go!" Belle cried out, but he didn't hear—or wouldn't.

"Jump!" Faith stood at the edge of Naomi's raft, ready to catch Belle as she had

Hannah.

"We're coming apart!" Charity cried. "Go!"

Chapter 4

Break Heart, Colorado
the same day

Sheriff Brady Fontana looked at his desk and despaired. He loathed paperwork, and his usual solution—handing over the onerous duty to his deputy—wasn't available. He'd lost the fool to gold fever and hadn't yet found a new one.

Deputy, that is.

He could do without the next man being a fool.

Still, that was no excuse for letting things pile up so badly.

More coffee would help, but sadly, he'd finished off the pot and was plumb out of

Arbuckles'. No time to go down to Tagget's to restock his supplies either. Mrs. Tweed's buggy was parked across the street in front of the Lilac Hotel.

This morning one of the hands from Nighthawk, Brady's ranch outside town, had delivered a note from his housekeeper. She'd be in town today and hoped he would join her at the Lilac Café at ten thirty.

She was right on time, as usual. The Lilac's brew was god-awful, but Brady's stomach growled eagerly at the prospect of a real breakfast. Roxanna couldn't mess up ham and scrambled eggs, could she?

A loud, ungodly snore boomed into the office from the cells in the back. Hotel Fontana, as some in town called the jail, was currently empty of prisoners, but not of guests. Brady rifled through several piles of this and that, found the spare key, and dropped it on the floor just inside the cell bars.

"I'm going out, Doc. If you leave before I get back, remember to lock up."

Doc Declan's muffled, miserable groan signaled he'd heard. Brady locked the office and left the usual sign out front:

NEVER A LAWMAN

SHERIFF OUT. INQUIRE WITH TED
GENSCH AT LILAC HOTEL.

The Lilac was the only real hotel in Break
Heart, conveniently located directly across
Main Street from the sheriff's office. The
owner, Teddy Gensch, was manning his usual
station at the front desk. His wife, Charlotte,
would be checking on customers in the café—
or, more likely, was in the kitchen pleading
with her niece, Roxanna, to do better.

"Morning, Sheriff." Teddy, a friendly man
in the middle of middle age, pushed up the
spectacles that had slid down his nose. He
glanced at the grandfather clock against the
wall, eyes twinkling. "What's still left of it."

Brady pulled out his stem-wound Patek
Philippe pocket watch and made a show of
checking the floor clock's time. "Right on the
mark, 10:37."

It was three years now since Brady had
brought his widowed mother out West for the
clean air. They'd stayed at the Lilac while he
negotiated the purchase of Nighthawk, his
ranch seven miles outside Break Heart.
Though it hadn't kept good time in years,
Charlotte Gensch's family heirloom had been
proudly displayed in the lobby. Timepieces of
every size and device were in Brady's blood,

and he had made two friends for life the day he fixed that grandfather clock.

Happier times. Optimistic times.

A world in which his mother lived, where Thalia would arrive any day now, and Brady would have laughed at the suggestion he take on the position of sheriff. That world had fallen apart.

He lived in this world now.

"Come along, Brady." Charlotte Gensch appeared at the open double doors that led to the hotel café. "I've put Hermione at your table."

Despite the loss of the Lilac's cook—she'd left town with Brady's deputy in search of their own El Dorado—the expansive café was jumping with locals and unfamiliar customers.

The town had been a stagecoach stop long before Brady moved West. Then last autumn the railroad completed its trunk line between here and Greeley. The tracks had been unusable through that first winter, but now the snows were melted and the ambitious, the devious, and the plain curious were once again on the move.

Most would stay in town briefly, then go on to establish homesteads or explore gold fields or the silver strikes near Leadville.

Some would stay and start businesses, supplied by the railroad and frequented by the homesteaders.

Break Heart was no longer a riverbank settlement. Seemingly overnight, it had become close to a bona fide town.

At his usual table by the window, where he could keep an eye on the street, sat a woman in her early sixties who looked a decade younger. Her hair, more gray than blond, was tucked up under a saucy straw bonnet trimmed with ribbons and satin flowers. Her gray-and-black-striped muslin day dress would be suitable for shopping in the most fashionable sections of New York. Her periwinkle blue eyes crinkled fondly when she saw him.

Mrs. Hermione Tweed, housekeeper extraordinaire—though of course she was so much more. Brady dropped his hat and jacket on the inside chair before sitting down.

"Thanks, Charlotte." He spoke with more enthusiasm than he felt as, without asking, the innkeeper produced a clean mug from her apron pocket and filled it with her nefarious brew. He eyed Mrs. Tweed's pot of tea longingly.

"The regular, I assume," Charlotte said. "Ham steak, scrambled eggs, hot biscuits and gravy?"

He didn't miss his housekeeper's little smile. When had he become so predictable? He nodded and looked around the café, crowded with more strangers than friends. "Looks like business is picking up now the snow's melted."

"Oh yes. Every day the railroad brings more would-be homesteaders from the East."

"Why the groan? You and Teddy must be happy with all these customers." Newcomers often stayed at the Lilac, as he had with his mother and Mrs. Tweed, until they found more permanent arrangements.

"Not if I can't keep my help," Charlotte huffed. "If Abigail Vanderhouten isn't coming through the front door, trying to lure my girls away with her bride book, Delilah Montgomery is coming through the back, enticing them with tales of easy gold to be made lying on their backsides at Sweet Dee's."

"Oh my word!" A woman at the next table dropped her fork. The utensil clattered onto her plate, drawing every eye in the café, but the attention didn't seem to bother her. Instead, she appeared to relish it and fluffed herself up like a righteous peacock—until Mrs. Tweed gave her the side-eye.

"It is challenging," Mrs. Tweed told Charlotte sympathetically. "There are so many opportunities in the West, for men *and* women. I'm quite gratified to have enough help at Nighthawk. Although"—she cleared her throat—"I would wish to add to the household staff should its master acquire a wife and children. A proper family to care for."

Mrs. Tweed looked at Brady pointedly, and Charlotte joined her.

"This is why you came to town today. To tell me I need to *acquire* a wife?"

"Partly."

"Well, it all sounds very nice." He looked at his coffee and added firmly, "But I'm not ready."

Mrs. Tweed would never give up her wish to see him married, but Charlotte knew when to let a topic go. "Last month we lost Maisy to the Break Heart Brides for a rancher in Nebraska, and now Abigail has our Trudy going to Denver to marry a stock agent."

"I didn't know that about Trudy," Mrs. Tweed said. "It sounds like Mrs. Vanderhouten's bride business is doing well."

"Too well." Charlotte sighed.

"Perhaps not well enough." Mrs. Tweed looked at Brady again, but before he could sulk, she and Charlotte burst out laughing. They knew their cause was lost, but they weren't going to let that rob them of their fun.

"Trudy's a good waitress." He tried to change the subject. "She'll be missed."

Trudy was practically the assistant manager where the café was concerned. Charlotte would feel her loss keenly. But losing Maisy had been the real blow, mostly because her replacement, Charlotte's niece Roxanna, was pretty much limited to scrambled eggs in the way of her cooking skills.

These days everything else on the menu was an adventure.

Charlotte hurried off to greet some new customers, and Brady noticed the shocked woman still watching him, her puzzled gaze fixed on the star above his shirt pocket.

"Ma'am." He hid his smile behind a sip of bad coffee.

Under her breath, Mrs. Tweed said, "I wonder if Miss Prim will be staying in town or moving on."

"I'll beg her on hand and knee to stay," Brady said, "if she's a qualified schoolteacher."

All manner of people were pouring into

the new state from the East. Some running from something. Most looking for something better. The West was strong, but not invulnerable, and Break Heart needed a goodly portion of its new citizens to be just like Miss Prim there. People with an appreciation for law and order, decent behavior—and yes, intolerance for establishments like Sweet Dee's.

If the town wanted respectability, it would inevitably have to sacrifice its unique characters. In Brady's experience, "good society" didn't value individuality. And on the surface, at least, it valued its schoolteachers over its bawdy house madams.

Charlotte's coffee was formidable as ever, and he finished his breakfast before getting through the first cup. But as soon it got anywhere close to empty, she showed up armed with a pot of the foul liquid.

There was a ruckus out in the lobby, and Ned Overstreet's girl burst into the café. "Where's Sheriff Fontana?" The filthy, skinny eleven-year-old scurried over to Brady's table and leaned against it dramatically.

Teddy Gensch had followed her, but he remained at the doorway, partly watchful and partly curious.

"There's a man!" The girl raised an arm to

her brow, her unruly hair escaping her braids.

Poor Charlotte jerked the pot away and spilled hot coffee all over her apron. "Sally Overstreet, when will you learn to mind your manners?"

Brady chuckled, but Charlotte had a point. This so-called bona fide town really needed a schoolteacher. Regardless, Jon Overstreet shouldn't be letting his kids run free. His wife dying of a fever this past winter was no excuse.

"At the river!" Sally nodded breathlessly. "A dead man!"

Chapter 5

"Bless us and save us," Mrs. Tweed said drily as the café erupted with gasps.

"Now, calm down, Sally." Brady laid his napkin over his plate and fixed the child with a wink. "We don't want to spook the tourists."

Break Heart Bend had come by its name honestly. The snowmelt this time of year meant a dramatic rise in the rapids and several weeks of treacherous flow. This past winter, the pack had been particularly deep, this spring unseasonably warm. Sally Overstreet was a dramatic kid, but the river had coughed up its dead on Break Heart's riverbank before.

"I'm afraid our discussion will have to wait, Mrs. Tweed." Brady got to his feet, grabbed his jacket and hat. "Thanks for breakfast, Charlotte." She'd put the bill on his tab. "Teddy, if you'd join me, I'd appreciate it."

He really needed to find a new deputy.

He and Teddy followed Sally out of the hotel as Damon Overstreet, her five-year-old brother, was coming up the steps. The boy huffed wearily and turned to follow them.

Brady made a mental note to talk to Jonathan about his kids. It wasn't safe, their running free, especially now that there were so many strangers in these parts. This dead man Sally found might have been alive—and up to no good.

"You all wait here a moment."

Brady crossed to the sheriff's office and went back to the cells. "Time to rise and shine, Sleeping Beauty. I'm going to need you to pronounce a death."

More paperwork.

Since becoming a state, Colorado had become awfully full of itself. All births and deaths had to be officially recorded now, certificates filed with the powers that be. Doc wouldn't mind. He could use the fee.

The doctor growled but roused himself. Brady locked up again, and he, Doc, and Teddy followed the Overstreet kids down

Main Street, stopping at Grayson's to have the undertaker join them.

At the riverbank, sure enough, the remains of a broken raft had washed up with a man's form sprawled akimbo over the cattycorner logs.

Doc turned the lump over—and it groaned.

"In my professional opinion, this isn't a body."

Devon Declan was a perverse and angry physician, and Brady, of all people, sympathized with his contrariness. But when there was a true need, the healer held sway over the curmudgeon. In fact, during a crisis was the only time Doc showed any sympathy or even awareness of other people's existence.

The victim came around after a second whiff of smelling salts, but the sounds he made were incoherent. There was a nasty gash over his eyebrow.

"The lad's in shock." Doc checked for broken bones, and the man shrieked in pain. Doc shrugged. "Possibly a cracked rib. He needs to be out of these wet clothes and warmed up before pneumonia sets in. Let's get him to my surgery."

"Sally, you take Damon home now,"

Brady said. "Where'd that scamp get to?"

"Aw, Sheriff—"

"Do as I say, girl. Your brother's too young to be—"

"Aeeeiiii!"

The big, blood-curdling scream came out of the small boy now making a beeline for Brady from the river's edge. Damon plowed right into him, wrapped his arms around Brady's legs, and wouldn't let go.

"A lady! She's dead for sure!"

"It's all right, son." Sometimes the main job of being sheriff in this town was soothing frayed nerves. "Where is she? Where's the lady?"

The kid pointed in the general direction of a boulder jutting up from the river's edge.

"Now this one's in shock." Declan squatted down to look at the shaking child, who immediately pulled away from Brady and buried his face against the doctor's chest. Doc heaved a put-upon sigh, but he let Damon cling to him while he patted the boy's back.

"She's here." Teddy was already on the spot. "Oh. *Gott im Himmel...*" He turned away and threw up.

It was a soul-crushing sight. Brady said a silent prayer and hoped the woman, who lay half-in and half-out of the water, had been killed instantly by whatever bashed in one side of her head. The river had pretty much torn the rest of her up, and it was all Brady could do not to lose his breakfast too.

The worst of it, she was carrying a child, five or six months along, by the look of her. He and Teddy pulled the body fully away from the water.

"She'll need a proper burial," Brady told Grayson. An image of Thalia lying on a travois and staring up at nothing flashed in his mind. "Send me the bill for the cost."

"I'll see to it, Sheriff." The undertaker covered the woman's face with his handkerchief.

Doc's arms were still occupied by the traumatized five-year-old, and with Sally leading the macabre parade, Brady and Teddy carried the undrowned man up to the infirmary located in an alley off the upper end of Main Street.

The fellow looked to be in his late twenties, a few years younger than Brady's thirty-one. Much younger than the dead woman. *What kind of man brings his wife on such a dangerous journey, and in that condition?*

Good thing he'd lived, because Brady wanted to kill him personally.

As usual, Doc's office was clean as a new

pin, in marked contrast to his disheveled person. Clear windows. Organized vials in dust-free pigeonholes. Shiny, intimidating medical instruments arranged neatly on spotless counters.

"Put him on that cot by the wall," Doc barked out, as if the sheriff and the innkeeper were his nurses. Meanwhile, he gently set the boy down on the raised examination table and had the cut on his chin cleaned up and bandaged within two blinks of an eye. "Now stay right there, Damon. You fall and break your leg, it'll be your own damn fault."

Neither kid seemed put off by the rough language. In fact, they seemed to relish it.

"Belle?" The stranger looked at Doc with unfocused eyes, then turned onto his side and retched. A vile stream of river water and who-knows-what-else spilled onto the pristine floor.

"Oh, Christ."

"Doc." Teddy shifted uncomfortably. "Must you use such language in front of the children?"

For his trouble, Teddy earned himself the squinty eye from Doc and gleeful giggles from Sally and Damon. Brady wondered if they heard the same, or worse, at home. Those kids surely needed a woman's touch in their lives.

"Where's Belle?" The patient tried to sit up but fell back from weakness or pain. "Did she make it?"

"She the pregnant woman?" Brady shifted to sheriff mode, beginning the investigation into what had happened. Belle must be the name of the dead woman at the riverbank. He ought to break the news to the fellow gently, but he was in no mood to be kind to a fool.

"Pregnant? No, that's Laura May. Mrs. Steele, Belle's mother. Why?" The man struggled to get a decent breath. "Oh dear Lord, am I the only one who survived?"

"What's your name, friend?" Teddy asked.

"McKinnon. Chet McKinnon. My ma and pa... my brothers. Are they...?"

"Your raft was broken up pretty bad, son. You came ashore on a couple of logs that were barely holding together."

Teddy was a gentle soul, for all the glad-handing and good humor he directed toward his guests. Brady was happy to let him deliver the bad news.

"Praise God I made it." McKinnon winced on the words and gingerly touched his ribs. "Am I going to die too?"

"You might. If you're damaged badly

enough internally and infection sets in."

Doc's abrupt manner told all. The fool would live.

"We found only one other lost soul," Teddy said. "The pregnant woman."

"Poor Mrs. Steele." McKinnon grimaced. "It wasn't my fault. I told Pa we never should have taken the river."

"Who is Belle?" Brady asked. "How many were in your party?"

Eventually, he got the story. Two families, thirteen people on three rafts, had come upon the rapids at Break Heart Bend. As McKinnon spoke, his mind seemed to clear. Though part of him knew all his family and friends were dead, like most survivors, part of him couldn't believe it.

"The Steeles—" McKinnon's eyes were wild. "The last I saw, Mr. Steele's raft hit the rocks and broke up. He went under for sure. But the other raft was still afloat. It's a passel of females. If they are alive out there, they'll be easy prey. Belle..." He looked at Brady. "Sheriff, you have to find them!"

McKinnon tried to rise, but the color drained from his face and he fell back.

"We will find them, Mr. McKinnon, have no fear." Teddy mercifully didn't add, *if they're out there.*

"Take Damon home now, Sally." Brady lifted the boy off the table and set him down beside his sister.

"Yes, Sheriff."

"I mean it. No stopping to explore."

"Yes, sir."

"Find your pa and tell him to saddle his horse and come to the sheriff's office."

He'd need every man he could get for the search party. Again, Brady felt the loss of his deputy. Doc would have to stay with his patient, but Teddy would gladly join the search. Jon Overstreet would grumble, then come along. But both were on the other side of forty. Though Jon was strong as an ox, Teddy wasn't in the best physical condition and was unlikely to hold up much more than a day. Grayson and his nephew could be counted on. For them, Brady thought darkly, it was a matter of business.

"My poor mother." Sounded like reality was beginning to sink in. Mr. McKinnon was crying now. "And Pa and Clayton and Daniel. Belle..."

The Lord really does take away. Life was loss more often than not, as Brady was witness. He surprised himself with a heavy sigh and headed down to his office to organize the search.

This Belle must be someone special, judging by McKinnon's tenderness when he spoke her name. Here was the reason Brady had agreed to become sheriff—certainly not from a love of paperwork. He couldn't save his own fiancée, but he'd save another man's, if the river hadn't killed her—or worse.

Of the animals living out near Break Heart Bend, the ones that concerned him the most were human.

Chapter 6

They came again to calmer waters and an inlet where the riverbank was wide enough to find purchase. Belle gave what strength she had left to help Naomi steer toward the shore, and as soon as it was shallow enough, the four of them jumped off—Belle, Naomi, Faith, and Luke.

Somehow they dragged their remaining raft up onto the dirt beach.

Dry land! When Mrs. McKinnon fell into the rapids, a kind of terror had seized Belle, a shock of understanding that she might actually die. But now a bird called out from the forest beyond this grassy meadow, and the ground beneath her feet was solid and welcoming.

She still heard the faint pounding of rushing water, somewhere—whether real or an echo imprinted on her mind, she couldn't say—but the world felt calm again, quiet. Safe.

And then Naomi's heartbroken whimper reminded her of what they'd lost. She embraced her trembling older sister. "We have to believe Charity and Hannah made it."

For their parents, there was no hope. Belle had jumped to Naomi's raft and safety just as hers had fallen apart. Pa and the chest he couldn't abandon went straight down. He never came to the surface again. Ma had gone over the side of Naomi's raft. Belle didn't know when.

In all the confusion, Hannah fell into the water too, but Charity's quick thinking saved her. In only her shift and shoeless, Hannah had kept her head above water until Charity could get to her—and true to her boasts, Charity really could swim!

The last Belle saw, they were together, heads above water, clinging to a broken log and inching toward the shore.

There absolutely was hope.

"There they are!" Luke took off running upstream along the shore. "Hannah! Charity!"

Belle saw the miracle: her missing sisters on dry land, making their way carefully along the riverbank on bare feet, dressed—like Belle—only in their underthings.

"Thank heaven."

"Everyone is accounted for then," Naomi said.

Accounted for, but not present. Belle said a silent prayer for Ma and Pa.

Everybody hugged everybody twice and more, laughing with the sheer relief of being alive. Naomi tore off the sweater she was still wearing and wrapped it around Hannah's quivering shoulders, and Belle thought ruefully of the lost shawl.

Immediately, she was ashamed of herself.

Charity had saved more than one life today by keeping her wits about her, and all Belle could do was find fault in something so unimportant? So unyielding and judgmental! She'd escaped Mrs. LeClair physically; now she'd have to purge the woman's severity from her own heart.

"Let's give thanks for our deliverance," she said.

They bowed their heads and waited for Faith to say a prayer. She knew the Bible better than any of them—*except Pa*, Belle thought. After a long silence, she looked up to see if something was wrong.

Faith let out an exasperated sigh. "Oh, all

right." She bowed her head, and took hold of Luke's hand on her left and Hannah's on her right.

Belle and Naomi shared a questioning look. *What was that about?* Everybody joined hands in a circle, and Belle reminded herself they were all shaken to their cores.

Both the ritual and the actual words Faith chose were consoling.

> *"They shall not hunger nor*
> *thirst; neither shall the heat nor sun*
> *smite them: for he that hath mercy*
> *on them shall lead them, even by the*
> *springs of water shall he guide*
> *them."*

She was unusually quiet and gentle in her delivery, with a degree of kindness in her voice never there before. As if the day had changed her.

But of course it would.

This day must change them all.

> *"And I will make all my*
> *mountains a way, and my highways*
> *shall be exalted."*

The sound of the river filled Belle's head and competed with the words of scripture. Were those rapids she heard, or a waterfall?

Or a memory? Would they find Ma and Pa's bodies? What had happened to Chet and his family?

> *"Behold, these shall come from far: and, lo, these from the north and from the west; and these from the land of Sinim. Sing, O heavens; and be joyful, O earth; and break forth into singing, O mountains: for the Lord hath comforted his people, and will have mercy upon his afflicted."*

Belle had come from far, but what now? She wanted to take the scripture to heart, but it was a struggle. How could any of them ever again be joyful and break forth into singing? They let go of hands and stood apart.

Despair isn't allowed, Belle told herself. Life must go on.

"We'd better take stock." Naomi pulled an apple out of her pocket, green with a red blush. It was the most beautiful thing Belle had ever seen.

Naomi, Faith, and Luke still had their clothes, and as they searched their pockets, Belle grew aware of her near nakedness. She hugged her arms to her chest and felt something hard inside her camisole—Wade's watch!

She blinked back tears. It was still there, surely ruined, but not lost. She glanced at the raft and the bolted-down trunk. Could his letters and photograph have survived all that water?

"Anyone else have anything?" Naomi asked.

It turned out they did.

Luke had a quantity of elk jerky he'd cajoled Pa into buying for him at the train station in Greeley. Faith produced a bag of butterscotch candies from a deep pocket in her skirt, treats she'd purchased there, thinking to surprise the family with them after tonight's supper. She spread her handkerchief on the ground, and the precious items were piled onto it. Luke added his pocketknife to the collection.

While Naomi sliced the apple and cut the jerky into bite-sized pieces, Belle went with Faith and Charity to inspect the raft for anything usable. The lean-to was gone, along with all the boxes of food and supplies, but the "treasure chest" remained.

Belle breathed in the clean air and fought the gloom threatening at the edge of her mind. She was so very tired!

"The chest is too well secured." Charity tugged at the lock. "But I think it would soothe Luke and Hannah to see their treasures."

It would certainly soothe me. "That's a very fine thought," Belle said. "I'll ask Naomi for the key."

"Wait." Charity grabbed her arm, her eyes large. She choked out, "Ma had the key, remember?"

Belle blinked and nodded, afraid to speak lest she fall into a crying jag that would never end. They found a few good-sized rocks, and the three took turns bashing the lock until it broke open.

Faith lifted the lid. "Everything..." Her face lit up. "Everything's fine, I think."

"Is your Bible dry?" Belle wasn't tall enough to peek over Faith's shoulders. "Do you see Charity's journal? What about my letters?"

Luke had dubbed the trunk the treasure chest because it contained the special personal items each of them had been allowed to keep and bring. Faith's was the Bible Pa had given her years ago. Now she carefully unwrapped the many layers of oilcloth she'd packed it in.

"I think it's undamaged." The leather binding looked dry. She leafed through the thin pages, every one covered—to Belle's mind, scandalously—with notes. None stuck together.

Luke ran over to join them, licking his fingers and wiping his hands on his drenched, filthy trousers—as if it would do any good. He peered into the chest. "Is my fortune still there?"

Belle dug out her brother's chosen treasure and caught a glimpse of her own peeking out at the bottom of the chest. "Still here."

Luke's "fortune" was contained in a maroon satin pouch on which Hannah had ornately embroidered LUKE, surrounded by flowers and leaves in gold thread. He opened it and dumped a half eagle onto his palm.

Pa had given him the five-dollar coin on his tenth birthday, much to Ma's dismay. She called it an outrageous and even dangerous extravagance for a child so young.

"Remember what Pa told you?" Belle said. "*It's good for a man to know he has a little more than he needs set by, just in case.*"

Charity barked out a laugh. "As if there was a day in Pa's life he had more than enough set by!"

It was meant good-naturedly, and they all smiled, recalling Pa's unyielding optimism despite his meager earnings as the church sexton and the devastation of his crops by locusts two years running.

Unbowed by the chronic austerity of unrelieved poverty, Jared Steele had been a happy man. He had all he ever wanted, the love of his wife and children. But he'd sacrificed his happiness, thinking to improve their lot, and had lost his life in the undertaking.

In the same vein, Wade had accepted a dangerous assignment for the good of his country—and lost his life doing his duty.

It was all so wrong, so unfair. Belle should love and admire both men for their sacrifices, but all she felt was anger. How dare they! How dare either put himself in a position to be taken from those who loved him!

"Here's my bundle, and Naomi's and yours." Charity handed over Wade's letters and hugged her journal and Naomi's mysterious packet to her chest.

She was right. The letters, Charity's journal, Luke's coin, Faith's Bible—these were material things, but it was indeed soothing to know all were intact.

It was good to see their little brother smile, holding the shining gold eagle with the liberty head on the other side. Faith had markedly relaxed upon assuring herself her

Bible was safe. Knowing that all the observations, secrets, and little tidbits of knowledge Charity had recorded in her journal over the years had not been lost, on this day of overwhelming loss, must be a consoling balm indeed.

And Wade's letters—Belle couldn't have borne it if they were ruined. Trembling, she opened the layers of oilcloth meant to protect them. "Oh!" Tears spilled out of her eyes.

"Oh, Belle," Charity said. "Are your letters spoiled? We never should have put your bundle on the bottom."

"No. No, they're dry. These are tears of relief."

All their treasures weren't mere things. They were also symbols. Reminders of home, of a world that was gone and could never be again, but that could be remembered and revered.

A world in which their parents, and Wade, were still alive.

"Come, Luke." In a rush of emotion, Belle pulled him to her and kissed his cheek. "Take Hannah her kit." She'd never understand why Hannah's treasure had been her sewing things—but the heart is a mysterious organ; one never knows what will speak to it.

Luke set the kit on the ground beside

Hannah, who lay sleeping on Naomi's knee. She let out a snore as loud as an old man's, and Luke burst out laughing.

How wonderful it would be to sleep. Belle's limbs ached and she was exhausted.

"It feels as though we've come through Scylla and Charybdis," Charity said.

The *Odyssey* had been one of Pa's favorites. More than once, he'd read it aloud to the family after dinner. Wade would have appreciated the reference too. Belle had been reading it again in Boston after he'd mentioned it in one of his letters.

"Yes," Faith said. "And for the first time, I sympathize with Odysseus's men. I'm hungry enough to eat one of Helios's sacred cows myself."

"I think this one must have found the Lotus Eaters." Naomi brushed a lock of hair away from Hannah's closed eyes.

Belle sat down in the circle and set upon her tiny portion of apple slices and jerky, devouring it all like the ravenous beast she was. "Oh, this is... delicious!"

Naomi nodded absently. She too was beyond worn out, Belle realized, past the end of her strength. Yet they couldn't all close their eyes, not just yet.

"What do we do now?" Charity said what

was in Belle's mind. "We have no food and we don't know where we are."

"Clementine is somewhere along the river." Faith said. "Maybe we should get back on the raft and—"

"Never!"

Belle spat the word out so ferociously Hannah sat up with a start and a disoriented whine.

"I'm sorry, Hannah. But I'll never go near a river again."

"It wouldn't work anyway," Charity said. "There are too many of us, and the raft lost a few logs. We'd sink it."

"We could go back," Luke said. "Walk back to that trading post."

"No." Naomi, Faith, Charity, and Belle said simultaneously, all with a shudder.

"Let's rest a while," Naomi said. "And then we'll move on. It's still early in the day. We'll keep close to the river. Clementine can't be far."

"Some of us no longer have shoes." Charity chewed on the last of her jerky and added drily, "I only mention it."

"I had a closet in Boston," Belle sighed, "one closet dedicated to footwear and stockings alone. Kid boots, carriage boots, riding boots, walking shoes. A pair of red-bowed silk evening shoes with gold embroidery even Hannah would approve of."

"Mr. LeClair must have been very rich," Hannah said dreamily.

"His mother was—is. She saw to it I was fashionably clothed and well shod—not, mind you, out of any concern for my happiness or comfort. She cared only to impress the ladies in her social circle. But oh, how lovely it would be just now to slip on my satin morning slippers. So soft, soft, soft."

"Why did you leave Boston? Why give up a life of sumptuous delights?"

Belle rubbed her chafed foot and smiled at her youngest sister's innocence. "Because the delights came at a cost, dearest. In exchange, I was required to obey Mrs. LeClair in all things." She chucked ruefully. "Believe me, I consider myself well out of it. Even if it means being stuck in the middle of nowhere with no food, no clothes, and no idea what to do about it."

"What's that?" Charity sat up and raised a hand to shield her eyes. All turned to follow her gaze to the edge of the clearing, where a horse and rider emerged from the trees. "Great thunder on the mountain, are we rescued?"

Another rider appeared. And another.

And a fourth.

"Or captured," Belle said. At this point she didn't much care which.

"Hannah, get behind me." Naomi got to her feet, her voice dark, and the alarm on her face set Belle on edge. "Now."

Chapter 7

Faith and Naomi stood with Luke between them to form a wary wall, one that failed to screen their nearly naked sisters from the four riders who emerged from the woods.

"Whadda we got here, boys?"

The first man through the trees walked his horse up to within a foot of Naomi. He pushed his hat back and grinned nastily, glanced at Faith, then returned to Naomi.

"Name's Frank Deckom."

Belle took it back. There *was* a difference between being rescued or captured.

Deckom surveyed the scene with a keen, acquiring eye, and when it landed on her, still sitting on the ground, his lips twitched with a not-nice smile that sent a chill to her bones.

She wrapped her arms around her knees.

"How do, ma'am." He actually leered. In a melodramatic play, it would have been comical. "That there is my brother Cole, my other brother Jessop, and our cousin, Red John."

Menacing attitudes aside, the brothers were bland-looking, everything about them the color of dirt: brown clothes, hair, horses. The cousin, Red John, lived up to his name, sporting flame-red hair. He rode a beautiful Appaloosa, light gray with black spots.

The poor horses, including the Appaloosa, were very ill groomed—as were the men, for that matter. They were nervous, tense. Like they hadn't eaten in a week and had just come upon four fresh hot cherry pies. Belle glanced over her shoulder. Maybe the river would have been safer after all.

"What's happened, ladies? You look plumb done in." Pleasant words said with a dark undertone. "Did Break Heart Bend earn its name again today?"

Break Heart Bend. Yes, that was the name for it.

"Yes, Mr. Deckom, I suppose it did." Naomi replied calmly, conversationally, as if they'd met strolling through Central Park and required directions to the main gate. "Sir, can you tell us how far it is to Clementine?"

"Clementine!" Deckom dismounted, and the others eased their horses closer. "Why, you're in the wrong neck of the woods, ma'am. Clementine is forty, fifty miles the other side of Greeley."

"Oh dear."

How could that be? Had Mr. McKinnon been given the wrong directions?

"That musta been some disaster to leave you ladies half-nekkid," Jessop said.

"You all better come along with us." Red John spat out a laugh. He fixed on Charity. "I wager Big Mama'll dress you up real pretty. Right, Frank?"

"Anything left over there?" Deckom ignored Red John and nodded at the treasure chest on the raft.

So that was it. These men were bandits. Belle had read of the exploits of outlaws in the Boston newspapers. The tales had always seemed far-fetched, the villains comically overdrawn. Now she wasn't so sure.

She *was* sure she didn't want to be dressed up by anybody named Big Mama. The image of the tall woman standing on the boulder and mocking the McKinnon boys came to mind.

As she shuddered at the thought, a glint

of metal flashed in her eyes. Charity had Luke's knife gripped behind her back, much good it would do.

"Leave us alone!" Luke cried out.

"Luke, no. Come to me." Belle forgot her state of undress and jumped up to pull her little brother into her arms. He wanted to be a hero and defend his sisters, but he was only eleven. She doubted these men had any respect for women or children, either one.

"Don't worry, darlin'." The leader came over to her, grinning. He smelled of sweat and tobacco and cheap liquor. "Frank Deckom isn't going to let one thing harm a hair on your pretty head. And you *are* a looker."

He shoved Luke away and ran a finger over her jaw. She thought she'd lose the apple slices and jerky churning in her stomach.

"They're all lookers, Frank." Red John dismounted, eyes still on Charity. "Every one of 'em, I'd say. It'd be a shame to let Big Mama have 'em."

"Your powers of observation are astounding, cousin." Deckom grinned. "I do believe the Lord has heard our prayers and brought the brides we've longed for."

Instinctively, Belle ran, but Deckom grabbed her wrist and pulled her against his chest. He put his hand behind her neck and crashed his lips against her cheek, barely missing her mouth. Disgusting!

She twisted and pushed. Adrenaline made her strong, but he was stronger. She could barely breathe, she was so afraid.

"I have gold!"

Oh Luke. No!

"Eh?" Deckom didn't let Belle go, but he paused.

Luke was holding out his hand, dangling his treasure pouch. "Gold."

"Bring it here, boy."

"Come and get it."

"Run, Luke!" She was so proud of her little brother—and terrified for him.

All the other men had dismounted now, and Cole Deckom caught Faith, hugging her from behind and laughing while Hannah screamed, "Leave her alone!" and beat her fists against his back. Jessop went after Naomi. She had a few paces on him, but he was fast. She didn't have a chance.

"This redhead will do me just fine." Red John already had hold of Charity. "We'll call our first little girl Carrots."

Luke backed away, taunting Deckom while Belle tried to dig her bare heels into the dirt. The blisters on her feet screamed as the outlaw dragged her along.

A shot rang out, and Deckom's hat flew off as the sound echoed over the water. He froze in his tracks.

"Aiee! What the—" Red John grabbed his bleeding cheek. Luke's knife had done Charity some good after all.

A second shot rang out, and now Belle saw where it had come from. Another rider came out of the woods, some distance north of where the Deckoms had appeared.

"Stand where you are, Frank Deckom." The man's voice, calm but deadly, carried an undercurrent of barely contained rage. "All you boys put your hands where we can see them."

He was so commanding even Luke raised his hands—then checked himself and put them down.

Two more riders appeared behind the man with the rifle, and then two more. All appeared to have bathed recently. Their horses were groomed. They wore looks of concern rather than predation. Definitely the rescuing kind, not the capturing kind. There was nothing menacing about them.

No. Belle had to take that back too— regarding the leader, at least. The man with the rifle was fixed on Frank Deckom, and there was murder in his gaze.

He clucked at his horse, a lovely buckskin quarter horse with a black mane and tail. She brought him forward at a steady pace while he kept his long gun trained on Frank Deckom. The mare's complete trust in her rider put Belle's fears to rest.

All would be well. This man would keep her family safe.

"You got no business here, Fontana," Cole Deckom said. "This ain't inside town limits."

A metallic click sounded over by one of the outlaws. "You might want to shut your mouth and do what the man says."

Faith!

Belle's sister had a six-gun in her hand, pointed right at Cole Deckom's heart.

"How'd you—" Cole grasped at his empty holster. "Why you—"

"I *will* shoot you." Faith stared at him, cold with rage.

Belle believed her. What a wonderous sight! But this Faith was as a stranger to her.

Faith moved her aim from Cole's heart to his face. "*According to mine anger and according to my fury; and they shall know my vengeance, saith the Lord God.*"

"Aw, wait a minute now, darlin'. I didn't mean nothing by it."

She closed one eye and cocked the

hammer.

"All right. All right." Cole's hands shot up and he stepped back, chuckling. "I surrender."

"Teddy, would you kindly relieve these weasels of their firearms?" Fontana kept his eyes on Frank. "Jonathan, keep them in your sights."

One of their rescuers dismounted. The kind-looking, middle-aged gentleman wore blued-steel spectacles and boasted impressive unruly muttonchop whiskers. He cheerfully disarmed Jessop, then moved toward Red John.

"Aw, come on." Frank Deckom was careful to keep his hands in the air. He'd gone from vicious animal to complaining child. "We need our guns."

"You should have thought of that before you attacked a pack of defenseless women—"

"Defenseless!" the cousin cried out.

"—and a boy."

Red John's hand was covered with blood from trying to staunch the wound to his cheek.

Fontana was not impressed. "Send a man to town tomorrow to file an order to show cause why I shouldn't confiscate these weapons. *One* man. I'll forward your request on to Denver, where I am sure it will receive a speedy review."

"Denver!"

"We're a state now, Deckom. Civilized. There's procedures."

Questions peppered Belle's relief. *Fontana.* Was that a first name or last name? What town? Was it close by? Was Fontana the mayor?

She took another look at him. He appeared about thirty, and he was strikingly handsome—in a blue-eyed, dark-haired, muscular sort of way. His manner was deadly serious and made him appear dangerous, but she felt no fear of him as she had of Deckom.

Rescued, then.

She couldn't stop looking at him. Staring at him.

She wrapped her arms around herself, again aware of her half-exposed chest. And suddenly she was acutely aware how filthy she was. She must smell as bad as Frank Deckom!

Enough. There was nothing she could do about it now, and their safety wasn't yet secure. She slowly moved closer to Deckom. "Keep your hands up." Her voice gave away her fear, but she kept to her purpose and unbuckled his holster belt.

"You can do that all the day long, darlin'."

"*You* can stop running your mouth, Frank." Fontana signaled his mare forward while still training his rifle on Deckom.

Belle relieved her tormentor of the holster belt and its pair of revolvers and moved away, out of his reach.

A glint of humor tickled Fontana's eyes. "Whoa there, Queenie."

At first, Belle thought he was insulting her, but then his horse stopped and she realized Queenie must be the mare's name. He kept his rifle trained on Deckom with one hand and with his other touched the brim of a Stetson shaped much like the one Wade had worn. "Brady Fontana, ma'am."

"Belle LeClair. I'm very happy to make your acquaintance."

She couldn't be sure, but for just a second his face seemed to go blank. He turned away from her to the middle-aged man who wore spectacles. "Teddy, you have the other guns secured?"

The whiskered man eyed Faith warily. She was still holding Cole Deckom's pistol, and he didn't attempt to take it from her. "That we do."

Mr. Fontana returned his rifle to its scabbard and dismounted, removing his jacket. "Allow me to offer you this, ma'am."

"Always the gentleman," Deckom muttered.

"You and your boys get on back to the Trading Post, Frank."

The Trading Post! Belle exchanged an appalled look with Naomi. These animals had come from that place. Thank heavens Mr. Fontana and his men had come along!

Her stomach fluttered at the thought of him draping his coat over her shoulders, but he just handed it to her, arm held out straight as if to keep as far from her as possible. She sighed, secretly embarrassed and feeling a bit ridiculous.

They say intimacy is the sweetest delight of a good marriage, and despite the brief and long-distance nature of Belle's union, there had actually been moments of tender closeness expressed in different ways. All a man's secret hopes and fears poured into his letters. Simple kindnesses, like ensuring there's honey for your tea when he knows you prefer it to sugar. Leaving a vase bursting with flowers by your bedside, blooms he picked for you himself. Tenderly wrapping his jacket around your shoulders when leaving a ball and finding the night unexpectedly cold.

As Brady Fontana impersonally handed

her his coat, Belle realized how lonely her world had become, stripped of her husband's loving care. She didn't know this man, but his coldness cut her like a knife and made her feel Wade's absence sorely. She covered herself with the jacket—and then suddenly froze as he stepped away.

Pinned to Brady Fontana's shirt was the unmistakable tin star of a man of the law.

Chapter 8

Abigail Vanderhouten considered the stock on the storeroom shelves of her shop on Main Street.

"Jane, what do you think?" she called out to the front. "I need something for the Miss Steeles."

Last night five—*count 'em, five!*—single sisters had arrived in town, orphaned on the rapids of Break Heart Bend and heroically rescued from the Deckoms by Sheriff Fontana. What a stirring scenario!

Abigail's romantic heart had leaped to pair the sheriff with one of the distressed damsels he'd saved—but only fleetingly. It was her business to know these things: where romance was concerned, there was no hope for Brady Fontana.

Not yet.

Besides, Abigail had a much bigger fish in mind.

"Will the four-buttons do?" The young ladies would need mourning, and it was impossible to possess too many gloves. *Please let them be of good character.*

"You'd think it was Christmas." Jane stood in the archway that led to the showroom, smiling wickedly. "Five potential brides, right here in Break Heart."

It did feel like Christmas, though Abigail was loath to say so. It was tricky running a respectable mail-order bride service, and she couldn't help salivating a little over this apparent bonanza that had fallen into her lap.

"In tragedy lies opportunity. Didn't the Bard, or someone, say that?"

"You realize they're in mourning."

"That should prove no barrier. They're in desperate straits, from what I hear. Marriage could be their salvation."

"If you say so." Jane used the stepladder to get to the boxes on the top shelves.

Now *there* was a tragedy of spinsterhood. Jane Stedman was young, fit, fashionable, and extremely good-looking—a lovely prize for any man, if only she wasn't so... strange.

Abigail blinked when she noticed the wooden handle sticking out of Jane's apron pocket. She moved to the other side of the worktable, though it was foolish being spooked by a mere child's toy. Of course she didn't believe in hexes or magic of any variety. And yet she couldn't forget what she'd seen. With her own eyes, she'd witnessed the weird little drum's effect, and she didn't want anywhere near that thing. Just in case.

What an enigma her assistant was. Two years ago when Jane arrived in Break Heart, traumatized and alone in the world, it had seemed an act of Christian kindness to offer her a room at the back of the store—if only to save her from Delilah Montgomery's clutches. Jane was strikingly handsome, well-spoken when she cared to speak, and very elegant. She would easily find a husband through Vanderhouten Brides, Abigail's mail-order bride business.

But Jane wasn't interested in marriage, and not even Abigail's sincere religious sentiment would have allowed her to hire Jane had she known then what the whole town learned later.

As it turned out, Jane was an extraordinary seamstress. Even magical, dare

Abigail say that word. If Jane Stedman had been a man, she could have held herself out as a tailor. The modiste business had doubled and doubled again soon after her arrival. Above all things, Abigail was a practical woman.

She learned to live with her dread.

"You must know I'm thinking of one of them for Mr. Morgan."

Preston Morgan, the wealthy owner of the Morning Star Ranch about fifty miles northwest of Break Heart, was in desperate need of a wife, but he would never put his name in Abigail's book. If he'd only say the word, she'd bypass the book and broker the match personally. He might do it too, if only she could find just the right bride for him.

"That poor man," Jane said. "If Mr. Morgan wanted another wife, by now he'd have her."

Abigail also learned to live with Jane's insistence on being treated as an equal, though it was very hard. What good was having an employee if she couldn't feel the pleasure of being the big bug in her own small domain? There was no end to Jane's opinions and suggestions—most of them spot on.

But *not* when it came to the owner of Morning Star Ranch.

"Victory doesn't come from wishing. I refuse to give up on Mr. Morgan. One day he'll thank me, you'll see. As the esteemed author tells us, it's universally known that a single man with a fortune needs a wife."

Jane frowned. She probably knew the real quote down to the exact word. Once again Abigail felt like an imposter—which she was, of course. But only one person in this town knew the real truth about Abigail Vanderhouten, and it wasn't Jane Stedman.

All Jane said was, "This year's letter already went out."

Every spring, Abigail wrote a personal letter to Mr. Morgan to remind him of everything he was missing and that she could supply a kind and upright lady to provide a mother's love to his two children and a wife's consolation to himself.

"No matter," she said. "Providence brought the Steele girls to Break Heart. As we speak, five single ladies are stranded at the Lilac Hotel with no guardian and no prospects. I mean to find husbands for them all. At least one must suit Mr. Morgan."

"Try these then." Jane held up a two-button fingerless lace glove. "We have five pairs in stock, all black."

"Very pretty. Very smart. But no." Abigail

shook her head. "They're extras from Ophelia's wake last week." A wake that had been an excuse for a wild night of drunken debauchery that was an embarrassment to the town.

"So?" Jane said. "Something pretty and smart will lift their spirits."

"But hardly appropriate for chaste females in mourning. We don't want the Miss Steeles to think we're uncivilized."

Abigail selected a more suitable style, the four-button black woolens, and took them out front to wrap in bright pink paper. "I'll be gone from the shop for a while."

"Happy prospecting," Jane said drily.

"Wish me luck."

"I always do."

Abigail stepped out onto Main Street, where her neighbor was sweeping the boardwalk in front of the place next door. She sighed inwardly at the dreary name, and not for the first time:

TAGGET'S GENERAL SUPPLY

She'd hinted oh so nicely that something more elegant—TAGGET'S EMPORIUM, perhaps—would be of benefit to Mae's business. Take Abigail's own establishment:

Never a Lawman

Abigail Vanderhouten, Modiste

Wasn't that lovely? The words tripped off the tongue, each one chosen with care. Last Christmas she'd even tried putting on a French accent to add to the allure—but dropped the affectation when Jane laughed at her.

Hints and suggestions were to no avail. Mae Tagget was a direct, and decidedly inelegant, sort of person in every way. EMPORIUM was beyond the reach of her imagination.

Not to say she was entirely normal. Who in this town was, when you got under their skin? Mae had her quirks.

For one, when her husband died of the same influenza that took Martha Overstreet this past winter, Mae had moved out of her lovely house on Church Lane to live above the store here. Not that Abigail minded. It was nice having her so close. But then Mae started wearing Stan's clothes. Certainly not normal.

But did Abigail say anything about it? No. God made secrets for keeping. Abigail Vanderhouten didn't ask. She didn't tell either.

"Morning." Mae yanked her broom out of the way and eyed the package in Abigail's hand. "I'll sweep your walk if you like."

"Thank you, Mae. That would be a kindness." Plain storefront and men's clothes notwithstanding, Mae Tagget was a good neighbor. "I'm off to take a little something to those poor girls Sheriff Fontana brought in last night. Black gloves, for mourning."

"Smart move. Butter 'em up."

Abigail cringed. Such a vulgar way of putting it. People didn't understand the finer points of the mail order bride business. She hadn't herself, at first. She'd stumbled into it without knowing at all what she was doing.

Like anybody, she'd read the ubiquitous newspaper advertisements for wives placed by lonely homesteaders on farms and ranches throughout the West who wanted to share their lives and labors. Not that she was ever interested for herself! But she did find the notices amusing.

One day during a final fitting, her customer was going on about a niece who was an orphan, already seventeen with no prospect of a husband in sight, and it gave Abigail an idea.

Ideas can be dangerous things.

She collected several newspapers and wrote to every man with a decent pitch, presenting them a list of questions to return answered, accompanied by twenty-five dollars, in exchange for her finding an appropriate bride. She figured if even one was fool enough to respond, she'd have twenty-five dollars and Mrs. Lucht's niece would have a husband.

They all answered. It was more money than she'd made the entire previous year.

Vanderhouten Brides was born.

She sat back, ready to collect easy money and unending gratitude. It hadn't been so straightforward. Jane was right to accuse her of prospecting. As Mae Tagget herself often said, you can't run a store without inventory! From that first flood of responses from eager would-be grooms, Abigail was always on the lookout for "appropriate" brides, the far more difficult side of the equation to solve.

And then there were gentleman like Preston Morgan of Morning Star Ranch. Eminently appropriate, but unwilling to step up to the task.

The work was more complicated—she discovered the hard way—than merely connecting any Tom, Dick, or Harry with any Ann, Beth, or Mary. More than pairing prosperous men with virtuous women. A truly successful match required something in addition to good character. A mutual compatibility in personality. A spark of recognition.

True, two sensible people who loathed each other could still make a bearable marriage. But two kindred spirits could create a lifelong bond for the ages, and that was a thing to see!

"It's a delicate matter," she told Mae now, "to convince a sensible female what a capital idea it would be to travel hundreds of miles through dangerous country to marry a total stranger."

"I reckon it'll take more than gloves this time. From what I hear, those girls were as naked as Lady Godiva when they rode up Main Street to the hotel."

"The poor dears!" Abigail could kill herself for going to bed early last night. She'd slept through the whole thing and found out about it only this morning from Jane. "You don't think Frank Deckom and his boys..."

"Oh, nothing like that. Sheriff Fontana got there in time. I heard the girls put up a good fight themselves. One of them pulled Cole Deckom's own gun on him! No, they lost their clothes to the river. It was shuck all or drown."

"Ah. Very practical."

"Our men lent 'em their coats, of course,

but the ladies' bare legs and feet were on display like a pack of tarts parading up to Sweet Dee's."

Sweet Dee's indeed. Abigail shuddered. "It's downright shocking the town allows that bawdy house to stay in operation."

"Now, now. Delilah does a lot of good hereabouts." Mae chuckled. She really was an odd duck.

Abigail wrinkled her nose at her inadequate package. Had there only been one or two girls, she could provide complete outfits from her window display, and bonnets and undergarments besides. But five? The Modiste wasn't a ready-to-wear shop. Aside from notions like stockings and gloves, everything was made to order.

She expected a shipment of stockings by train any day. Gloves would have to do for now.

Mae grew serious. "Sheriff's pretty sure the dead woman Sally found is the mother."

"You sure know a lot for a Tuesday morning."

"Saw Brady coming up from the undertaker earlier." Mae shrugged. "We chewed the fat a spell."

Abigail bid Mae good day and hurried on. There wasn't a moment to lose. The girls might decide to go back to where they came from. Or worse, a certain person might have already talked to them, promising golden apples and silver sugar plums working at the bawdy house.

Sometimes Abigail wondered if heaven had sent her to Break Heart to save the innocent from Delilah Montgomery's clutches. She picked up the pace.

Chapter 9

At the Lilac Hotel, Abigail found Charlotte Gensch at the front desk and was greeted with a knowing smile. "I reckoned you'd show up last night. I suppose you mean to procure those poor girls for Break Heart Brides."

"It's *Vanderhouten* Brides." How many times did she have to remind people? Break Heart was a terrible name for a bride business! "And I am no *procuress*. My matches are respectable."

"If you say so." Charlotte grinned and came around from behind the desk. "Lily Rose might say different."

"No need to bring that up." Abigail looked over her shoulder, as if mention of the very name was bad luck.

In the early days of Vanderhouten Brides, Lily Rose Chapin had answered an impressive listing in the bride book from a gentleman in Arizona. On the way to her new husband, Lily Rose's stagecoach was robbed just outside Kingman, the bandits' faces covered by handkerchiefs. She'd pled her case, and miraculously one of the outlaws took pity and gallantly returned her boxes and handbag and even her traveling money.

The next day when she went to the church to meet her husband-to-be, she recognized a scar over the man's eyebrow—the same scar she'd seen on the gallant bandit who'd let her go! She feigned illness, fled, and returned to Break Heart.

Abigail would never forget waking to a commotion in the middle of the night and coming downstairs to find Lily Rose banging on the front door of the shop. She'd stood there on the boardwalk, bawling out her tale loud enough to reach the angels in heaven.

"I offered to find Lily Rose another husband, no fee on either side. It's not my fault she went to work for that... for that woman."

"Nobody holds it against you."

"Nobody lets it go, either."

To Abigail's mortification, Lily Rose had

gone to work at Sweet Dee's—not upstairs, thank goodness, but tending bar. It was hard to forget the story when Lily Rose herself took such delight in telling it.

Another reason it would be such a feather in Abigail's cap to find a good wife for such an upstanding citizen as Preston Morgan.

"Have the Miss Steeles come down? I brought a little something to welcome them to town."

"That's... nice." Charlotte's attention shifted past Abigail to Sheriff Fontana, now emerging from the hotel café.

"Ladies." He must have just finished his breakfast.

Abigail's knees went a little wobbly. Funny how a mere word could be so... unsettling. Brady Fontana's voice was deeply male. It rumbled through her bones and set her nerves aflutter, and the man's guarded nature only made her want to scream at him to open up and tell more. She might be a resolute spinster on the cusp of middle age, but she was still a woman.

Not that she'd ever experienced the pleasures of marriage. She only called herself "Mrs." because it made people take her more seriously and bolstered her own self-confidence.

But confidence was the last thing she felt around Break Heart's sheriff. The man was a puzzle. Frightening and attractive in equal measure, and wound tight as a spring.

For his own good, he should be in her book, but she'd never offered. After two years, he still grieved his dead fiancée. Without asking, she knew what his answer would be and, tragically, that she'd be powerless to change it. But the day would come when Brady Fontana let love into his heart, and Abigail hoped dearly she'd be there to see it.

He looked at Charlotte. "Have the Miss Steeles come down?"

Abigail caught her breath, too surprised to believe her ears. When a man spoke of a lady he was sweet on, his voice betrayed a certain vulnerability, and something of that quality laced the sheriff's question.

Brady Fontana's interest in one of the Steeles was definitely more than professional.

"I don't expect they'll leave their rooms today," Charlotte said. "They've been through a terrible ordeal."

How disappointing. "The poor dears," Abigail said. "Something's got to be done about those Deckoms. Don't you agree, Sheriff?"

Fontana's face darkened. The Deckoms had been a blight on Break Heart in the early days. The sheriff had run them out of town soon after he'd first put on the star—with the inexplicable assistance of Jane Stedman's magical drum—but not far enough away.

The gang lived like border ruffians, having established their Trading Post upstream on the White Feather River, where they sold tobacco, liquor, and female pleasures. It was a true house of trugs, nothing like Delilah's place, which Abigail had to admit had an air of class about it.

"They're a nest of vipers," Charlotte said. "Delilah Montgomery is a veritable Florence Nightingale compared to Big Mama."

Big Mama. Abigail could loathe Delilah and still disagree. "I shudder to think of that monster getting hold of the Miss Steeles."

The sheriff's jaw worked every muscle. He tended to be protective of all Break Heart's citizens, but there was something more at work here.

"Are they pretty, do you think?" She watched his face. "The Steele girls?"

Most men answered such a question with enthusiastic yeses, no matter the objective truth. Not because they were liars or stupid but because deep down they thought it was true. Most men were more tenderhearted and willing to adore the female of the species than people gave them credit for.

Brady Fontana was not like most men. His inner workings were a mystery. But outwardly, he was utterly straightforward. *When* he gave you an answer to a question—and he often didn't—he told the truth.

"I can't rightly say." His eyes narrowed, as if he disapproved of the question. "When I saw them, they were covered in mud from head to toe. I couldn't tell you how they might clean up."

Would nothing melt that man's heart? Discombobulate that cool self-control? Break Heart's sheriff was ninety-seven percent righteous discipline and three percent barely controlled turmoil.

That three percent scared Abigail more than Jane and her drum ever would.

"Oh—here they are after all." Charlotte indicated the staircase.

"Oh... my."

Three young ladies dressed in exceptionally fine—and familiar-looking—mourning clothes descended the stairs. The first was simply lovely, Abigail's personal ideal of femininity.

Hair the color of corn silk. Eyes like

bluebells. Skin flawless. Softly rounded cheeks. A heart-shaped mouth that smiled sweetly. A figure to rival Aphrodite. Perfection. How unfair to mere mortal women when a goddess walked among them!

But no matter, so long as the goddess was among the Vanderhouten Brides.

Mr. Preston Morgan wouldn't have a chance.

Chapter 10

"Morning, Miss Naomi, Miss Charity." The sheriff was his usual model of gentlemanly manners and steely reserve, but even he softened a little when he turned to the golden-haired beauty. "Mrs. LeClair."

Mrs. LeClair! Abigail's heart sank.

Mrs.!

Confirmed by the gold band on her left hand. Oh, the angels in heaven were cruel!

"Sheriff Fontana."

The frosty tone was a surprise. What could the lady possibly have against the man who'd rescued her and her family from certain ruin and unimaginable degradation?

Perhaps Abigail had been too quick to assume sweetness and kindness must naturally accompany such physical perfection. Better, then, that Mrs. LeClair was already taken. She sighed. Something too good to be true usually wasn't.

The sheriff started to turn away, but the goddess wouldn't let him go. "Mrs. LeClair is my mother-in-law. Please call me Belle."

"Yes, ma'am."

"Ma'am?"

He swallowed, then said, "Belle."

Abigail bit her tongue, but she couldn't stop her eyes from going wide. *The sheriff has a sweet spot for Mrs. LeClair!* What a tragedy! And how utterly unsurprising. Of course the man who'd sworn off women would entertain thoughts of one he could never have.

Inwardly, she tsked. *Men!*

But still, how very interesting. Brady Fontana was the one man every single lady in town sighed over—and not a few of the married ones—while he refused to leave the fortress he'd built around his heart. This was the first Abigail ever saw him smile at a woman fondly.

She looked to Charlotte for confirmation, but her friend appeared oblivious to the whole thing. Abigail sighed again. No one understood these things the way she did.

"Criminy, I'm ravenous!" The words rang

out over a great galumphing sound, and a fourth girl came clomping down the stairs. Already smiling, her blue eyes—so dark you might think they were purple—brightened further when she spotted Charlotte. "Good morning, Mrs. Gensch. The maid said your hotel has a café—and I can smell the coffee even now. Heaven!"

Charlotte beamed, Sheriff Fontana's eyebrows twitched, and Abigail felt her own lips pinch involuntarily at the thought of calling the Lilac's coffee *heaven*.

The young ladies moved on through the lobby.

Overall, Abigail was pleased. Her first impression was of gentle spirits, hopefulness, curiosity, and underlying goodness. Her heart went out to them all. Even cool Mrs. LeClair must be made allowance for. She too had lost her parents to Break Heart Bend.

Abigail's designs on the Miss Steeles had been entirely mercenary, but now that she'd seen them, she felt a strong desire to set them up with good men who would truly deserve them.

They were greeted at the café entrance by the head waitress, Trudy, Vanderhouten Brides's latest triumph. As the ladies started to follow her, Sally Overstreet rushed in from the street and ran to Mrs. LeClair, yanking on her skirt to pull her aside. The two spoke briefly, then Sally nodded and ran off again, and Mrs. LeClair disappeared inside the café.

The lobby felt suddenly very empty.

"Brady, didn't you wish to speak to the Steeles?" Charlotte asked.

"It can wait. No point ruining their breakfast." With that, the sheriff left the hotel.

"Now, Charlotte." Abigail got down to business. "Tell me everything you know."

"I see that hungry look. Now that I think about it, I shouldn't let you in my hotel, the way you rob me of my workers."

"Charlotte Gensch, you don't fool me. You're as happy as I am to see Trudy find a good husband."

Charlotte was teasing. No one would argue being a cook or waitress was a better life than having your own home, a husband to love and care for, and the joy of your own children. At least, no one with any sense.

And Charlotte was a model of good sense. "The redhead is Charity, and the oldest—the serious one with dark brown hair—is Naomi. And then Mrs. LeClair, of course."

"Just my luck the real beauty is married. Will Mr. LeClair be joining them?"

"There's no Mr. LeClair. Belle's a widow."

"How wonderful!" The angels could be kind too.

"Abigail Vanderhouten, that's a terrible thing to say."

"Oh, you know what I mean."

It was sad—of course it was sad!—but people died all the time. From disease, by misadventure, encountering roving outlaws ready to murder a stagecoach full of travelers for their luggage.

Survivors must choose: go mad brooding over all the death in this world, or get on with the business of living—always made sweeter when love was in the mix.

Abigail moved to the entrance for another look. In her experience, there were two kinds of widows, those eager to marry again and those with nothing good to say about the institution. Mrs. LeClair didn't carry herself as a woman ill-served by marriage. Mr. Morgan would definitely be getting a second letter this year.

And if he still wasn't interested, maybe cool Belle LeClair was the one to finally melt the block of ice encrusted upon the sheriff's heart.

Abigail could dream. If she was one thing, she was a romantic.

"And the raven-haired clodhopper with the freckles and violet eyes?"

"That's Faith." Charlotte chuckled. "Teddy says she's quite handy with a Peacemaker."

"Jane mentioned something about that." There was nothing wrong with being *quite handy* with firearms. Faith Steele would appeal to a man just getting started, one who cared more for a practical wife than an ornamental one.

"She took Cole Deckom's six-shooter off him without pulling a thread."

"Goodness."

"Impressive. Still, I shudder to think what might have happened if our men didn't show up when they did."

"I thought there were five ladies."

"I suppose Hannah is still upstairs with the brother, but never mind her. She's not old enough to interest you."

"They have a man among them?" Darn. That could be a problem. Brothers often felt responsible for sisters. Believed they knew what was best.

"Luke is eleven."

"I am relieved to hear it. Now one last thing, Charlotte. Do explain how they came by those outfits."

Abigail had recognized the girls' mourning clothes immediately, for she and Jane had made them. Mostly Jane, if she were honest.

"Thought you'd notice." Charlotte chuckled. "Delilah and Lily Rose brought the dresses over last night, along with a passel of unmentionables and boots and slippers to try on. They even had things for the boy."

"How generous." Abigail looked down at her sad little package. At least the girls hadn't been wearing gloves.

"Don't pout," Charlotte said. "You know Delilah loves to make a show of being a benefactress. And her girls only wore the dresses once, for the wake."

Ophelia's wake. And to think Abigail had rejected those lovely lace gloves for the Steeles because they were associated with the bawdy house—and that wake.

Such an extravagance. Delilah had loved that horse, and when it died last month she'd paid for a funeral and a musical parade up Main Street and made all her girls wear black. A ridiculous, outrageous display. But Abigail had accepted the commissions for the mourning clothes—though it went against the grain to give Delilah the satisfaction.

"Don't worry about Delilah either,"

Charlotte continued. "She won't be getting her hooks into the Steeles. They're good girls. Teddy says their father was a sexton, and their uncle back in Minnesota is a minister."

"That explains their excellent deportment." Abigail had been observing the Steele girls talking to Trudy. You could tell a lot by the way someone treated maids and waitresses. "Not so elegant as to give off airs, but refined enough to be welcome at the best tables in town."

"Do we have those?" Charlotte laughed.

Abigail kept her counsel about Mr. Morgan. Technically, his table was nowhere near town. Though she had never seen it—nor the man himself, for that matter—it qualified as the best table in the county by dint of his reputation alone.

And wouldn't the lovely Mrs. LeClair improve the standing of any table? If the cattle baron of Morning Star Ranch couldn't be stirred by this exquisite exemplar of femininity, then he must be made of the same ice that bound Brady Fontana. What were the odds of that?

Yes, Abigail was quite pleased. Each of the Miss Steeles would do quite nicely for some lucky fellow. Even the galumpher.

True, Charity Steele's hair was the

unfortunate color of a copper kettle. Now, some gentlemen were partial to red hair, believing it signified an independent nature, but most found it off-putting for the same reason.

However, Charity was very pretty, and there was a mischievous glint in her blue-green eyes that even her current sorrows hadn't vanquished. It bespoke an undaunted spirit that required a worthy lover. And though Abigail loved the moneymaking aspect of her business, she loved the challenge of making a good match even better.

Faith made her chuckle inside. The girl was all angles and a bundle of nervous energy, but with her raven-black hair and spattering of freckles beneath those bright eyes, she too was very pretty—when she stopped moving long enough to get a fix on her. She would give some young fellow a delightful run for his money.

"Naomi would make the best wife, I think."

Why would Charlotte say that? Abigail gave the oldest girl another look. She looked to be past twenty-five and unremarkable, even a little dowdy. "The best wife, maybe. Not the most appealing bride."

"Black isn't her color. A cheerful calico print will brighten her up nicely."

"I see you've chosen *your* favorite."

Charlotte was a good judge of character. She might be on to something, so Abigail looked again. Most men wanted blushing brides, pretty young things to flatter their egos and make them feel young and powerful. But wise men knew beauty fades. They cared more for kindness, resilience, and the willingness to take on the hard work necessary to make a good life in the West.

Everything Abigail knew of Preston Morgan indicated he was no fool.

Perhaps... yes. Naomi Steele *could* be lovely, if she would let go of the cares life had thrown at her and find a reason to smile.

But smiling or not, Belle LeClair was simply stunning.

"Not to pry, Charlotte, but can you really afford to put them up? I heard they were left with absolutely nothing."

"Not nothing," Charlotte said. "Naomi paid a week in advance for their rooms. She was appalled at the notion of their being freeloaders."

"Commendable." No wonder Charlotte liked Naomi so well. "It bespeaks good character."

"She means to send a telegram to her uncle today and have him send the fare for the train back to Minnesota."

Time to sigh again. "Why are things never easy?"

Abigail would have to move fast, before the Steeles bought their train tickets. Something had made them believe Colorado promised a better future than Minnesota. She would show them it still did.

But not right this moment. Sheriff Fontana would return soon to speak with them, and she had a good idea why. She didn't want to introduce herself just at the moment they learned their mother's body had been discovered.

"Charlotte, would you kindly give these gloves to the Miss Steeles with my compliments?" She handed over the package. "And ask them to join me for supper tonight here at the hotel dining room. Six o'clock. My treat. I do hope dear Roxanna will be up to it."

Mrs. Abigail Vanderhouten could be a benefactress too.

Chapter 11

The town was called Break Heart. Of course it was.

Ma was dead, her body washed up from the river. Chet McKinnon had been found nearby, alive though seriously injured. He was the one to send the sheriff and his men to search for Belle and her family. Neither Belle's pa nor the rest of Chet's family had been seen.

Sheriff Fontana and his men had brought Belle and her family—what remained of it—to a hotel on the main street where they'd taken two rooms that were a luxury after this past week. As she went downstairs with Naomi, Charity, and Faith, Belle's emotions were all in a jumble.

Upstairs, Luke slept as if dead to the world. Hannah was awake but fitful, unwilling to come out of her room. She'd barely spoken a word since their rescue, and Belle and the others had decided they'd best not push their fragile little sister.

Her heart skipped a beat. Sheriff Fontana was in the lobby, talking with one of the hotel's owners and another woman. Their eyes met, and her first thought was that he was as handsome as she remembered. Then he looked away.

What did she expect? The man showed her yesterday what he thought of her, and now she tried to show him the same disinterest, babbling something foolish about Mrs. LeClair. Anyway, she had no business having any kind of feelings about any man, lawman or not. Wade hadn't been dead a month.

She headed to the café with her sisters, and as a waitress met them at the entrance, a little girl rushed in from the street and grabbed Belle by the skirt to pull her aside.

"Are you Belle?" the girl said breathlessly. "He said you were the pretty one with the golden hair."

"He?"

"Mr. McKinnon. The man from the river."

"Ah."

"He wants to see you."

"All right." Belle was secretly ashamed of herself—she hadn't given Chet a second thought, and the poor man had lost everyone. "Tell Mr. McKinnon I'll be there soon, in about an hour."

She found the others in the busy café, where the customers' relaxed chatter blended with the clinking and tinkling of utensils, a scene so cheerful and lacking in peril that it lifted her spirits. The place was clean and pleasant—although she gasped at the sight of a gigantic ram's head with dramatically curved horns mounted high on one wall.

She wasn't in Boston anymore. This strange new world was strange indeed. But though it hadn't even been a full twenty-four hours, she knew she liked it here. The hotel staff were hard-working, efficient, and friendly, willing to chat at the drop of a hat about anything under the sun. Boston's oppressive adherence to propriety and class divisions was indeed a world away.

There seemed no distinction between people here. And while the men tipped their hats and smiled at Belle and her sisters as men do everywhere, the women of Break Heart seemed quite different to those Belle had known in Mrs. LeClair's circle or in Minnesota.

Mrs. Montgomery and Lily Rose, Mrs. Gensch, and even Trudy, their waitress, carried themselves with the independent self-confidence Belle had seen in the ladies of the New England Women's Club, to which she had dearly wished to apply, and of which Mrs. LeClair had heartily disapproved.

There was excitement in the air. With each breath, Belle drew more optimism into her lungs. A sense of all things being possible, if only you were strong enough, brave enough, and willing to reach out, grab your future, and hold on for the ride. This was the allure of the West.

It was intoxicating.

It wasn't just this country that was different. *Belle* felt different. She might brave anything here.

Outside, a passing wagon rolled by, revealing the sheriff's office across the street. A warm feeling washed over her, and she didn't fight it. It was only natural to feel gratitude toward the man who'd saved her and her family from an unspeakable fate.

Never mind how the musky scent of his coat had made her feel cared for and safe. Or how she'd been so terribly disappointed when he lifted her up onto Mr. Overstreet's horse instead of his own for the ride to town.

But still. None of that changed the fact Brady Fontana was the sheriff of this town. By the very nature of his job, he could be dead tomorrow. She hardly knew him—that's how she meant to keep it.

And he obviously intended the same.

He'd left the hotel, but even now, against her will, he was in her thoughts. It had been a pleasant surprise to see him so soon after yesterday, but for the life of her she couldn't say why. It couldn't be his smile, because he didn't smile. It couldn't be his friendliness, because he was curt and stoic. It couldn't be his flattery, because nothing of the sort crossed his lips.

But she couldn't deny Brady Fontana made her light up inside when she saw him and fade again when he went away. In a world constantly shifting around her, he felt as steady as a rock.

She shuddered to remember the disgusting men they'd escaped. Belle was no Greek hero, but she'd passed through the Scylla and Charybdis of river rapids on the one side and outlaws on the other and was still far from journey's end—and in worse straits than Odysseus, for she had no Ithaca to return to.

In running away from Boston, she had once again acted in haste and must face the consequences. It was one thing to get away from Mrs. LeClair, but now she had to figure out how she was going to actually support herself, let alone scrape up an extra twenty dollars to send to her mother-in-law.

"That Peacemaker had a fine feel to it." Faith was watching the jail too, and there was something like longing in her eyes. With a shock, Belle wondered if her sister had been equally moved by the sheriff.

"I wish you would stop thinking about that pistol," Naomi said. "It's unladylike."

"Oh Naomi, no." Belle hadn't escaped Mrs. LeClair merely to encounter her embodiment in the person of her own sister. "Let Faith be. In New York society, it's considered the height of femininity to be an excellent archer. You never know. The West's equivalent might be target shooting with a six-gun."

"Thank you, Belle." Faith smiled broadly.

Naomi blew out a sigh, the signal she'd given in. "After we eat, I'll find the Western Union office," she said. "We should let Uncle James know what happened."

Belle's stomach clenched at the mention

of their uncle's name. The sooner Naomi wrote to him, the sooner he'd want them to come home. "Wouldn't a letter be less dear?"

Then she remembered the reason they could afford to stay at this hotel, and her anger at Naomi came flooding back.

When the rescue party brought them here last night, Luke had again offered up his treasure, this time to pay for their accommodations. That's when Naomi revealed she'd been wearing her petticoat with coins sewn into the hem all along. Charity had given her a mighty tongue-lashing, and well deserved.

Naomi would have drowned if she'd fallen in the river!

On the other hand they'd now be penniless in a strange country if she hadn't worn that petticoat. It was confusing to be so furious with someone yet so relieved by the very thing that aroused your fury.

"I mean to ask our uncle to wire us the train fare home," Naomi said.

Oh... Disappointment flooded Belle to her bones, followed by panic. *I can no more go back to Minnesota than I could to Boston.*

"He won't like that," Faith said.

No, he wouldn't. Their uncle, James Steele, was a penny-pincher in the extreme.

"Train fare for five?" Belle said. "Plus the prospect of five more mouths to feed? He'll be aghast."

"Don't kid yourself. He'll love it," Charity said drily. "He'll feed on it for years, lord it over us that Pa never should have left and aren't we grateful to be dependent on his goodness."

"True." Naomi's lip curled ever so slightly. "He'll preach a sermon on recklessness our first Sunday back."

"Would to God ye could bear with me a little in my folly." Faith grinned.

"Here we are." Trudy set a tray of mugs, milk, sugar, and a coffeepot on the table, distributed the cups, and filled them in a whirlwind of activity, all to a purpose, a big smile on her face despite being overwhelmed with customers.

As she poured out the hot coffee, she recommended the scrambled eggs, hotcakes, and ham steak. "Roxanna does her best." She sounded apologetic. "But you can't go wrong with the simple fare."

Start simple, build on that had been Dottie's maxim. She would thrive, working in a place like this.

Trudy left to put in the order, and Belle asked Naomi, "How long do you think we can stay here on... on what we have?" No point in saying *on what you nearly killed yourself over.*

"I'm not sure." Naomi chewed on her lip. "Maybe a week? If we don't eat much."

A week! Belle's heart sank. She'd hated her mother-in-law so relentlessly trying to control her life, but she couldn't stomach returning to Uncle James's constant sermonizing, in and out of his pulpit.

Or the locusts. Or the poverty.

If she was honest with herself, she'd married Wade *in part* to get away from Minnesota. She loved her family but had never seen any future for herself there.

Evangeline would be happy to have her in New York, but that would be exchanging one woman's charity for another's. Evie was the most fun and generous person Belle had ever met, and though she couldn't bear being dependent on anybody ever again, the best place for her might be with her friend—at least temporarily.

"Great thunder on the mountain!" Charity choked out as she set her mug down with a *thunk.*

Belle took a sip of her own coffee, then tried not to retch as she reached for the milk.

"Good morning, girls." Mrs. Gensch appeared at their table. "How is every little thing?"

"Just peachy!" Charity pasted a smile on her face, and Belle and the others followed suit. The Gensches had been very kind to them, and no one wanted to hurt her feelings.

But good grief, this coffee was bad.

"I hope you're rested and ready for the world." It was hard to credit that this lady was Ma's age. She seemed a decade younger, so full of vigor. She handed Naomi a package wrapped in pink paper. "A gift from Mrs. Abigail Vanderhouten."

"How kind," Naomi said. "But who is Mrs. Vanderhouten, and why would she think of us?"

"For I was an hungred, and ye gave me meat: I was thirsty, and ye gave me drink: I was a stranger, and ye took me in."

"Don't mind Faith. That's her way." Charity rolled her eyes. "A verse for every occasion."

Faith shrugged. "It's a habit."

"There are worse habits, my dear." Mrs. Gensch patted Faith's shoulder. "Mrs. Vanderhouten was in the lobby when you girls came through earlier. I meant to introduce you, but she had to go. She owns the dressmaker's shop on Main Street. In fact, she made the mourning clothes you're wearing, and she thought you might also need gloves."

Last night two ladies from the town had come to the hotel with a provision of nightclothes, undergarments, shoes, and the mourning clothes they were now wearing, but Belle hadn't heard that name mentioned.

"That was awfully thoughtful," Charity said. "My hands are cut up after all that grabbing at rocks and splintered logs."

Belle sympathized. Her hands weren't in as bad shape as Charity's, but she was terribly bruised and battered all over. This morning she could barely move when she tried to get out of bed. A long soak in a hot bath last night had helped, and she'd love another one today.

"Please thank Mrs. Vanderhouten for us," Naomi said.

"You can yourself tonight. You're all invited to be Abigail's guests for supper, here in the dining room. She means to convince you to stay in Break Heart."

"If only that could be." Naomi smiled wistfully, as if Mrs. Gensch had suggested they fly to the moon on gryphon's wings.

Mrs. Gensch chuckled and said something about Mrs. Vanderhouten's powers of persuasion, then moved on to her other guests, leaving the sisters to ponder their next moves.

It was a relief to know they'd have dinner paid for tonight. But more than that, if this Mrs. Vanderhouten wanted them to stay, it must be for a reason. Maybe she had something in mind that would make it possible.

The table had gone quiet. Faith was staring out the window, absently tapping her cheek with one finger, and Charity and Naomi seemed lost in thought.

Naomi looked up. "We have to go back, don't we? There is nothing for us here. We have no real money, no clothes, no friends, no protector. Ma and Pa are... are gone." Tears welled in her eyes, and Belle realized all her sisters felt the same way about going back to Minnesota.

"What about homesteading?" she squeezed Naomi's arm. "Chet McKinnon told me you only have to be twenty-one and a citizen, male or female, to stake a claim. We can still do it."

"Can we improve the land and pay the fees?" Naomi said. "All our money for seed and stock and tools and materials to build a shelter is gone. We have nothing."

She was right. Dismay clamped down on Belle's heart. These past months, she'd lived in relative luxury, but she'd missed her sisters so much. She wouldn't part from them again if she could help it.

"I can't go back to Mrs. LeClair," she said. "And Uncle James? How can you think of living under his roof? The man's a bully." Belle had had enough of bullies.

"He is," Charity said. "How did Pa turn out so gentle and good?"

"Pa's a—*was* a dreamer," Naomi said. "Uncle James is a realist."

Faith scoffed. "Pa spent all his time in Ecclesiastes and the Song of Solomon. Uncle James prefers Timothy and the Apocalypse of John." Still gazing at the sheriff's office across the street, she added, "I would rather not live under Uncle James's... thumb."

"*I* would rather stay here in Break Heart." Charity picked up her coffee, wrinkled her nose, and put the cup down again.

"I don't disagree. I just don't see how." Naomi placidly sipped her own coffee. She had a marvelous power to accept things as they were.

Their food came, and as they ate, the sentiment at the table was palpable. Could they possibly stay? Everyone here had been very kind, and kindness was such a healing thing. It renewed Belle's faith in people. Made

her think one day, very far in the future, she
might be happy again.

Of course that had nothing to do with
Brady Fontana's steadying presence, or the
way she had felt so safe when he was near. He
was a sheriff. An officer of the law. At any
moment, word could echo through the streets
that he'd been shot in the back by the relative
of someone he'd arrested or killed while
raiding the hideout of an outlaw gang or
ambushed while protecting payroll money on
the train from Denver.

Okay, maybe Belle had read too many
adventure stories.

But Wade's murder wasn't a story, and
Break Heart's sheriff had living, breathing
enemies. That awful Frank Deckom, for
instance, obviously had it in for him. One of
those two might survive the other, but she
didn't see both living to a ripe old age. The
very vital Brady Fontana, whose gaze was
fierce with heat, could be lying cold in the
grave next week, next month, next year.

Belle considered the big-horned sheep up
on the wall. The noble-looking beast, strange
and wonderful, seemed to issue her a
challenge. Could she become as free and
independent as the Colorado women she'd
met so far?

Uncle James was a proud and vindictive man who wouldn't offer a place in his household twice. There would be no going back. But somehow she had to do it.

It was another snap decision, but the words Belle said next came from a place deep inside, more real and more true than anything she'd ever known. She felt excited, nervous—and more than that, powerful.

"I'm staying."

Chapter 12

"I'll find a way." Belle bubbled with excitement. She didn't know how, but she was going to stay in Break Heart. "I can find employment."

"You could teach the mysterious Roxanna how to make coffee," Charity said under her breath.

"Maybe we all could," Faith ventured. "Find employment, I mean."

"If we didn't have Luke and Hannah, maybe," Naomi said. "But they're too young to be left on their own while we all go out to work."

"Hannah is fourteen," Charity said. "Maybe this Mrs. Vanderhouten who made these dresses needs an assistant seamstress."

"About Hannah," Belle said. "I'm worried. She's not herself."

"She'll be all right." Charity waved her hand. "None of those Deckoms laid a hand on her, fortunately."

"If one had, he'd be a dead man today."

"Faith!" Belle and Naomi said simultaneously.

Charity just laughed. "We were lucky to have a shootist in the family."

"I suppose Hannah could work." Naomi returned to the subject at hand. "But Luke is only eleven."

"He should be in school," Belle said more forcefully than she'd intended. She'd seen children younger than Luke put to work in Boston. Not healthy work on family farms, either, but grueling labor in factories and slaughterhouses. Dangerous, back-breaking drudgery that wore grown men down. It was a disgrace.

"Uncle James could give Luke a stable home," Naomi said, apparently thinking along the same lines.

"He could," Charity answered sharply. "And he'd raise our sweet, tenderhearted brother to be just like him."

That gave everyone pause, and Faith again turned to the window. Eyeing the sheriff's office across the street, she said, "Let's at least wait a few days before we decide. Give ourselves a chance to learn more about this town."

"Three days," Naomi agreed—much to Belle's surprise. "We should split up, two and two, and see what's here. And I need to find the telegraph office."

"I can't join you until later," Belle said. "That little girl who grabbed me in the lobby brought a message from Chet. I promised I'd visit the infirmary this morning."

"*Chet*, is it." Charity's grin reminded Belle of their conversation on the river before they hit the rapids. *Has Chet McKinnon made you an offer?*

"It isn't like that." She rolled her eyes. "One of us should let him know he's not alone in the world. We lost Ma and Pa, but we still have each other. Chet lost everyone."

"Here he comes again." Faith nodded toward the café entrance, where Sheriff Fontana stood. He removed his Stetson and headed toward them, acknowledging nods and greetings from customers along the way.

"He doesn't look happy," Charity said.

Faith grinned. "I think that's just his natural face."

"Morning again, ladies."

Belle remained perfectly calm. The sheriff didn't look at her, and she was sure it was intentional.

"I'm sorry to have to ask, but I wonder if one of you would be willing to identify the body washed ashore near where the children found Mr. McKinnon."

Naomi paled. "Children?" she said distractedly.

"Yes, ma'am. Sally and Damon Overstreet. Mr. McKinnon has already said it's your mother, but it's best to confirm this with her family. With statehood, there's more paperwork."

The sheriff flinched apologetically as he mentioned paperwork, but Belle didn't mind. Even death, she supposed, was subject to the requirements of recordkeeping. She'd been spared all that with Wade—an aspect of Mrs. LeClair's controlling personality to be glad of.

Sally Overstreet, he'd said. The girl who brought Chet's message was named Sally. She'd put Belle in mind of the street urchins of Boston. Break Heart must have no school if its children were left to run around like that.

"I must warn you, it isn't a pretty sight," the sheriff said gently.

Faith blotted her eyes with her napkin.

Handkerchiefs, Belle thought absently.

How many small, mundane items would they discover missing as time went by? This morning she'd sorely grieved her lost toothbrush and Dottie's paste. Did they sell those things in the West? She'd noticed a general store last night when they rode through the town. She'd visit it sometime today.

Naomi sat stunned, stoic as always. She was the oldest, born just before Ma turned seventeen. The two were so close that Naomi had always seemed more a second mother than an older sister.

Belle couldn't let her shoulder this burden. "I'll—"

"I'll do it." A tear ran down Charity's cheek. She covered Naomi's hand with her own. "If you take on one more thing, you're going to fall apart."

It wasn't like Charity to think of someone else, especially Naomi, whom she always took for granted—and not only as a source of extra clothes. The brush with death was changing them all.

"Charity's right, Naomi. You're worn out with worry and responsibility. Why don't you go back upstairs and get some rest?" Belle said. "I'll ask Mrs. Gensch to send breakfast up for Luke and Hannah. Uncle James can wait."

Faith stood up. "I'll go with Charity while Belle checks on Chet." She squared her shoulders and looked at the sheriff. "Let's get it over with."

Chapter 13

After seeing to Luke and Hannah's breakfast, Belle walked out of the Lilac Hotel to a day so beautiful it made her angry. How dare the world go on living and breathing when Ma and Pa never would again?

She glanced across the street where Charity was following Faith into the sheriff's office. Sheriff Fontana had said he needed to pick up a certificate for the undertaker to sign.

Suddenly Belle regretted being excluded from the others. It was like being locked out of Wade's study, though in this case she'd done it to herself. Her curiosity was piqued. What would Sheriff Fontana's office say about him? Would it reveal something of what lay behind his hard façade?

She sighed and glanced up Main Street. Chet was expecting her, though she'd given no particular hour when she'd be there. She automatically pulled out her pocket watch, forgetting it had been ruined by river water. It made her uneasy not knowing the exact time, not hearing the rhythmic *tick tick tick*.

No matter. Chet wasn't going anywhere. She crossed the street. She'd accompany Faith and Charity to the undertaker, then visit him after.

Entering the sheriff's office, she suppressed a gasp at the unruly mess, the last thing she'd expected. The sheriff dressed so fastidiously! He was at his desk, riffling through a mountain of papers. Next, he opened and closed several drawers, then looked in the pigeonholes that covered the wall behind him. When he saw Belle, his cheeks pinked.

"Mrs. LeClair." *Not Belle.* "You've decided to accompany your sisters."

"I can visit Mr. McKinnon after."

The sheriff held up his hands as if in surrender. "Ladies, I apologize for the disarray. I can't find where my former deputy put the blank forms."

Belle said nothing about the *disarray*

being an adorable contrast to his formidable self, but Faith didn't hold back.

"*Judge not according to the appearance, but judge righteous judgment.*"

Good old Faith, but the poor man! He couldn't know the Bible quote constituted friendly teasing on her part.

"Never mind. It'll turn up." He picked up his hat. "Let's get you all down to Grayson's."

The walk through town was a pleasant revelation. They'd arrived in Break Heart long after dusk, their progress illuminated by the lights of establishments still open at the late hour. The raucous saloon hadn't made a comforting impression.

Pa had always said the "Wild West" was an idea romanticized in overzealous stories meant to sell newspapers. Now, in the light of the new day, Belle suspected he'd been right all along.

Despite its name, Break Heart was a pretty little town and more developed than she'd expected. They passed a newspaper office, and she made a mental note to stop by on her return to inquire whether they had a telegraph. Not that she particularly wished to contact her uncle, but it would save Naomi some legwork.

In addition to the newspaper, saloon,

hotel, and sheriff's office, Main Street boasted a general store, a dress shop—ABIGAIL VANDERHOUTEN, MODISTE—livery stables, and more. Finding employment here began to seem not completely irrational.

In front of the dress shop, a short man leaned on a broom, conversing with a young woman with extremely pale skin and dark chestnut curls half-hidden under a Neapolitan bonnet with an effusion of purple, black, and white ostrich feathers. This wasn't Mrs. Vanderhouten—whom Belle had glimpsed at the hotel—but her day dress was as elegantly tailored as anything from New York. She must be a customer.

"I think that man with the broom is a woman," Charity whispered.

On a closer look, Belle agreed. Break Heart was becoming more interesting by the minute. She considered going over to introduce herself, but Charity linked arms with her and pulled her onward.

They passed a shoemaker's small shop and came to GRAYSON'S HOUSEHOLD FURNITURE at the end of Main Street. In one window a sign read:

CHAMBER SETS ~ PARLOR SETS
ROSEWOOD AND WALNUT ROCKING CHAIRS

Never a Lawman

And in another:

UNDERTAKER ~ METALLIC CASKETS
ROSEWOOD AND WALNUT COFFINS

Sheriff Fontana showed them the way to a back entrance where the undertaking portion of the business was conducted. Mr. Grayson was waiting for them, and he got right to the point.

"The gravedigger should be finished by noon."

"Gravedigger?" Charity said.

The awful smell of death hung in the air, and Belle became acutely aware of the body on a raised table near the back wall, laid out in a clean, pretty cotton dress.

This was a mistake.

"We didn't expect to find family." Sheriff Fontana spoke softly and kindly, but with no less strength. He'd be someone to lean on, if he weren't so cold. "I chose an agreeable place for her in the churchyard near a wild plum tree in full blossom."

"She ought to be in the ground today." Would the undertaker be so efficient and businesslike if someone he loved were lying on that table? "But I do have formaldehyde on hand if you'd rather send her home."

"No!" Belle hadn't meant to speak so

loudly, but the mere mention of the stuff sickened her.

"Belle's right," Charity said. "We should bury Ma here in Break Heart. Then when we find Pa, they can rest in peace together."

Belle looked to Faith. She seemed diminished, shrunk into herself, and her silence was terrible. She offered nothing from scripture and refused to step any closer to the body.

For Naomi's sake, Belle felt she should do something. Kiss their mother goodbye. But instead of moving forward, her feet stepped back, seemingly of their own volition.

She couldn't do it.

It was Charity who rose to the occasion. She went to the body. "It's Ma. But... it isn't."

Belle felt the walls closing in. She couldn't breathe, couldn't stay.

She fled.

Outside she came to a small garden and took a seat on a wrought iron bench under a trellis bearing red and white roses. She faced a simple stone altar which contained a vase of fresh-cut lilies and a hurricane lamp with a candle burning inside. The altar was carved with scripture:

PRECIOUS IN THE SIGHT OF THE LORD

IS THE DEATH OF HIS SAINTS

"Oh Ma." Belle buried her face in her hands and let the tears flow.

Someone sat down on the bench beside her and gently laid a clean handkerchief over her knee. She knew who it was, but she refused to stop crying or pay him any mind. His presence was a comfort, actually. If she didn't look at him or speak, maybe that spell wouldn't break.

She dabbed her tears, blew her nose, cried a little longer, and when she was cried out she sat up straight. No need to be rude.

"Thank you, Sheriff. For the handkerchief, and for the rescue yesterday. For all your kindness."

"It's my duty, ma'am. Part of the job."

"I wonder." Belle scoffed. "You must be so often in danger that you no longer appreciate the risks you take."

"I assure you there wasn't much danger in searching for your family. I only wish we had reached you sooner. Before the Deckoms did."

"You knew those men?"

"I did. I do. I can banish them from the town limits, but not from the wild, sadly." He offered no more on that subject. "I'm very sorry about your parents."

"Thank you. I should have kissed my mother goodbye, but when it came to it, my courage failed me."

"It has nothing to do with courage."

"I've seen my share of the dead—nothing compared to your line of work, I'm sure—but it never affected me so strongly until my husband died."

He stilled even more, if that were possible.

"You're a widow."

He sounded surprised. But then, how would he know different? Absently, she touched the wedding band under her glove. She hadn't been wearing gloves when he found her—or this morning, before breakfast.

She nodded. "My husband was a Special Deputy US Marshal." She found herself smiling. "Like you, he grumbled over the mountains of paperwork involved. He wrote once to me that none of the job was so glamorous as the newspapers make it sound."

"To which I can daily attest."

"But then he was murdered, hardly a mundane event. In the Dakota Territory. A coward shot him in the back in a town called Deadwood."

"Ah, Deadwood. Where Hickok met a

similar fate."

"Wild Bill Hickok?" Belle looked up. "I didn't know. I... I think that makes it worse, somehow."

"I'm sorry. I shouldn't have said."

"Oh no. Please don't be. I'd rather have learned that information from you than elsewhere."

Belle wondered if she was being too familiar. This man was very easy to talk to, and it felt so good to talk about her feelings freely, without fear of judgment.

"Wade was a man of such vital force that I—well, I guess I harbored a notion he was invulnerable. When we learned he was killed, his mother insisted he be sent home to be buried. He'd been preserved with formaldehyde, and it was horrible. The body was a... a wretched *thing*, if you understand my meaning."

The sheriff nodded. "It's consoling to think they're just sleeping, waiting for us beyond the veil." His gaze was on the scripture carved on the altar, but it was like he was looking through it. "A body that's suffered a violent death doesn't cooperate with that pleasant illusion."

"No."

Did this man mourn someone in

particular? Had his heart been broken? Was there a story buried beneath all that self-control? Belle shouldn't let herself care, but she was intrigued. She wanted to know more about Sheriff Brady Fontana.

"When I saw the wretchedness of Wade's mortal remains, I knew beyond all doubt he was truly gone. Free and in heaven. Knowing that, it freed me too—from his mother, I mean."

"Sounds like a formidable woman to me."

"That's one word for it."

"Yet you left her. I'd say that took courage." He actually smiled. It was... nice. "Mr. McKinnon says you all are from Minnesota. Why was your husband in Deadwood? If you don't mind my asking."

"My family is from Minnesota. Wade was from Massachusetts. Boston, to be exact. We met when he came to my town on a special assignment for the Service."

Fontana grunted fondly. "My sister says if two people are meant to be together, fate finds a way to make it so."

"And if they're meant *not* to be, does fate find a way to separate them?"

He flinched. She'd meant herself and Wade, but her words had hurt him somehow.

She moved on. "Ironically, my husband

was never particularly interested in law enforcement. He took the position at his mother's insistence. She had political ambitions for him and saw it as a step toward his one day being appointed to the United States Senate."

"Very grand."

"Quite. Mrs. LeClair was highly ambitious regarding her eldest son. I'm afraid I didn't fit into her scheme for him." If only she'd allowed Wade to follow his heart's desire, he might be alive today. "When she learned he was to marry against her wishes, she refused to come to our wedding. I was too far beneath the family dignity, you see."

"I doubt that, Mrs. LeClair."

"Please call me Belle. In my mind, Mrs. LeClair is not a very nice person."

"I can understand that. Belle then, but I hope you'll call me Brady."

Before she could respond, her sisters and Mr. Grayson joined them. It was agreed they'd bury their mother at three o'clock. The church was at the edge of town, a twenty-minute walk from the hotel, and Mr. Grayson would deliver the coffin to the churchyard before then.

Belle felt more at ease with Sheriff Fontana and looked forward to continuing their conversation on the way back to the Lilac, but he seemed to go out of his way to avoid her. Then Faith said something about his messy office, and the two struck up an animated discussion regarding pigeonholes that lasted all the way to the hotel.

"Good day." He touched his hat to them all without quite looking at Belle and crossed the street. From the hotel veranda, she watched him pick up a sign from the bench in front of his office and disappear inside.

It shouldn't bother her, but she felt somehow cheated.

"I'm not going back to Minnesota." Faith linked her arm around Belle's waist. "No matter what Uncle James says. No matter what Naomi decides."

"Oh, Faith! I feel the same," Charity said. "But how can we stay? We've lost everything."

"I heard Mrs. Gensch say that Trudy, the waitress in the café, is leaving to be a mail order bride."

"Great thunder on the mountain, you don't mean to be a mail order bride!"

"Never." Faith laughed.

"A waitress?" To Belle that sounded worse.

"I have something in mind." Faith looked

determined. "I'll say no more until I know if it can be."

"Aren't you mysterious!" Charity said. "I don't know what I'll do. Find a job, I suppose. I know I'm never getting married." Her eyes went wide. "There. I've said it out loud."

"I can understand not wanting to marry, although I believe I would have liked it," Belle said. "But a woman must have money of her own to live decently without a husband." She thought of Evangeline in New York, an heiress, the only grandchild of a man who'd made a fortune speculating on land along the route of the Erie Canal. Evangeline had dozens of suitors, and she could afford to—and did—reject every one.

"I never thought about it," Faith said. "I always assumed I'd marry someday. I want a passel of kids. But I could never be a mail order bride and marry a stranger."

Belle said, "I wouldn't mind marrying again."

"You and Sheriff Fontana seemed to be rubbing along nicely," Charity said.

"You don't wish to marry, but you like playing the matchmaker." Faith looked away, as if she couldn't care less what Belle might say about the sheriff.

"We were only talking about Ma," Belle

said. "I don't think he likes me. Besides, I'd rather have someone who isn't going to get himself killed, thank you very much. I already told you. *If* I marry again, it won't be to a lawman."

Chapter 14

Jane Stedman was inside Tagget's, but Brady stifled the urge to retreat. After two years, it still rankled him to be near her—and the fact it did rankled him more. But he was here for a reason, and he wasn't going to let his demons drive him away.

"All right, five pounds of sugar." Mae Tagget emerged from the backroom. "I'll put it on Abigail's tab." As she set a bag on the counter, she noticed Brady. "There's himself, at last. You're out of everything, I'd imagine."

"Just about. If I had any prisoners right now, I'd have to give them Charlotte's coffee."

"We can't have that." Mae chuckled. "I'm sure our fine new state laws don't abide torture. Don't let me forget there's a letter from your sister and one from England for Mrs. Tweed. They've been sitting in the back a couple of days."

Jane fixed on Brady with the same amused look as earlier when she'd watched him escort the Steele sisters to Grayson's. Sure enough, she wasted no time in giving him grief about it.

"That was a pretty gaggle of geese you were ushering down the street earlier." The woman was on a futile mission to make him forget Thalia.

"A pleasant day to you too."

Jane Stedman was an odd thing. If a man could get past her strange demeanor, she was actually pretty—though nothing like Mrs. LeClair, who was all gentle softness and golden light. Jane was rather the opposite, solid and briskly handsome, with chestnut hair and blue eyes so dark they were nearly violet.

It was her attitude that put people off, male and female alike. If she had been a man, she would have made a terrific preacher, all fire and brimstone before the final judgment. She seemed to enjoy the heck out of the rumors she had supernatural powers.

The first time Brady saw her, he'd just stepped out of Tagget's, having come to town from the ranch for his mail. She was riding up Main Street on a bay gelding, perched behind a frail-looking young man so light and airy it seemed he might float away on a breeze.

Physically, Doc Declan and Jane Stedman were a study in contrasts, but on that day their eyes had been similarly crazed. They'd both been dressed splendidly, in what would be considered the height of fashion back East. But where Dr. Declan's clothes were relatively clean, Jane had been covered in blood from her feathered straw bonnet to her lavender kid leather boots.

Then Brady saw what their horse was dragging, and his thoughts were for nothing else. He'd raced to the travois hitched to the gelding, where lay another woman, dressed equally fine, a thin line of dried blood at her throat and a gaping, fatal wound to her abdomen.

Jane Stedman was the last soul on earth to make Brady forget Thalia Merrick. He could never see the living woman without picturing the dead one on that travois.

No one in Break Heart knew the whole story—both Doc and Jane had been too traumatized to give clear accounts—but over time some of the nongrisly details had emerged. Jane and Thalia had met on their journey west, their stagecoach had been attacked by vicious outlaws, and Dr. Declan had happened upon the aftermath, too late to save anyone.

Perhaps he'd saved Jane from herself. When he found her, she was sitting on her heels, covered in blood, a dead man on the ground before her and a blood-drenched knife in her hand. The man had been practically butchered—by Jane, from all appearances.

She never said anything to refute the story. Quite the opposite. She seemed to take peculiar delight in the stories that spread about her superhuman strength and supernatural powers and to revel in supposedly giving people the evil eye.

But with Brady she always had something to say. She seemed to think being with Thalia at the end gave her the right to speak to him however she liked.

Guess he thought so too.

He put up with it, didn't he?

"You be careful, Fontana." She wiggled her fingers mysteriously. "I see your future. One of the geese in that gaggle is going to make the heartbreak you wear on your sleeve feel like a schoolboy's puppy love."

"Button it up, Jane." He didn't believe in

superstition, and he didn't discuss his love life with anyone. "The Salem witch act doesn't hold water with me."

She lifted her chin haughtily, and he held her gaze until a glint of humor flitted through her eyes. She opened her mouth, but Mae cut her off.

"Leave the poor man alone, dear. He's here for sugar and salt, not courting advice."

"That may be, but I know what I know." Jane huffed and turned away.

"I'll take five pounds of Arbuckles', Mae—ten if it won't deplete your stock."

Brady rattled off the rest of the supplies he needed. Though Nighthawk, his ranch, was only seven miles north of Break Heart, since becoming sheriff, he'd lived in town above the office and took most meals at the Lilac Hotel. The godawful coffee there had forced him to learn to make his own, and he could also make decent beans and somewhat edible cornbread with the office stove. Sometimes a man just wanted to eat a meal in private.

He'd do it more often, if he was a better cook.

Mae made a list, and while she went to the stockroom for what wasn't on the shelves, Jane continued to give him the side-eye. He wasn't about to give her the pleasure, but if he was honest with himself, she might have a point.

One of the Steele sisters *had* sparked something he'd thought long cold. An ember. A small ember. The way McKinnon talked about her, Brady had at first assumed they were engaged. Then when he heard her full name, he figured she was married. Safe either way. Off-limits. *Mrs. LeClair*. McKinnon had said nothing of her being a widow.

Jane was still watching him knowingly.

"Don't you have some hems to sew or something?"

She just laughed. "Mrs. V is in a swoon with her book. I stay away from her when she's like that."

"I reckon that's wise."

He hadn't thought of that. Women were scarce, and the four older Steeles were prime calico—good possibilities for Abigail's mail order bride business. Lively girls and pleasant company, if what he'd seen so far held true. And all of them good-looking.

Frank Deckom and his boys had probably been sincere in their desire to make the Steele girls their brides. When it came to women, men could be desperate. And hopeful. And stupid.

Though he'd denied as much to Abigail,

Brady had noticed Mrs. LeClair's beauty right off, even covered in dried mud. But that wasn't it. There was something serene about her that had moved him, as if she carried a deep sorrow inside with admirable grace. At the time, he'd assumed it was for the loss of her parents.

He'd fought hard not to stare. Filthy or not, he'd never seen such fancy underthings. He had no idea fine ladies had such interesting layers. It was clever of her and her sisters to shuck their heavy clothes when their raft started coming apart. Probably what saved them from drowning.

Of course he'd offered her his coat for cover. What gentleman wouldn't? Then like an idiot, he'd stopped himself from helping her into it. A warning had sounded inside. Touching her would be too sweet, and too dangerous.

Seeing her again this morning, his emotions had been all over the place. Emotions he'd thought were shut down for good. When she said she was going to visit McKinnon, he'd been seized by jealousy.

Jealous of that sniveling excuse for a man!

Brady had no proof, but he had a strong feeling Chet McKinnon had been no hero in yesterday's disaster at Break Heart Bend. He acted more relieved to be alive than devastated to learn his family and friends hadn't made it.

Jealousy had dissolved into happiness when Mrs. LeClair changed her mind and joined her sisters to go to Grayson's.

Then embarrassment kicked in when she walked into his office and witnessed its messy state.

He found himself searching for a reason to invite her out to the ranch. Show her how he'd really meant to live—before his life went to the devil.

Then mortification became tender concern when she fled the undertaker. To his credit, Grayson had done a respectful job preparing Mrs. Steele's body for burial, but of course Mrs. LeClair would be repelled by the sight no matter what. Brady was grateful she'd only seen the "good" side and was spared the full extent of the damage done by the river's wrath.

Unable to stop himself, he'd followed her out to the memorial garden. So lovely, and so sad, she had indeed suffered. When she said she was a widow, it was as if the church bells had started pealing—and that had terrified him.

Even now he wanted to retreat, back

away, and lock up the gate to his heart. But it was too late. He'd accidentally let her in, and talking with Belle LeClair, or just sitting together, not talking, had eased his pain more than anything these past two years.

"Better act quick." Jane's voice pulled him from his thoughts. "Mrs. V already has plans for those girls. She's got that Mr. Morgan up at Morning Star Ranch in mind for the pretty blond one."

And all the better for her.

Relief washed over Brady. What was he thinking! He had no right to entertain notions about any woman. He didn't deserve love. If it wasn't for him, Thalia would be alive today. Being alone was his punishment, and being sheriff was his penance.

"I can give you seven pounds of the Arbuckles' now." Mae came back from the storeroom, pulling a handcart stacked with the popular one-pound bags of pre-roasted and ground coffee beans. "You can have another three when my next shipment comes in around the first of the month."

"That'd be fine. Appreciate it." Brady helped load the rest of his order onto the handcart.

"I'll come up for the cart later after I close the store." Mae had had a stock clerk for a while after Stan died, but she was running the general store all by herself these days. Brady wasn't the only one losing people to gold fever.

"Don't trouble yourself, Mae. I'll return the cart on my way down to the church for the burial."

That gave him an idea.

"If you're still looking for help here in the store, you could do worse than hire Faith Steele. Coming back from Grayson's, I had an impressive conversation with her about filing and organizing. If she were a man, I'd have asked her to be my deputy right there on the spot."

Chapter 15

Finding the infirmary wasn't easy. Belle finally stumbled onto it in an alley off Main Street, up a ways from the hotel. The sign in the window's lower corner was so small she nearly missed it.

INFIRMARY
DEVON DECLAN, PHYSICIAN

It made her smile. Break Heart's storefronts were as straightforward as the people of the town seemed to be.

Though perhaps not everyone. Sheriff Fontana wasn't at all straightforward. In fact, the man was a downright mystery. A study in contradictions.

Everything about his person was impeccably neat, and yet his office was a terrible mess.

He conducted himself with iron-like control, but a cauldron of emotion roiled below the surface.

And when the dead body of a complete stranger washed up on his town's riverbank, he put as much thought and kindness into choosing a final resting place as if it had been his own dear mother. Sheriff Fontana was a mystery, but one thing was clear: he was a good man.

"Hello?" Speaking of contradictions, what a contrast the infirmary was to the sheriff's office!

All was sparkling clean, even the floor. Vials of potions and pots of ointments were labeled and arranged on dust-free shelves and cobweb-free pigeonholes. Fresh towels and bandages sat neatly folded and stacked on a counter beside a tray laid out with gleaming instruments of medical torture that made Belle shudder.

On the wall were two certificates. One declared that Devon Kenmare Declan, Medical Doctor and Chirurgiae Magister, was a graduate of the school of medicine at the McGill Faculty of Medicine of Montreal,

Canada. The other proclaimed his membership in the American Medical Association.

Impressive!

But where was everybody? From the injuries the sheriff had described, Chet couldn't have left the infirmary already.

"Is anyone here?" Out of habit, Belle again reached for Wade's broken watch. As she shook her head at herself and returned the watch to her pocket, a clock on a shelf chimed the hour. One o'clock.

She was late.

A door opened in the back, and Belle caught her breath as a strange-looking creature came toward her. He was exceedingly thin and two or three inches taller than her. His complexion was youthful and clear, but his eyes were old. He could be twenty-five. He could be thirty-five. *He could be a fallen angel.*

On first impression, he seemed quite frail, but as he drew near, she sensed his wiry, angry strength. Unruly straw-blond curls reached his collar and framed a cherubic face with haunted cornflower-blue eyes, fair skin, pink cheeks, and soft-looking lips. His clothes were of excellent quality, nicely tailored, and hopelessly wrinkled, as if he'd slept in them.

As if the inverse of Brady Fontana stood before her.

"You must be Mrs. LeClair." Like the sheriff, this man's gaze was intense. Ferocious, even. If he *were* an angel, he'd be an archangel. A righteous warrior like Michael. Or Gabriel, the voice of the Lord God himself. She should be frightened, but instead she found him extremely interesting.

It was because of the river. Surviving the ordeal *had* changed her.

"Please call me Belle. I take it you're Dr. Declan?"

"I am. But call me Doc. Everybody does."

His voice was scratchy, as if he'd been screaming too long and too loud. Also like Sheriff Fontana, the doctor struck Belle as having no patience for wasting time or suffering fools. She should write and tell Wade how she admired the first and was intrigued by the second.

She caught herself. For just one moment, she'd forgotten Wade was gone. Would it ever end, this surprised shock of remembering, followed by the sadness of accepting his loss all over again?

"Your Mr. McKinnon is in the—"

"He's not *my* Mr. McKinnon." She hadn't meant to be abrupt, but it was jarring to so quickly shift from thoughts of Wade to thoughts of Chet—and the second didn't compare well to the first.

The doctor raised an eyebrow. "I stand corrected."

Had Chet told him differently? *Great thunder on the mountain!* Belle remembered Charity's words. *Has Chet McKinnon made you an offer?*

He hadn't—though he'd hinted at it plain enough.

To be honest, marriage would solve all Belle's problems. She didn't love Chet, but what married couple was madly in love from the start? She and Wade had been an exception. Love had struck them both at first sight, like lightning bolts.

He'd been staying with the mayor while on assignment from back East and was invited to the Cranston wedding reception. Around ten o'clock, he asked her to dance. At midnight he asked for her hand.

Love like that only happened in fairy tales. In real life, love grew over years of building a good life together. That's what she'd always been told.

Her fairy tale was over, no happy ending. She accepted that. But she couldn't accept the epilogue on offer: to become a duplicate of

Wade's mother, join the female do-gooders of Mrs. LeClair's social circle, and marry Wesley. *No.* Belle shuddered. Her handsome prince was gone, but she wasn't about to become a Sleeping Beauty or Rapunzel, locked away from the world.

If the river had taught Belle anything, it was that she meant to live, and to live fully. She knew for a fact Wade would have wanted it that way. He'd said as much in his last letter.

Chet McKinnon was just the kind of man she ought to build a new life with. A farmer or rancher. A hard life, yes, but a safe one. She'd be mistress of her own household, not a boarder with a room in the house of her husband's mother and a maid who reported her every movement.

Marrying Chet had everything to recommend it.

"At all events," Dr. Declan said, "he's in no condition to receive you. When you weren't here by eleven o'clock, he became agitated and I dosed him to calm him down."

"I did tell Sally I'd visit this morning. But then my sisters and I were asked to identify my mother's body."

"You have nothing to explain." The doctor's voice softened. "I reckon Mr.

McKinnon was getting on my nerves more than he was any real danger to himself. He'll awake soon."

That didn't sound right. Belle wasn't familiar with medical ethics, but it couldn't be proper to medicate a patient for the doctor's convenience. Still she couldn't very well judge when she'd done the same with Finola in order to make her escape. She chuckled to herself.

The doctor narrowed his eyes. "I was making coffee before you arrived, and I can promise it's drinkable. Let me offer you a cup. My patient might come around before you're finished."

Now that he mentioned it, there was a wonderful smell of fresh coffee in the room. And not burnt either.

"That sounds lovely Dr.—Doc."

He motioned her to a little table set against the wall and filled two cups from the blue-and-white speckled pot sitting on a pristine, bright red stove. "How do you take it, Mrs. LeClair?"

"Do please call me Belle. Milk if you have any, but black is fine too. Thank you." In spite of the doctor's prickly manner, she liked him. Maybe because of it. "I confess I wouldn't mind stopping a few minutes. I have to be at the churchyard at three for the burial, then we're to have dinner at six with Mrs. Vanderhouten."

He set a mug before her and took the other chair at the table. "My condolences on your loss."

"Thank you. At least we have a body to bury. I haven't much hope we'll ever find my father." Again the weight of the loss hit her, and she blinked back tears.

"Let me get you a clean—oh. I see you're equipped."

She had tucked the sheriff's handkerchief in her sleeve, intending to ask Mrs. Gensch to launder it. "I'm a veritable fountain today. Sheriff Fontana lent me his earlier at the undertaker's."

"Brady is a resourceful man." Was the doctor trying to hide a smile? "Dinner with Abigail, eh? She's got her hooks out for you already."

"Hooks out? Is she looking for help in her dress shop?"

Belle thought quickly. She couldn't do the fancy work required of a professional seamstress. Hannah was the one who possessed talent with a needle. And if Mrs. Vanderhouten needed help with the books, that would be more along Faith's line of interest.

Belle remembered her sister and the sheriff talking about filing and paperwork and him smiling at Faith—though in an amused, big-brotherly way. Belle would have to be a mean cat to be jealous of that.

And besides, she had no feelings whatsoever for Brady Fontana. She refused to entertain thoughts about a lawman.

Her immediate problem was finding a job. She briefly wondered if Dr. Declan might need an assistant, then dismissed the idea when she realized it would entail actual nursing.

Being a wife was really the only thing she was fit for. She glanced at the door to the back room.

"I don't know about dressmaking," Dr. Declan said. "I was referring to Abigail's side business. She brings together would-be brides and husbands. I don't doubt she's salivating over the prospect of matching you and your sisters with the men she keeps in her book."

"But we're in mourning." Belle wondered if the waitress Trudy had found her husband-to-be through Mrs. Vanderhouten.

"Let's just say I've found these parts far less strict about that particular convention. Out here men are in urgent need of wives, and decent women are in need of protection."

Belle and Evangeline had laughed over advertisements from men out West desperate for wives, and at the time she'd dismissed the idea as rather horrible. She wasn't laughing now. In the new light of changed circumstances, the notion sounded perfectly sensible and worth considering—not for herself, but for Naomi and Faith—and even Charity, despite her opinion of marriage.

"What do you mean by a book? I thought men advertised directly in newspapers, and ladies answered, and that was that. I had no idea a business could be made of the enterprise."

"Abigail investigates her gentlemen to ensure they are what they seem. They pay for a spot in her book, then ladies read the pitches, so to speak, and choose who they like. Abigail coordinates a correspondence between the parties until they decide to do the deed."

"You seem to know a great deal about it." Was the doctor's name in Mrs. Vanderhouten's book?

"Patients are foolish creatures who treat me like a confessor priest. I hear far more than I like."

"Well, it sounds complicated—but also less risky than what I'd imagined."

"The West can be brutal on a single woman with no protector. Better Abigail get to you than Delilah Montgomery—not that you or your sisters would entertain any offer that woman would make."

"Mrs. Montgomery? But she's been so kind. She gave us these mourning clothes. Does she have a business?"

"Indeed. She runs the bawdy house up the hill."

"Goodness!" *Bawdy house.* Belle swallowed a smile. They really did call them that!

The doctor looked at her for a moment, and then his pale skin pinked.

"What?"

"You'll hear it soon enough. Might as well be from me."

"Can it be so bad?"

"Delilah had a horse named Ophelia that pulled her carriage around town, and last month she died—the horse, that is. Dee loved that horse. She gave it a funeral with a full New Orleans-style parade and music and a wake that lasted till dawn the next day. For the occasion, she had mourning dresses made up for all her girls."

"Oh my." Belle's hand went to the high collar of her muslin jacket. "I suppose that explains things."

The black fitted jacket with long sleeves came only just below the bust, like an old-fashioned spencer, elegant and modest, hiding a gown underneath which—now obvious—had been designed to display the feminine form to best effect. The bodice was quite décolleté, with tiny cap sleeves and bared arms.

"Still, it was good of her to help us in our need."

Dr. Declan refilled her cup. "If it's any consolation, Abigail made the dresses, and she's entirely respectable."

"I wouldn't have thought... I don't mean to truck in gossip, but things I overheard at the hotel gave the impression she and Mrs. Montgomery were rivals."

"To the bitter end. But Abigail isn't one to pass up a dollar. She can appear silly on the surface, but she's as practical and enterprising as Delilah."

"Running two businesses seems proof of that."

Belle almost asked if Dr. Declan was in Mrs. Vanderhouten's book, but stopped herself. Then she wondered if Sheriff Fontana was—and all her feelings raged against the possibility.

"With so much to do, then perhaps she

needs an assistant."

"She has one. An excellent seamstress." The fierceness went out of the doctor's eyes, and the haunted, vulnerable look returned.

Break Heart was certainly turning out unlike anything Belle had pictured when she'd imagined life in Colorado. She'd seen herself on a farm like so many in Minnesota, the only difference raising beef cattle instead of dairy cattle. She never expected to meet such a variety of interesting people.

It was exciting.

"Jane Stedman's the reason I ended up in Break Heart." The doctor's expression smoothed and he stared off into space. "I had been heading for Denver to set up as a physician."

Belle remained silent, sensing he'd keep talking only so long as he forgot he had an audience.

"I came upon a terrible scene. A stagecoach had turned over. One horse was dead, another dying, and the other two nowhere in sight. The driver and passengers were mutilated, violated in ways I'll never forget."

Belle's stomach revolted. There was more violence in *The Odyssey*, but this was different. This was real.

"I followed a whimpering sound through the trees and found Jane sitting on her heels, quivering. A dead man and a dying woman lay on the ground nearby, both covered in blood. Jane held a bloody knife which she pointed at the woman and beseeched me to help her."

The doctor squeezed his mug between his hands.

"I tried to save the poor dear, but she'd lost too much blood. Her last words were 'Tell Brady I'm so very sorry.' And then she was gone. Can you imagine? She apologized for being murdered."

Brady. Sheriff Fontana.

"If only I'd arrived a few minutes earlier, I might have saved her. I might have saved them all, somehow."

Belle understood now what haunted Dr. Declan. "But you saved Jane Stedman."

He looked up quizzically, as though forgotten Belle was there. Then, strangely, he laughed.

"Jane saved herself. I warrant the devil himself would quake in her presence. If people knew..."

If people knew what? Belle waited, to no avail.

The spell was broken. Doc blinked and shook his head.

"I saved no one." He blew out a deep breath. "The dead woman was named Thalia Merrick. She was coming out West to be married, traveling in the same stagecoach as Jane, and they'd become friendly on their journey. Jane asked me to help her take the body to Thalia's fiancée in Break Heart. How could I refuse?"

"It was good of you to do it, all the same."

"As I said, the West can be brutal. It takes courage and grit to survive, whether the danger comes from outlaws or Mother Nature."

"When I was caught in the rapids, all I could think was *I will survive this. I want to live.* The same when Frank Deckom and his gang attacked us. But I don't blame the West or wish I was back in Boston."

"Boston." Doc chuckled. "This must seem a different world altogether after that beacon of culture and moral clarity."

"Very much so. But I like it here. It feels right. *I* feel right here, as though Break Heart is where I was always meant to be."

"I felt the same when I arrived. The town needed a physician, I figured there were plenty medical men in Denver, and so I stayed."

"Belle?" The voice beyond the back door

was muffled but recognizable.

"There's your—I mean *my* patient. You'll be saved from my jawboning."

"I enjoyed your jawboning, Doc." Belle wasn't used to such informality, but it felt natural to call him Doc. In truth, she felt quite at ease with the man, and more so after he'd shared such a personal story. The coffee and gossip had been a tonic, a reprieve from her own worries.

She excused herself and went to the backroom, where she found Chet in a narrow bed, propped up against pillows.

"Aren't you a vision?" He smiled and glanced at a pitcher and glass sitting on a chest against the wall.

"Let me get you some water."

"You're an angel, darlin'."

Belle chuckled as she handed him the glass of water. "You already sound like a westerner." She pulled a chair over to the bed.

"I aim to make it so." He finished the drink in three gulps and handed her the glass. "I aim to make a lot of things so."

She hadn't noticed before how direct he was, but then anyone would seem so compared with Sheriff Fontana. "I'm glad to see you feeling better."

Chet McKinnon was young and strong, and his quick physical recovery wasn't surprising, but his spirits were so much higher than she expected. She'd been afraid he'd be overcome with grief. Maybe he hadn't yet accepted that he'd lost his entire family.

He reached out for her hand.

"I won't pussyfoot around, Belle. I've admired you from the moment I first clapped eyes on you. Why, I've never seen a better-looking woman in all my life, and I don't want to chance it you might get away from me a second time. Belle, will you be my wife?"

Chapter 16

It was a solemn, sorrowful occasion, and Brady struggled to suppress a smile watching Faith Steele glower at Parson Hood. The poor man had done his best to bury Mrs. Steele properly, but it seemed in Faith's opinion he'd sorely missed the mark.

The preacher closed his prayer book and studiously avoided the girl's squinty eye. The sisters moved away from the grave, and Brady and the Graysons grabbed a few of the extra shovels the gravedigger had hopefully provided.

"Sheriff Fontana, can I help, sir?" The boy, Luke, shuffled his weight from foot to foot, looking a bit lost and unsure what to do with himself.

"That would be appreciated, son." Whenever Brady felt overwhelmed by life's twists and turns, he found hard work not exactly a cure, but it was surely a treatment. He gestured toward the extra implements.

Luke picked up a shovel, but before he could start in, Hannah came over to speak to him.

"Lend me your treasure pouch, will you?" She was the youngest of the sisters and very quiet. It was hard to know if her rectitude was natural. She might be still shaken from yesterday's ordeal. She'd lost her parents to the rapids and barely survived herself, only to be attacked by a gang of outlaws.

The Deckoms had to go.

He didn't despise them for what they were. No use despising rattlesnakes or black widow spiders. Best just to rid the world of them. The Trading Post might be outside Break Heart's jurisdiction, but it still infected the town.

The boy removed the satin bag he wore around his neck and handed it to her. "Be careful with it."

"Thank you, brother." Hannah gave Luke an awkward hug and went to join her sisters. The boy heaved a sigh too great for his young age and solemnly joined in the work of burying his mother.

"Good man," Brady said. Then he noticed that Belle LeClair had been watching the whole thing.

She mouthed *thank you* and started walking toward him. He nodded and kept shoveling. It was a small thing, and the right thing, to include the boy, but it gave him a warm feeling to know she appreciated the gesture.

Belle. He shouldn't think that way, even though she'd asked him to use her given name. She was only being polite.

And *Mrs. LeClair* was safer.

"You were right, Sheriff." Suddenly she was there beside him. "The wild plum tree is lovely, and so full of blossoms. It was a real kindness choosing this resting place. A consolation, truly."

"Then I'm glad." His handkerchief peeked out from the edge of her sleeve. It shouldn't give him so much pleasure to see it there. "I'll be sure Luke gets back to the hotel safely if you ladies want to go now."

"Oh." Her smile fell as if he'd dismissed her. "Thank you." She turned away.

He leaned on the shovel and watched her depart from the churchyard with her sisters, hoping she'd look back. But if she did, he'd only smile like a fool. Better she feel pushed away rather than encouraged; if she got close, he'd only hurt her worse in the end.

Parson Hood had pitched in, and with so many at it, the grave was soon covered and Brady and the boy walked back to town. They passed Abigail's place. Hannah was there, talking to Abigail and Jane.

The rest of the Steele sisters were inside Tagget's. Belle saw Luke through the window and motioned for him to go inside while she avoided looking at Brady.

"I better go in," Luke said reluctantly.

Brady walked on, trying to push down a jumble of emotions. It would be good for that whole family if Abigail brought Belle and Pres Morgan together. Morning Star Ranch was well regarded, one of the most successful spreads in the state. Brady had met the rancher in Denver during meetings regarding statehood, and he'd been impressed—not by the man's wealth but by his temperament and character.

Morgan was decent, intelligent, and had good judgment. His men were loyal out of admiration and satisfaction with their situation rather than fear and desperation for a job. He'd be a good father to Luke, he'd see the other sisters were taken care of, and he'd treat Belle with respect. It would be the very best thing for her.

And yet... At the very thought, a primal *no!* rang out in Brady's mind. At the office, he finished storing his supplies, then grabbed a broom. If only he could sweep these emotions away as easily as the dust. Somehow he had to get Belle—Mrs. LeClair—out of his head.

***

"My name is Hannah. Hannah Steele. I was wondering if... if you might... you might be looking for..."

The trembling young girl in the front room dressed in familiar mourning clothes couldn't possibly mean she wished to find a husband. She was no more than fourteen, if that. Abigail didn't truck in child brides.

The girl squared her shoulders and started again. "I was wondering if you might need a seamstress."

Ah. A more palatable inquiry.

But equally unlikely to end in satisfaction.

Every female worth her salt could put together serviceable cloaks, dresses, aprons, nightgowns, and the like, but it took more than a passing skill with a needle to be a professional dressmaker. And Abigail was a modiste! It took some talent and a lot of discipline to perform the same perfect stitch over and over and over to the point of sheer boredom and aching fingers. Then get up the next day and the next to do it again.

As if making an offering, the girl held out a small pouch made of cheap satin that Abigail would ordinarily dismiss immediately, had she been anyone else.

"You say you're one of the Miss Steeles?"

This must be the one who'd been upstairs this morning. It wouldn't do to offend her older sisters by turning her away without a hearing. And besides, fourteen-year-olds become sixteen-year-olds in due course. While Jane made a show of looking at the ridiculous pouch, Abigail gave Hannah a second look.

She *was* pretty. Indeed, she might possibly one day rival Mrs. LeClair's beauty. But did she have to tremble so, like a frightened kitten? And that expression! The last thing a man wants is a bride who looks congenitally horrified and slightly nauseated, no matter how creamy her complexion, how blue her eyes, or thick and luxurious her hair.

"I'm so sorry about your terrible ordeal, little one." What was this? Jane never spoke to anybody with kindness. "Those Deckoms are blackguards."

"Yes, they are." The girl nodded and choked out the words.

Jane never touched anybody either, or allowed herself to be touched, but now she squeezed Hannah's forearm in sympathy. "I heard you were very brave fighting them off."

Hannah met Jane's gaze, and when she did her eyes glistened.

Jane smiled. "This embroidery is rare neat work."

Well, didn't that beat all! It was simply nowhere in Jane Stedman's nature to praise another's work. If Abigail had been in motion, she would have stopped in her tracks.

"Let me see." She examined the item with new eyes. The material itself was indeed of low quality, but the needlework... "This is very fine."

The intricate leaves and vines reflected talent which could, if appreciated early enough in its development and properly guided, become real artistry. Abigail looked at Jane. Would she possibly consider taking Hannah on as an apprentice?

"I was so scared."

"I know." Jane the Terrible actually put her arms around the girl. "Let me show you a secret. Something silly that the Deckoms are all more scared of than you ever were in your life. You won't believe it when you see it."

Abigail's heart raced when Jane pulled that infamous drum from her pocket. To think she carried that bedeviled mojo on her person! *Oh dear. Oh dear.*

"That's lovely," said Hannah Steele.

Not the word Abigail would use for it.

Jane laughed—a creepy, ungodly cackle.

The small two-sided drum was mounted on a stick, one face plain and the other with a painted rose at its center. Jane twisted her wrist back and forth, back and forth, back and forth, and the two beads hung on leather strings on either side b-beat, b-beat, b-beat against the faces.

Abigail was sure the rose grew redder with every turn.

***

Tidying up, Brady started with the cells. As usual, the one where Doc had slept the other night was already clean as a whistle. The man was a farrago, one moment a frustrated mess, the next a focused warrior battling his twin enemies, disease and injury.

He'd established a custom of sleeping it off at the jail either after imbibing too deeply up at Sweet Dee's or when he feared to be near his copious supply of laudanum when he was in a certain mood. Brady didn't mind. He was the last to judge another man's method of keeping his demons at bay.

Brady had demons of his own.

Strangely, today at the churchyard he hadn't thought once about Thalia. He'd even forgotten to visit her grave. It seemed his demons lost their power when Belle LeClair was near. Her smile was the warmest he'd seen in years, her manner and voice so accepting and understanding. Just being in her presence made him feel better.

There was a flash of black outside the window, and his heart skipped a beat. Was she coming to talk to him again? Maybe he should put on a pot of coffee.

Clomp! Clomp! Clomp!

Wait. That racket coming up the porch steps couldn't be Belle LeClair. Her step was light, refined. Ladylike. A Deckom must have come to town to collect their guns.

Brady glanced at his Winchester, mounted on the rack across the room. His Colt was in its holster, hanging from the hat stand. The Deckom pistols were locked away in the shelves below the rifle rack.

The door flew open, and in a whirlwind of black, a she-devil appeared in the middle of the room. Faith Steele. Brady laughed at himself.

Sort of.

"Sheriff Fontana, I have a bone to pick with you! Mrs. Tagget just told me you told her she should offer me a job at her store."

"Yes?" Brady was confused. Why would that make her angry? "I thought you ladies wanted work in Break Heart."

"But I'm going to work for *you*."

No. "But Mae needs—"

"*You* need me. Vain to deny it. This office is a disgrace. *But if any provide not for his own, and specially for those of his own house, he hath denied the faith, and is worse than an infidel.*"

Well!

Brady had no answer to that.

"I'll be here tomorrow bright and early," she continued. "If I haven't convinced you of the obvious by the day's end, then I won't be able to account for myself."

Chapter 17

When Belle returned to the hotel, there was some time yet before they were to meet Mrs. Vanderhouten for supper. She went upstairs and lay down for a nap, but sleep didn't come.

She stared at the ceiling, listened to the street sounds from the open window, and considered her life.

What was wrong with her? Now that Chet had proposed, she didn't want him. She felt nervous and trapped, like when Mrs. LeClair had revealed the plan to foist her off on Wesley.

Belle was self-aware enough to know she'd never be happy settling for what she didn't want. But that wasn't the problem—it was easy knowing what she didn't want. For instance, no one in their right mind would want to marry one of those Deckoms!

Nor Wesley LeClair.

Nor, apparently, Chet McKinnon.

"Belle Steele, you're a real piece of work," she said aloud.

Mrs. LeClair had often complained she was too obstinate, like Lady Catherine de Bourgh lecturing Elizabeth Bennet on her lack of respect for the proper order. But Elizabeth had stayed her course, remained true to herself, and in the end was rewarded with Mr. Darcy.

Belle had obstinately married her own Mr. Darcy, even when his mother didn't approve. But now her Mr. Darcy was dead, and she saw no clear path to the right next step.

What if, heaven forbid, the Mrs. LeClairs and Lady Catherines of the world were right? Should the "proper order" be Belle's guide? Whether it was her guardian angel or merely common sense, all signs pointed to her marrying Chet McKinnon.

On the practical side, he wasn't a lawman. And he possessed the means necessary to fund a homestead, no small thing. He'd told her that instead of selling the family farm in Minnesota, his father had rented it to a cousin, intending to sell when he was ready to prove up his claim in Colorado. Chet was heir to that farm in its entirety.

He wasn't rich by any means, but he was well fixed to become a prosperous man—with hard work and time. And extra hands were always needed on a farm, which meant Belle could provide a home for all her sisters and Luke.

On the petty side, Chet was young and handsome, and he was a good dancer. She'd known him all her life and had danced with him at more than a few weddings and church gatherings.

He said he cared for her. She didn't return his feelings, but Evangeline would say that fact was a mark in favor of their union. *It's better the man care for you more than you care for him. Otherwise he'll always have the upper hand.*

Being an heiress, Evie lived in a world where wealth and connections were more important than character or talent or even animal attraction. Down here on the ground below the clouds, a woman of no fortune purchased security and comfort with the coin of her freedom.

With Wade, it had never occurred to Belle that this might be a bad bargain.

With Chet, she wasn't so sure. She'd

told him she needed time to think about his proposal. He wasn't happy about it, but to his credit, he'd agreed.

Outside, a familiar *stomp, stomp, stomp* sounded from across the street at the sheriff's office. Faith ascending the porch steps. Again Belle fought a twinge of jealousy.

Which was somewhat irritating. She wasn't interested in Brady Fontana, not in that way, and yet this morning after leaving the undertaker she'd felt like an abandoned child when the sheriff had avoided her and walked back to the hotel with Faith instead. Later it shouldn't have hurt so much when he recoiled from speaking to her at Ma's graveside. But it did.

She should marry Chet and be done with it.

She tossed and turned a while longer, then slept dreamlessly until Charity woke her.

The grandfather clock in the lobby was chiming six o'clock when they all came downstairs. It felt good to be on time. Mr. Gensch intercepted them. He must have had a good idea what Mrs. Vanderhouten meant to talk to them about, because he invited Luke to join him and Mrs. Gensch for dinner.

"Instead of listening to a bunch of

cackling hens, how'd you like to dine with me and Charlotte? After supper, I'll teach you how to whittle a whistle."

Such kindness only strengthened Belle's feeling that Break Heart was where she belonged.

Trudy led them to a small dining room off the main café. "Mrs. Vanderhouten thought you'd like some privacy."

"That was kind," Naomi said.

"She's the very soul of kindness." Trudy's friendly smile was tinged with a bit of mischief. That settled it. Belle had no doubt Mrs. Vanderhouten wanted to see what kind of brides the Steele sisters might make.

There was bread and butter on the table and a carafe of red wine, courtesy of the Gensches. Trudy handed out menus, recommended the lamb, and left them to wait for their hostess.

"I don't know about everybody else, but I'm not wearing this at the table. It's not like we're in public." Faith whipped off her spencer and hung it on one of a double line of hooks along the wall that must be for hats and coats.

Belle decided to keep Dr. Declan's tale of their mourning clothes to herself. What purpose would it serve to tell the others?

Hannah's fingers paused at her spencer's top button. She seemed unsure whether to take it off and reveal the gown beneath, the first to show off her changing figure.

When her age, Belle had seized on any excuse to wear her first fancy gown, with Ma forever pulling the sleeves up after Belle would inch them down over her shoulders. Hannah, in contrast, had kept her spencer buttoned all the way to her throat.

She'd been subdued about everything since the Deckoms' assault, though this evening she seemed different. Not so wounded. Lighter. Perhaps Charity had been right, and Hannah would quickly get over the attack.

At all events, in Hannah's place, Belle would have jumped at any excuse to throw off the outer jacket in order to display her developing female charms. Removing her own spencer now, she wished the sheriff could see her. *I must have something of the hussy in me.*

"I have news," Hannah said. "I met Mrs. Vanderhouten earlier, and she gave me a job."

"What?" Naomi's shock spoke for everyone.

"I don't want to go back to Minnesota

either. When you were all talking with Mrs. Tagget, I went over to the modiste and showed Mrs. Vanderhouten Luke's treasure pouch, and Jane Stedman said if Mrs. V didn't hire me to do fancywork she would be very sorry indeed."

"Mrs. V?" Naomi raised an eyebrow.

"That's what Jane calls her."

Hannah appeared as enchanted as Dr. Declan with Mrs. Vanderhouten's assistant. Considering what Doc had said, Belle wondered if it would be safe for her little sister to work so closely with such a character.

"Jane says Mrs. V's employees always call her that, and now I should too since I'm a modiste-in-training."

"*The hand of the diligent shall bear rule.*" Faith winked and chucked Hannah's chin.

"Well done, Hannah!" Charity lifted her wineglass, and all repeated the toast, even Naomi.

"Well done, Hannah!"

"You're young yet to be employed," Naomi said. "You must make sure you don't neglect your studies or work too many hours in a day."

"But you should be proud of yourself," Belle said, "doing your part for the family."

As she ought to do hers by marrying Chet.

"Belle, dear," Naomi said softly. "How did you find Mr. McKinnon?"

"Better than expected." Belle's stomach clenched. It hadn't felt right to tell the others about Chet's offer at Ma's graveside, and she still wasn't ready to discuss it. **"Dr. Declan wants to keep him another day, just to be sure there's no infection or internal bleeding."**

"I'm sure he didn't object to another day in bed," Hannah said drily. She never did like Chet.

"I had quite a chat with the doctor today." Belle didn't want to talk about Chet. "What a strange fellow he is, and a regular gossip!"

"Do tell." Faith smiled like the cat who ate the cream. She was hiding something, Belle could tell. Why had she gone to see the sheriff earlier?

"For one thing, this place isn't as sleepy as it appears. Why, last month the town had a funeral for a horse! Except it sounded more like a celebration, with a parade up Main Street and musicians and a wild wake at Sweet Dee's that lasted two days."

"That's the local bawdy house," Charity said knowingly. "It's run by Mrs.

Montgomery, who brought us these clothes last night."

"How did you know that?" Faith said.

"Mae Tagget told me after you tore out of the general store with a bee in your bonnet. I don't understand you, Faith. I thought you wanted to stay in Break Heart."

"And so I do, but I don't want to work in a store."

"Good. Then you won't mind I asked her to hire me instead."

"Charity!" Naomi looked stunned.

Wasn't that just like Charity, to take what had been put on offer to someone else?

"Why not? I can be a hard worker."

Belle snorted but was instantly sorry. The river accident had changed her. Why shouldn't it affect Charity as well? True, Charity could be a real flibbertigibbet, and it was irritating how she always borrowed other people's things without asking. But she was also smart and kind and had certainly proved brave.

"I'm sorry." Belle squeezed her sister's hand. "That was nothing to laugh at."

"No need to apologize." Charity laughed gaily. "You're right to doubt me. But I do feel different now."

"Everything's different now." Naomi

spoke quite seriously. "And this is different country than we've been used to."

"It certainly is," Belle said. "Dr. Declan told me Mrs. Montgomery is highly respected in Break Heart. She's even a member of the town council." A devilish imp seized her and she added, "She and Mrs. Vanderhouten compete for ladies."

Naomi choked on her wine. The idea of procuring females must call for more tolerance than she was ready for. But then she said something remarkable. "I suppose we can't judge. I've read that in the West there is only one female to every three or four males. I imagine a lot of good, single men get lonely."

"As well as the bad ones." Hannah shuddered, and again they remembered their narrow escape from the Deckoms.

Sheriff Fontana was a single man. Belle couldn't help but wonder if he availed himself of Sweet Dee's offerings or if there was a particular girl there he preferred. Or perhaps he had a proper sweetheart among Break Heart's denizens. And though she had no business entertaining an opinion on the subject, she didn't like either possibility at all.

"I have to confess I'm still judgmental on that subject." Charity shook her head. "I'd rather be a wife than one of those painted ladies."

"And if Mrs. Vanderhouten has her way, that's just what we'll all be." Faith looked sideways at Charity, and with a twinkle in her eye she continued. "*Then shall the kingdom of heaven be likened unto ten virgins, which took their lamps, and went forth to meet the bridegroom.*"

They both burst out laughing.

"*And five of them were wise,*" Faith continued. "*And five foolish.*

"Which five do you think we'll be?" Charity said through giggles.

It felt so good to laugh. It seemed to Belle she hadn't really laughed in years.

"Well, well. Isn't this a lovely sound?" A woman on the young side of middle age entered the room. "My mama used to say innocent laughter is God's favorite music."

She carried a large hand-bound volume that made Belle think of the albums of photographs Mrs. LeClair kept.

"Good evening, ladies. Hello again, Hannah."

Hannah stood properly, as if she'd matured a few years in an afternoon. "This is Mrs. Vanderhouten."

"I'm delighted to welcome you all to

Break Heart—though I'm very sorry for the circumstances that brought you to us. I do hope you've settled in and your rooms are comfortable."

"We have, Mrs. Vanderhouten," Naomi said. "Thank you for giving Hannah a chance—and for the kind gift of the gloves."

"Oh, pish! The gloves were nothing. And your sister is a real talent. Glad to have her on board." She sat down and laid the book on the table. "But let's have none of this *Mrs. Vanderhouten* business. Why, I'm only ten years older than you, Miss Naomi." She already knew their ages.

Trudy came in then, and they all ordered the lamb. After which Mrs. Vanderhouten started in, asking all about Belle and her sisters. The woman sure didn't pussyfoot around. By the end of the meal she'd ascertained far more than their ages.

They ordered strawberry cake for dessert—with tea instead of coffee. Belle couldn't help noticing how very dry the cake was.

"Now tell me, ladies. How would you like to find some fine husbands?" She patted the book that had been sitting on the table throughout the meal. "I have plenty of successful men of good character to choose from."

Naomi started to answer. "That's very kind, Mrs.—Abigail. But—"

"I'm never getting married," Charity blurted out. "And Hannah is only fourteen. Even Faith is only nineteen."

"Nonsense!" Mrs. Vanderhouten ignored Charity's first statement. "I'll grant you fourteen is too young, but I've certainly seen brides at sixteen, even fifteen when the stars align. Seventeen is the best age to marry. Nineteen is all right. Any older, and you start to worry about being considered on the shelf. Too many ingrained habits."

"Then at twenty, I'm done for," Charity said happily.

"At twenty-five, I must be an old maid." Naomi was more rueful.

"In some people's minds, my dear." Mrs. Vanderhouten was a smart woman, Belle gave her that. She didn't argue with Naomi or try to flatter her. "But a gentleman of quality appreciates that a mature woman can be a pearl beyond price, and why would you settle for less than such a gentleman?"

On the other hand, a little flattery might do Naomi some good.

"What about you, my dear? You must miss the joys of marriage." Mrs.

Vanderhouten homed in on Belle like a hawk on a rabbit. "Why, you're exquisite. You could have your choice of any gentleman in my book—and one in particular whom you won't find there. I have only quality bachelors, mind you, fully investigated and vouched for."

"Belle's already taken," Charity said.

"Charity!" Naomi frowned.

Mrs. Vanderhouten's face fell. "Is that so?"

"No." Belle glared at her sister. "Not exactly." She felt the world closing in on her again. "I'm not quite ready to risk marriage again. Not just yet."

There. Hearing the words out loud, they rang true.

"Belle lost her husband not two months ago," Naomi said. "It's too soon."

"I see. Again, my condolences. But you'll rally, my dear. Mark my words. And marriage isn't a sorrow. The right husband brings all the happiness in the world. There, I see that smile. Your first marriage was a success, I take it."

Mrs. Vanderhouten wasn't easily put off.

"If you call four days a success."

"Charity, really!" This time it was Faith who objected to their sister's tactlessness.

"It's too soon for any of us to think of marrying." When Naomi made up her mind about a thing, that was that. "We're in mourning for our parents, and Belle is in mourning for Mr. LeClair too."

"I'm sure you know best." Mrs. Vanderhouten made a tactical retreat. She set aside her half-eaten cake, wiped the corners of her mouth delicately, and placed her napkin over her plate. "I'll intrude no further upon your grief, but let me leave this for your perusal." She patted the book again. "You may have a change of mind after you've had time to really think about the way things are for you now."

The way things are.

Mrs. Vanderhouten departed, but her words hung behind in the air.

"Well, that was brutal." Charity pushed the last bit of cake around on her plate.

"But to the point," Naomi said.

Everything had changed. In Colorado they had nothing. No money, no friends, no relations... which was why Naomi had at first assumed they must return to Minnesota.

But Belle could see in her older sister's eyes the same decision everyone else had already made. Life with Uncle James couldn't be borne. Hannah had found a job. The rest of them had to do the same.

"By the way, in case anybody was curious, Mrs. Tagget accepted my offer," Charity said. "I start at the general store tomorrow morning."

"That's wonderful, Charity." Belle lifted her glass to her sister.

"And I start my new job tomorrow," Faith announced. "I'm Sheriff Fontana's new deputy."

Chapter 18

Belle woke to the sound of sniffles. Faith was gone. Charity was at the desk in the corner, holding a fountain pen and staring at a sheet of paper.

"What is it? What's wrong?"

"I asked Mrs. Gensch for paper and pen to write to Uncle James about Ma and Pa."

"But you loathe Uncle James."

"I didn't want Naomi to have to do it."

"Who is this responsible young woman, and what have you done with my sister?" Belle threw on a wrap provided by Delilah Montgomery and went to the desk. Over Charity's shoulder she saw their parents' names on the page, written over and over again:

Laura May Whitworth Steele

Jared Steele

Charity looked up and smiled through her tears. "I don't know what came over me. I started writing their signatures and couldn't stop."

Belle squeezed her shoulders. "Pa always said if you were of a criminal bent you'd make a master forger."

"At first it was comforting, but then it hit me. They'll never write their names again."

"Oh, Charity." Belle kissed the top of her sister's head. "Let's go downstairs. You'll feel better after some breakfast."

"I'll write to Uncle James later." Charity brightened. "After work. Do you think Mrs. Gensch will be insulted if I ask for tea instead of coffee?"

In the café, Belle exchanged a wave with the little girl, Sally, who'd delivered her message to the infirmary. She was there with her brother and their father, Mr. Overstreet.

Naomi, Hannah, and Luke already had a table near the front window, where the sheriff's office was in plain view. Faith must be there now, her first day at her new job.

Belle was still befuddled by Faith's announcement. Deputy? That couldn't be right. The sheriff *did* need his office cleaned up and his papers organized. A clerk, more like. Not a deputy. Whatever her title, she'd be with Sheriff Fontana every day.

"You're not serious." Charity took a chair next to Naomi, who was browsing through Mrs. Vanderhouten's book.

Belle was equally surprised. "I thought you weren't interested in being a mail order bride."

"I wasn't. Hannah was looking through this when I came down."

"Great thunder, Hannah. You—"

"I was just curious."

"I'm relieved to hear it. We'll have no child brides in our family," Belle said, and they all laughed.

"That's just it. *Our family*," Naomi said. "I don't want us to split up. Faith and Charity and even Hannah have found employment here in Break Heart. And Belle, I expect you'll marry Chet McKinnon and homestead close by."

Belle felt her face warm. The angel on her shoulder whispered *yes indeed*. But the devil on the other shoulder chanted *not yet, not yet, not yet*. She could hear Mrs. LeClair's voice between them: *Why must you be so stubborn?*

"Anyway, I'm thinking that Mrs. Vanderhouten could be right. Maybe I can find a local man who's set up well enough to take Luke along with me." Naomi smiled. "And Hannah, when she's not slaving away for her new employer.

"Don't be noble and self-sacrificing on my account," Hannah said. "I can make this into a real profession, just you wait and see."

"I don't doubt it. But I've cared for you two all your lives, and I'm not stopping now." Naomi closed the book. "Sadly, I see no one who fits the bill."

"I can work too," Luke said. His treasure pouch was draped across one shoulder by the leather thong Ma had given him from her sewing basket back in Minnesota.

"Don't be tempted to spend that half eagle," Belle said. "Pa meant you to keep it."

She was suddenly struck by how bereft they were of worldly goods. It had been much easier to disparage worldly goods when there was a surplus of them!

At this moment, their only clothes were these on their backs, generously donated with the nightgowns and wraps. Her donated shoes had already given her blisters, not that she wished to complain.

They had no home, would soon run out of money, and their only hope lay in the kindness of strangers and a book of lonely men. *We really do have nothing.*

She should march up to the infirmary right now and accept Chet's offer. He'd take Naomi and Luke and anyone else willing to supply the backbreaking labor required to get a homestead going.

"You can go to school," Naomi said to Luke. "That is if Break Heart has a school. Hannah too."

"Yes." Belle wrinkled her nose at the bitter coffee. "School would be better."

"And for your information, I have no intention of being self-sacrificing," Naomi said. "I just think I should explore all the possibilities."

"Do *any* of the men in the book look promising?" Charity said.

"Not really." Hannah rolled her eyes as Naomi opened it again.

"Look, there's Faith." Luke nodded at the sheriff's office.

Their sister had emerged with a broom and started sweeping the porch.

"She was up and gone at an ungodly hour," Charity said. "I'm glad I don't have to be at the general store till eight."

Belle wished her watch wasn't broken. She'd forgotten to look at the time when they came through the lobby, and not knowing made her anxious.

She wondered if Sheriff Fontana had already been in and gone. Mrs. Gensch had mentioned he ate at the Lilac most mornings. Belle knew he lived across the street because last night, when she turned out the lamp, she'd noticed a light burning in a room over the sheriff's office.

His back had been to the window, and he was taking off his suspenders, which had struck her as silly in so serious a man. It was rude and wrong to keep watching, but she couldn't stop herself. Then he bent down and blew out the light, leaving her yet again secretly scandalized by her own brazen self.

Maybe he'd start having breakfast at the sheriff's office now.

With Faith.

Faith finished with the porch and went back inside. Charity had been watching her, frowning the whole while. "I don't see how that's any different from working in a store." She turned to Naomi. "Mrs. Tagget said she badly needs help. I could ask if she'd hire you too."

"That won't work. I need something

where I can keep Luke with me, especially if there's no school here. Yes, Luke. I don't want you running all over town, getting into trouble like those Overstreet children."

"Great thunder on the mountain!" Charity spit out the bite of muffin she'd just taken. "These are as bad as the rolls we had with last night's supper. And that cake! Belle, I'm dreaming of your wonderful currant scones."

"And her chocolate cake," Naomi said. "I hope you didn't fall out of practice living with Mrs. LeClair."

"Quite the contrary," Belle said. "In Boston, the kitchen was my refuge, though Mrs. LeClair hated it when I cooked. She didn't want her friends thinking she'd made a servant of me."

"I'll wager she had no objection to eating your lemon tarts," Hannah said.

"Remember how the neighbors used to tell Ma, *be sure Belle makes something for potluck*?" Charity said. "I could swoon, thinking of that peach cobbler you made once for Luke's birthday."

"Warm with ice cream," Luke added dreamily.

"I promise to make one for you as soon as peaches are ripe." Belle frowned. In what kitchen? They were going to have to find a place to live, and they didn't have a stick of furniture. Maybe they could find a boarding house with kitchen privileges. "They must have peaches in Colorado."

"Of course we have peaches in Colorado." Mrs. Gensch happened by with more of her dastardly coffee. No one could accuse her of being stingy with the thick, bitter brew. "Mr. Overstreet there grows the best fruit. You wouldn't believe how sweet."

"He's a farmer?" Naomi turned to get a better look.

"He has orchards about two miles southeast of town." Mrs. Gensch nodded. "Peaches and cherries, plums, and persimmons too. Though who knows what his harvest will be like this year, poor man."

"Why 'poor man'?" Charity asked.

"His wife died this past winter," Mrs. Gensch said. "Left him with the two kids to raise and one less pair of hands around the house. And don't I understand how he feels! Abigail Vanderhouten has stolen my Trudy away for someone in that infernal book. She's the best waitress I ever had, the ungrateful girl."

"Don't believe her." Trudy came up behind her employer and set down a pretty little pitcher of milk for their coffee. "Mrs. Gensch is a sweetheart and very happy for me and Gus. She and Mr. Gensch gave us a load of sheets and towels and a full set of dishes for a wedding present."

"I can be happy for you and sorry for myself at the same time," Mrs. Gensch said with a fond smile. "And sorry for Mr. Overstreet besides."

"Mr. Overstreet should advertise with Mrs. Vanderhouten," Charity said.

"He has." Mrs. Gensch said simultaneously with Naomi, who pointed to a page in the brochure.

Naomi said, "The notice describes his orchards—peaches, cherries, plums, and persimmons, and that the gentleman in question has a boy and a girl."

"No luck then, I take it." Charity said.

"Could be he was too honest in his description." Mrs. Gensch's cheeks pinked. "Not that Jonathan Overstreet isn't a decent man. Pays his account every month on the very day the bill is presented."

I must remember never to tell Mrs. Gensch my personal affairs. Belle examined Mr. Overstreet more keenly. She was willing to believe he was honest, but he didn't strike her as particularly good. He ignored his children terribly. His face had been stuck in a newspaper throughout their breakfast, and it stayed there now as the little boy jumped down from his chair and dashed out of the café.

A loud crash and an anguished "oh no!" erupted from the kitchen, followed by woeful crying.

"Ach, what has that Roxanna girl done now?" With a harried sigh, Mrs. Gensch rushed away, Trudy on her heels.

"I'm not sure how honest Mr. Overstreet is." Naomi read quietly from the brochure.

> *"Gentleman thirty-seven years of age with two adorable children and excellent producing orchards seeks strong and virtuous young lady for marriage who isn't afraid of hard work. I am tall, in robust health, and have dark brown hair. I promise to be a good provider and loving husband."*

"Oh dear." Belle watched Sally race after her brother. The poor thing couldn't be older than Luke, and she seemed to be the responsible one in that family.

"Mr. Overstreet isn't much taller than I am, as I remember," Hannah said. "He's certainly half a head shorter than you,

Naomi."

"And brown hair?" Charity added. "I suppose there's more brown than gray—what's left of it."

"And he's forty-two if he's a day," Naomi said.

Belle wondered how accurate any of the advertisements were. "Still it's rather sweet. 'I promise to be a good provider and loving husband.' He sounds sincere."

"I hope he is," Naomi said. "For his future wife's sake."

The man folded his newspaper and tucked it under his arm, then followed his children out of the café. He appeared again on the street outside, headed in the direction they'd run off to.

Naomi stood up and looked at Belle, then Charity, a strange light in her eye. "I'll be right back."

She rushed out of the café and caught up with Mr. Overstreet.

"Here comes the noble self-sacrifice," Luke said, while Belle, Hannah, and Charity craned their necks to watch from the window.

Belle had no idea what was in Naomi's head, but it sure looked like she was making a proposal of some kind. She looked at Charity.

"She wouldn't..." *Would she?*

"They're definitely having an earnest conversation," Charity said.

Then Naomi and Mr. Overstreet shook hands, and Naomi headed back to the hotel with a smile on her face.

Charity looked at Belle, stricken. "Naomi never smiles."

Their older sister returned to the table, added milk to her coffee, and drank it without wincing.

"Well?" Belle, Charity, Luke, and Hannah all said at once.

"I'm Mr. Overstreet's new housekeeper and governess to Sally and Damon," Naomi said. "And Luke, you can be with me while I'm working and help in the orchards alongside Sally come harvest time." She looked at them all. "It's something."

"I couldn't do it." Charity stood up. "I'd rather haul fifty-pound sacks of sugar all the live-long day than watch a passel of kids." She winked at Luke. "But you have the patience of Job, Naomi. It sounds perfect for you."

"You've always been wonderful with children," Belle said.

"Speaking of sacks of sugar, I hear them calling. Hannah, are you ready to go?"

What a topsy-turvy world!

Belle had been first to declare she'd stay

in Break Heart, and now Faith, Charity, Hannah and Naomi were fixed for work. Everybody had a job of some kind but Belle. Maybe God *was* telling her to marry Chet McKinnon.

"Miss Belle, could I talk to you for a minute?" Trudy had returned, and with an anxious look on her face. She motioned her head as if she wanted to speak in private.

"Of course." Belle followed the waitress toward where the commotion in the kitchen was still going on. "What is it?"

"Normally, I wouldn't presume." Trudy stopped at the end of a short hallway just before a pair of double swinging doors. "Only I heard you talking about wanting a job, and the others were saying how good a cook you are."

"I do. And, well... Yes. I am."

Trudy grinned and grabbed Belle's hand. "Then come with me."

She pushed through the doors into a massive operation that put Mrs. LeClair's kitchen in Boston to shame. But then, this kitchen had to serve the needs of a hotel, not a private home.

But the mess! Sheriff Fontana's office had nothing on this place. Everything was in shambles, and something was burning somewhere—maybe more than one thing—while a young woman wearing a splatter-covered apron cried over a fallen cake.

At least, Belle assumed the lumpy concoction on the worktable was supposed to be a cake.

"I can't do it, Aunt Charlotte!" sobbed the cook, who looked to be about Belle's age. "I try! I try so hard. I'm just no good at it."

"There, there, Roxanna." Mrs. Gensch put her arms around the girl and patted her on the back. "I know you do your best, my love. Now dry your tears. We'll think of something."

"I've thought of it already," Trudy said cheerfully. She winked at Belle.

Belle was already bubbling with excitement. *Could it be possible?*

Aunt and niece looked at the waitress hopefully, and Belle saw from Mrs. Gensch's expression that she was as kind to her employees as she was to her guests.

"Belle here is a wonderful cook," Trudy said. "Mrs. Gensch, if you're as smart as I think you are, you'll have Roxie take my place as waitress and hire Mrs. LeClair to run your kitchen."

Chapter 19

Run the kitchen? Belle's stomach fluttered with excitement—this was perfect. Not only employment, but something she was suited to. Then fear kicked in. Running a hotel kitchen would be far more complicated than merely baking a lot of cakes.

But even if she didn't need the income, she would want to try. Just to see if she could do it.

"Oh yes, Aunt Charlotte!" Roxanna was saying. "I'd much rather be a waitress."

Mrs. Gensch's brows scrunched together. "I don't know..."

"Well, you better figure it out pretty quick," Trudy said with a laugh. "My train leaves for Denver at 1:27, and there is no way on God's green earth I'm disappointing my Gus."

Belle held her breath. All her life, she'd been a good girl, kept quiet, and hoped people who cared for her would notice her desires and see she got something close to what she wanted.

She'd wanted Wade the instant she saw him, but she'd waited for him to approach her, to ask her to dance, to ask for her hand.

She'd wanted to be left alone with her grief over Wade, and when Mrs. LeClair wouldn't cooperate, Belle suffered in silence until by chance an opportunity arose to run away—and even then, instead of standing up for herself, she'd sneaked away at dawn, to avoid a confrontation.

Now she wanted to never again depend on the luck of someone noticing her needs or including her in their plans. That wasn't being good. It was being a coward! If she wished to be treated as if she had a mind and heart of her own, Belle was going to have to behave as though she actually did.

She *wanted* this.

She wanted to run the kitchen at the Lilac Hotel Café in Break Heart, Colorado, more than she had ever wanted anything.

More, even, than she'd wanted Wade.

Oh.

My.

Yet another shocking bit of self-discovery to push to the back of her mind.

She didn't wait for Mrs. Gensch to decide. "I'd be so grateful if you'd give me a try. I'm sure I could do you proud."

She could at least get the kitchen cleaned up and put in order, and she could make just about everything she'd seen on the menu better than poor Roxanna had done, though it wouldn't be very nice to say so.

"People say I make a wonderful peach cobbler." She hadn't seen any kind of cobbler on the menu.

"Well..."

"Auntie?" Roxanna spread her hands over the disastrous cake and batted her eyelashes.

"Yes, I see your point, dear." Mrs. Gensch burst out laughing. "All right then. But on one condition, Mrs. LeClair. That you call me Charlotte."

"If you'll call me Belle?"

"Fair enough. Belle."

"Wonderful!" They shook hands. "Thank you. Charlotte."

Belle started mentally listing all the things she would make and thought of the customers enjoying her creations—and the look on Sheriff Fontana's face when he tried her peach cobbler. Luke wasn't the only fan of that dish.

But peaches weren't yet in season. What else would he like? She'd have to see what was in the cellar, take stock of the ingredients on hand, determine the kitchen's budget—

"*Hola?* Is Señora Gensch here?"

Belle, Trudy, Roxanna, and Charlotte Gensch all turned as one unit toward the kitchen doorway. How long had that frightened-looking girl been standing there? She couldn't be more than sixteen years old.

Her voice trembled. "Señor Gensch sent me... to see about work in *la cocina*."

Belle's hopes faltered. Mr. Gensch had sent this girl in for a job. In fact, it sounded like he'd hired her already.

"Who are you, my dear?" Charlotte Gensch said. "Where did you come from?"

"Carmelita Ramon. I escaped Sweet Dee's while Mrs. Montgomery was asleep."

"That sounds remarkable," Trudy said.

She was a brave girl. Or desperate. Belle smiled inside. She and Carmelita had more in common than wanting this job.

"Oh my." Charlotte Gensch paled and her hand flew to her throat. "Oh dear. One of Delilah's girls? What was Teddy thinking?"

"No, no, *señora*! I'm not—"

"The Lilac's reputation! We can't have that." Charlotte shook her head. "Besides, if I hire you away from Sweet Dee's, she'll kill me."

Carmelita's eyes went wide. "If I go back, she'll kill *me*! She wants to make me work upstairs, but I'm not like that."

Against her own best interests, Belle couldn't help defending the girl. "Mrs. Montgomery won't kill you because you don't want to... work upstairs." She surprised herself being able to say those words, let alone think them. "Or because you'd rather work for someone else."

But was that even true? Naomi had cautioned them things were done differently in the West. After all, the madam of Break Heart's bawdy house was a member of the town council. Belle looked to Trudy for confirmation.

"All right, all right. Let's all calm down and get this settled." The waitress took over matter-of-factly. She was going to be missed. "Carmelita, where are you from? And how did you end up at Sweet Dee's?"

Carmelita hesitated, as if considering how much to tell. "I came from Santa Fe. There was an advertisement in the newspaper for a cook at the Sweet Dee Hotel—"

"Hotel!" Roxanna snorted.

"—in Break Heart, Colorado. Mrs. Montgomery said I could work in *la cocina*—in the kitchen. She was very kind. Gave me food and a place to sleep and a new dress." She indicated the cotton calico frock she was wearing. "But then she told me I was too pretty to keep in the kitchen and I had to go upstairs with a man."

"Bless us and save us," Charlotte Gensch muttered.

"I told her no, I wouldn't do it, and she locked me in a closet! She said I couldn't come out until I promised to behave."

Belle steadied herself against the worktable. She wasn't an innocent. She was well aware the world was unkind to unprotected females. But this was monstrous.

"I cried and cried and pounded on the door, but she didn't care. Then later it got quiet, and I pushed against the door again. I guess I broke something because it opened right away. That lady, she was blocking the other door out to the hallway, snoring away in her chair."

Carmelita had the room in thrall. Belle started. An older man stood in an open doorway she hadn't noticed before, located at the far end of the kitchen. He wore a full white kitchen apron and had a towel thrown over one shoulder. His salt-and-pepper hair was slicked back—from steam, it seemed, rather than pomade. He appeared fascinated by Carmelita's story.

"So I climbed out the window and jumped off the balcony. A kind man on the street saw me. Señor Gensch, it was. He said what on earth are you doing, and I told him everything that happened. He sent me here. To you."

She gave Charlotte Gensch such a pathetic look Belle would have laughed if the whole thing weren't so awful.

"You'd better give this girl a job, Mrs. Gensch," Trudy said, "if only for the entertainment value."

"Yes," said the older man. Everybody looked at him, and his face turned red. He seemed surprised that he'd spoken out loud. "Carmelita tells a good story."

"And you need more than Belle here in this kitchen," Trudy went on. "Most of Roxie's trouble comes from not having enough help. If Carmelita can chop an onion, I'd say grab her while you can."

"I can chop an onion! And chilis and carrots and potatoes. And pluck chickens. I make a flan you won't believe. It will melt in your mouth, that I can promise you!"

Belle had no idea what flan was, but Carmelita's enthusiasm made her want to try it.

"You must hire her, Auntie. I think it's your Christian duty."

"Don't tell others what they owe God, Roxanna dear. It's unseemly." Charlotte Gensch rubbed her chin nervously and looked from Carmelita to Trudy to Belle to the older man and back to Carmelita. She sighed. "But I take your point."

"Carmelita's funny." The man nodded enthusiastically.

"I'll take that into consideration, Sudsy." Charlotte's fond smile made Belle even more curious. Who was that fellow?

"I've already cleared out of my room. Carmelita can stay there." Trudy turned to Carmelita. "You'll have to be up at first light every morning to light the fire in the stove and get the water boiling for Sudsy *and* for coffee."

"No problem at all, señorita. I'm a hard worker. Anybody will tell you."

Belle had her own ideas about the coffee, but this wasn't the time. With everybody else, she looked to Charlotte for her decision.

"All right then. But Carmelita, you must stay away from Sweet Dee's so as not to rile Delilah. I have no idea what I'm going to tell her."

"Hurrah!" Roxanna twirled a towel, and Trudy clapped her hands in approval.

Carmelita took over for Roxanna straightaway and went to work on the breakfast orders. She knew her way around a kitchen, all right, so much so that Trudy was able to take Roxanna aside for a quick lesson in waitressing before leaving for the train.

Belle spent the next few hours taking stock of the kitchen and planning what she'd cook for the next few days. That night's supper would be the last Roxanna cooked at the Lilac.

Belle was upstairs in Naomi's room when Charity and Faith returned to the hotel from their first day at work with more wonderful news.

"We have a place to live!" Faith said.

"Mrs. Tagget has offered to rent her house to us," Charity said. "She hasn't lived there since her husband died, but she doesn't like leaving it empty."

"We can have the rest of May and June rent-free if we're willing to give it a spring cleaning and haul her personal things up to the attic," Faith added.

"And we can use her furniture," Charity went on, "and move in as soon as we like."

"Fontana says it would suit us perfectly," Faith said.

"Oh does he?" Belle wasn't sure how she felt about Faith and Sheriff Fontana discussing personal things. The topic of whether a house would suit seemed rather intimate.

"Let's go look at it now," Charity said. "Mae gave me the key. She'll be there later, after she closes the store. The Lilac's been ace-high, but I can't wait to get a good night's sleep away from the noise of town."

Belle couldn't argue with that.

Faith said, "The sooner the house is ready, the sooner we can move in."

Belle's feet ached from being on them all day in ill-fitting shoes, but she didn't care. "Let's go."

A house with all its furnishings! It was the final necessity in securing their place in this strange new world made up of a seemingly infinite variety of characters. Kind employers. A damaged, haunted doctor. An eccentric widow who wore men's clothes. A professional matchmaker. Outlaws frightened by a mysterious seamstress. A sheriff Belle trusted to keep everyone safe.

She'd gone from East to West; from the illusion of wealth to real, earned wages; from a certain, gilded dependency made and controlled by others to an unknown, wild independence that she'd have to work very hard to keep.

She could have all this, and on her own terms. She didn't have to marry any man in order to survive in this world. If she married Chet McKinnon, it would be because she *wanted* to.

Belle had no idea what the future would bring.

And she couldn't wait to find out.

RACHEL BIRD

Chapter 20

The Little Church of Break Heart Bend was a lovely whitewashed clapboard structure nestled into a picture-perfect meadow at the southwest end of the town's undulating topography. It was impossible to imagine the soaring, transporting rhetoric of Boston Trinity's Rector Brooks fitting inside the Little Church, but the only other style of preaching Belle had ever known was Uncle James's lengthy and fiery exhortations against the fires of hell, which would be as inappropriate in this sweet place as screaming at kittens.

A square bell tower loomed above the double doors at the front entrance. Inside were two rows of sturdy oak pews with a wide aisle between them leading to a simple altar at the center. Looking from the pews, a pulpit was raised modestly high off to the left.

A lovely Mason & Hamlin reed organ stood against the opposite wall, the bench occupied by a severe-looking woman about thirty years of age. Her brown hair was parted at the center and pulled back into a plain chignon from which no curl or errant strand might dare escape.

With a serious, workmanlike expression, she began a dour hymn, pumping and fingering as if the very notes she sent out into the world would weave a spiritual net, gathering souls both witting and unwitting.

Belle prepared for a service in the style of Uncle James.

She was wrong. Parson Hood's sermon was decidedly *not* fiery, inoffensive—other than, apparently, to Faith—and gratifyingly short. He entreated his flock to do their best in their labors, avoid temptation in their pleasures, and practice the Golden Rule in their daily lives.

He also said a special prayer for Belle's parents and the lost members of the McKinnon family. It was an unexpected and consoling kindness. Belle could tell even Faith was touched, because she stopped commenting under her breath on the preacher's misquoting of scripture.

The congregation finished singing "Blest Be the Tie That Binds," and after the final benediction, to the accompaniment of the resolute organist, Belle and the others filed outside to another lovely day.

She glanced longingly at Mae Tagget's house, easily seen up a little hill from the churchyard where many of the congregants gathered. She couldn't wait to get back to it and get to work. Sheriff Fontana had been right. The house suited them perfectly, situated here at the far end of town, away from the bustle and noise of establishments on Main Street that never closed their doors.

Why, when they'd opened the windows to let in the fresh air, Belle had been delighted to hear birdsong.

All the house had needed was its dust and cobwebs cleared away, the rugs beaten, the slipcovers shaken out, and moving whatever Mae wanted up to the attic. With all hands on deck after their jobs yesterday, they'd worked until long past dark, but it was a big house, and there were still things to be done.

"Clever of Chet McKinnon to leave town for a few days," Charity said.

"Very convenient," Faith agreed. "But I'm

sure he'll be happy to come to dinner as soon as it's offered."

"He had homestead business in Greeley," Belle said. "Besides, he's of no use just now. Dr. Declan forbade him to lift anything heavy because of his ribs."

"I can be of use." Sheriff Fontana came up behind Belle and joined their circle. Why did he have such a manly voice? The back of her neck tingled. "Allow me to lend a hand."

"Why, Fontana," Faith said, "I almost mistook you for a dude."

Belle turned toward the sound of his voice and caught her breath. Faith wasn't quite on the mark. Sheriff Fontana looked nothing like a flashy Eastern pretender. His appearance was sophisticated but understated.

He wore a black woolen vest subtly embroidered with roses in black and wine-red satin thread under a charcoal suit, and the draping gold chain of a fine pocket watch showed behind the unbuttoned jacket. The collar of his white linen shirt was appropriately stiff under a wide black necktie knotted in a loose but neat bow.

His thick dark hair had been tamed and brushed back off his face—though one errant strand had broken free.

Brady Fontana could pass for a man of fashion in any Boston salon of Mrs. LeClair's choosing, and yet he couldn't hide his western vigor. Was this his usual Sunday best, or had he dressed to impress her?

Aren't you full of yourself! Belle chided herself.

"Steele and I can move the heavier objects," he told her, tilting his head at Faith. "I've learned she's stronger than she looks."

"A gallant offer, Fontana," Faith responded. "But you'd better go change out of that fancy rig into something you can get dirty."

Maybe he'd dressed to impress *her*!

At first, the sheriff had called his new employee *Miss Steele*, but she'd objected, saying no prisoner would take a Miss Steele seriously when she brought him his breakfast. Belle suspected she really just wanted to be called Deputy Steele. The sheriff then dropped the "Miss" and called her plain *Steele*. She'd decided to return the favor.

Fontana and Steele. Belle wasn't envious of the budding friendship between those two. Not a jot.

People lingered in groups, engaged in friendly conversation and stealing glimpses of Belle and her sisters. It was to be expected, their being new in town. Mae Tagget grinned at Charity and wiggled her fingers in a surreptitious greeting from where she stood with the Gensches, Mrs. Vanderhouten, and Jane Stedman.

Mr. Overstreet chased after Sally and Damon while sending Naomi pathetically hopeful glances, which she studiously did not notice. It was her free day, after all.

Parson Hood introduced them to the organist, Miss Hortensia Hood, his spinster sister. She'd come from back East to keep the preacher's house. "Someone had to do it."

Most of the people Belle didn't recognize. Notably, Dr. Declan wasn't present.

There were plenty of children.

"I'm surprised there's no school in town," Belle said. "Certainly the number of children in this congregation alone shows the need."

"You'll get no argument from me," Sheriff Fontana said. "I was planning to propose hiring a schoolteacher at the next town meeting."

"Sally and Damon Overstreet are in desperate need of schooling," Naomi said. "They've had no lessons since their mother passed, and I'm not qualified to teach."

"Luke and Hannah need schooling too," Charity said.

"I'd rather apprentice to Miss Stedman." Hannah wrinkled her nose. "I can read history in my free time."

"You're the sheriff. Why do you care?" Luke frowned, as if something had just occurred to him. "Do you have any kids?"

"Sadly, I don't." Sheriff Fontana put a hand on Luke's shoulder. "But Break Heart is my community, and I want it to flourish. That doesn't happen in a town filled with ignoramuses. Or should that be ignorami?"

Luke and Hannah both laughed and admitted they didn't know the answer.

"Also, I'm the sheriff. Having a school is a matter of the children's safety as well as their education."

"I'd like to help find a teacher." A swell of civic feeling hit Belle. "In Boston, Mrs. LeClair was always volunteering me for committees on public improvements that never improved anything but the reputations of the ladies heading the committees. Bringing a schoolteacher to Break Heart would actually do some good."

She could indeed be useful as well as ornamental!

"I would appreciate that, truly." His look of gratitude warmed Belle inside.

His attention shifted past her to a group

of ladies, including Mrs. Montgomery and Lily Rose Chapin, who stood away from the main crowd near the edge of the graveyard. Belle had already guessed the ladies were from Sweet Dee's. They'd been together at the back of the church, though Mrs. Montgomery and Lily Rose had taken a pew near the front, bold as you please.

Remembering Carmelita's story, Belle reconsidered the bawdy house madam. She'd been so kind to the Steeles yet so cruel to the young cook. There was indeed a hardness about the woman that her smile couldn't disguise. Maybe she was like Mrs. LeClair, dispensing kindness or cruelty according to the receiver's status in society.

It was a relief Carmelita wasn't here today. She wouldn't like seeing Mrs. Montgomery. She'd agreed to run the kitchen on Sundays so Belle could have the day free. She told Charlotte she was Catholic anyway and it just didn't feel like church if she couldn't hear Latin or go to confession.

Lily Rose's attention had been on the sheriff, but a couple of times she stole a glimpse at Belle. *She's sweet on him.* It was obvious to anyone with eyes. He acknowledged her smile with a quick nod.

"Ladies." He nodded to Belle and her

sisters. Then to Luke. "Young man." The two shook hands. "I'd best do as Steele here instructed and change into working clothes. I'll see you at the house in, say, an hour?"

He took his leave without speaking to Lily Rose, and against her will, Belle was glad—then immediately ashamed of herself when she saw that Lily Rose's cheeks were burning with either hurt or embarrassment.

Belle made her way over to the ladies from Sweet Dee's, and an audible gasp erupted from Mrs. Grayson and Hortensia Hood. Even Mrs. Vanderhouten pursed her lips, and Belle realized her mistake.

It must be considered unseemly, at least by some, to speak to such women. She understood. Mrs. LeClair would be appalled too. But weren't all equal at church on Sunday, if nowhere else? Anyway, it would be wrong to snub the women who'd been there for her family in a time of great need.

Lily Rose glared at Mrs. Grayson in defiance, while the other girls stood wide-eyed at Belle's approach and Mrs. Montgomery smiled as if the virtuous women of Break Heart and the painted ladies of her bawdy house met politely in public every day of the week.

Today, Belle noted, the ladies bore no hint

of paint, and their dresses were modest calico cotton prints.

"Mrs. Montgomery, Miss Chapin." She spoke loud enough for Mrs. Grayson to hear. "I wanted to thank you again for thinking of my family. I don't know what we would have done without your kindness."

Lily Rose's eyes narrowed, as if doubting Belle's sincerity, but then she relented. "It's a terrible thing for a female to be stranded with nothing." Her eyes stayed on Belle, but she seemed quite aware that Mrs. Vanderhouten had moved closer and was listening. "I know *I* didn't like it."

Chapter 21

Monday afternoon when everyone returned to the Lilac from their various employments, the Steeles collected their few belongings and checked out. The Gensch's were delighted for them—Teddy slapped his forehead and wondered aloud one more time why he hadn't thought of Mae Tagget's place in the first place.

Naomi settled their bill, Faith and Charity each grabbed a handle of the treasure chest, and they set off. Aside from a few stray ends to take care of, Mae Tagget's house was ready and waiting.

Yesterday after church, Belle hadn't seen much of the sheriff. She and Charity worked outside at the back of the house, beating rugs and shaking out curtains, while he'd been inside the whole time, moving furniture and hauling things up to the attic. With his help, the heaviest work had been completed by the end of the day.

The place was a good-sized dwelling, with five family bedrooms and servants' sleeping quarters both in the attic and downstairs off the kitchen—which made Belle sad. Mae and her husband must have hoped for a large family, but children never came. Or worse, they'd had children who didn't survive infancy.

She hung her spencer next to the others on the row of hooks in the front vestibule, then went around opening windows to let in the fresh air. She couldn't decide which she needed more, new shoes to save her poor feet, or a new dress, something comfortable to work in made of a lighter fabric and with a respectable neckline.

From the parlor, the church was partly visible, though Ma's grave was hidden beyond a dip in the yard. To Belle's surprise an empty, dissatisfied feeling came over her which she couldn't account for.

"I think it was very good of me to share." Hannah came downstairs after inspecting the curtains Belle and Charity had hung in the room where she'd volunteered to double up with Luke.

"*God loveth a cheerful giver.*" Faith winked.

"It was a generous gesture," Naomi said.

"It's generous of me too," Luke pointed out.

"It was, wasn't it? I'm quite mature, you see, now that I'm a modiste-in-training."

Belle said a silent prayer of thanksgiving on seeing her sister's smile. According to Naomi, Hannah was still having nightmares about the attack by the Deckoms. During the day, however, she was starting to reclaim her old self, and Belle felt a well of gratitude toward Jane Stedman for bringing Hannah out of the shell she'd begun to crawl inside.

Maybe Doc was right and the seamstress was something of a magician after all.

"Besides," Hannah said, "it won't be long before Belle marries Mr. McKinnon and I'll have her bedroom."

Everybody stared at Belle.

"I..."

She still hadn't mentioned Chet's offer to anybody. Had he said something to Dr. Declan? And had the doctor passed it on? What a hypocrite she was! She enjoyed listening to Doc's gossip, but it was immensely unpleasant to be its subject.

In truth, she still hadn't decided on her answer. It was nice to think she didn't have to marry if she didn't want to. But when it came down to it, maybe she did want to. She'd told Charity on the river she wanted children someday. A husband was a necessary ingredient in that recipe!

Maybe the cause of her empty feeling was the fact that this house, nice and as comfortable as it was, would never truly be hers, not if she stayed here another twenty years.

After spending the first twenty years of her life in one house, she'd moved three times this past year: to Mrs. LeClair's, to the Lilac Hotel, and now to this house on Church Lane, but not one of the homes could she call her own. Not that she wasn't filled with gratitude, but she'd never be happy until she had her own home.

Another argument in favor of accepting Chet's proposal.

"I haven't given him an answer."

"Then I take it he's asked," Charity said. "Aren't you a cool cucumber! You said nothing."

"Hello!"

She was saved from having to say more by the knock at the front door, which had been left wide open. Mae Tagget came in with Sheriff Fontana behind her. He was no less handsome in his regular workaday clothes, and Belle caught herself smiling stupidly.

He hung his hat on a hook in the vestibule, avoiding her eye. Had he overheard the talk of Mr. McKinnon's proposal?

Had it bothered him?

There was nothing she could do about it. And anyway, it would be ridiculous to pretend Chet hadn't asked her to marry him. She could have turned him down on the spot and put an end to the subject. But she hadn't, and there it was.

She really was a hypocrite! She didn't like Brady Fontana thinking she was engaged to Chet McKinnon, even though she might well accept Chet's offer.

Even though she had no desire to be more than friends with the sheriff.

Right?

"We come bearing gifts." He conquered whatever had bothered him and smiled, and it sent butterflies through her stomach. "Housewarming presents."

He'd brought a hand-pulled wagon loaded with what he called a few incidental supplies, but there were more than a few, and they were hardly incidental. Sugar, flour, salt, lard,

Fleischmann Yeast Company packets, and something called Arbuckles', which she found out was coffee beans already roasted and ground and ready for the pot. He'd brought oil for the lamps, too, and even some luxuries like lemons and spices.

"Since you enjoy cooking," he said by way of explanation when she held up a jar of cinnamon and another of nutmeg. "I wasn't sure what you'd want in your pantry, but it's good to have a stock of necessary things."

What a puzzle he was. How odd that a single man who spent his days chasing outlaws and keeping the public peace should think about things "necessary" to a well-stocked kitchen. It was... attractive.

Belle's sisters descended on him with effusive thanks. Faith ribbed her boss with a verse about exceeding all the kings of the earth for riches and wisdom. He took the kidding in stride.

"You're someone's hero now for sure." Charity winked at Belle and held up a crock of honey.

Sheriff Fontana said quietly, "Faith mentioned you prefer honey in your tea." His face was a blank, which Belle had discerned was his version of blushing. "Just tell me where you want these things stored."

"Belle can show you," Faith said without guile. "She's the kitchen expert in this family."

It was the difference between Break Heart and Boston, summarized in one exchange. Mrs. LeClair had been embarrassed by Belle's activities in the kitchen. Her family here not only loved eating her cooking, they were proud of it.

"Say, Luke, you want to give me a hand?"

Luke jumped at the chance. It was the second time the sheriff had paid particular attention to him, including him in the task at hand. He seemed to understand that a boy needed to be noticed by the men in his life, and Belle felt another swell of gratitude.

It seemed every day was full of signs she'd done right to leave Boston. Still, she had a nagging feeling she shouldn't have gotten away so easily. She had to send that twenty dollars back as soon as she could.

"Lemons!" Luke lifted one of the boxes from the handcart. "And oranges too!"

"But how can that be?" Belle was wonderstruck.

"They're from California. With the railroad, we can get just about anything now." The sheriff sounded proud of his town.

That was attractive too.

"Can we have lemonade?" Luke held a lemon to his nose and closed his eyes.

"Yes, of course." Belle did the same. Heavenly! "I'll make some after everything is put away."

"I have a gift for you too, of a kind," Mae Tagget said. "The passel of frocks and things in the attic. Half I never wore before, and all I'll never wear again. You're welcome to them, if they're not too old-fashioned for you young girls. Some of the fabrics are very fine, and I'm told Hannah here is a magician with needle and thread. If you can pull them apart and put them back together to suit, you're welcome to them."

"What a blessing!" Naomi said.

And what a relief. Now with her first pay envelope Belle could order some underthings from Mrs. Vanderhouten.

And visit the shoemaker.

She thought wistfully of all her lovely things back in Boston. Her satin morning slippers, riding boots, dancing shoes, walking shoes, and evening slippers alone had taken up an embarrassing amount of space in her closet. She would often change outfits three or four times a day, depending on how many appointments her mother-in-law had made and whether they were dining formally. She wondered if Mrs. LeClair had given all her clothes away.

Or burned them!

Sheriff Fontana raised an eyebrow at her chuckle, but she shook her head and looked away. She could hardly explain she'd been thinking longingly of lost stockings and fans and other luxuries.

In all her life she'd never thought so much about money as in these past two weeks. Till now, she'd gone from utter dependence in her father's house to utter dependence in her mother-in-law's. In both circumstances—one with never enough and the other with an overabundance—money matters were not considered her province, and she'd had no reason to question the order of things.

She'd even forgotten to ask Charlotte Gensch what her pay would be, and now she was embarrassed to. She'd just have to wait until payday to find out.

Somehow she doubted it would be enough to get everything she needed right away, even after all these thoughtful presents, but after Mae Tagget's generosity with her dresses, Belle would surely be able to buy some footwear that didn't give her blisters.

"That would be wonderful," Hannah was

saying to Mae. She hesitated and looked at Naomi. "Would it be so very bad to come out of mourning early?"

Belle had been in mourning for two months now, since the news of Wade's murder. A year was the very minimum considered proper to mourn a husband, but that was in her old world. She was ready to put away the black.

And she had Wade's blessing to do so. She eyed the lantern oil and thought of his letters. With her own room again and the privacy that afforded, she looked forward to reading through them tonight after she retired.

She made a simple dinner and invited Mae and Sheriff Fontana to stay. They gathered at Mae's large cherrywood dining table, and when Luke said grace, Belle had to wipe away a tear.

"What is it, Belle?" Hannah said. "Are you feeling sad?"

"Quite the opposite." She squeezed her little sister's hand. "I'm just so glad to be with my family." In Boston she'd missed the simple joys like sitting down to a meal at the end of the day, giving thanks for their blessings, sharing troubles and victories alike.

By their easy banter, she could tell Mae and the sheriff were good friends. True to form, he didn't say much about anything, and even less about himself, but Mae Tagget was a different kettle of fish.

By the end of the evening, they'd learned that Brady Fontana had brought his widowed mother west from Philadelphia for the air a year before becoming sheriff, that he had a ranch outside Break Heart which shared a boundary with Mr. Overstreet's orchards, and though he lived in town he'd kept his ranch hands and household staff on "so the place wouldn't go to rack and ruin."

"Brady's right. That's why I'm so happy to have you girls move in," Mae said. "I can't bear to think of living here without my Stan, but I don't want the house to fall apart either. Houses are meant to be lived in, and they will be—if not by the living, then by the dead."

Mrs. LeClair could use a dose of Mae Tagget's philosophy. The house in Boston was slowly becoming inhabited by Wade's ghost— kept earthbound by a mother who refused to accept that he was gone.

Belle wouldn't allow that to happen to her family. Her parents' ghosts mustn't hang on too long.

"Hannah, I do think it would be good to put away your mourning. We all should. Wade once wrote me that if anything happened to him he wanted me to go on with my life. I believe Ma and Pa would feel the same."

"I agree." Naomi surprised her. Belle had expected her to fight the idea more than anyone. She'd been so close to Ma. "Of course we'll remember them, but we mustn't be maudlin about it. They brought us to Colorado to start a new life, and we honor their memory by doing just that."

The sheriff turned away with a stoic but pained look. Belle could kick herself. She hadn't even thought of his fiancée. It was two years now since her death. He must have loved her very much.

Chapter 22

Brady woke late, his body protesting the new day. In the middle of the night, he'd been called to Sweet Dee's to break up a disturbance and didn't get to bed till first light. Law enforcement was a young man's game, and it was becoming harder to ignore that he was no longer fresh as a daisy. He never used to notice when he didn't get a full night's sleep.

At thirty-one he wasn't an old man by any means, but Luke's question after church on Sunday had set him thinking about his mortality. *Do you have any kids?* It was this job, not his age, making him soft. More paperwork and public relations, less chasing bad guys. Brady sat at a desk three hours for every hour he was in the saddle.

And time *was* passing.

Do you have any kids? No. Nor a wife. He didn't even live in his own home.

That's just how he wanted it. Right? It wasn't his guilt over Thalia alone that kept him unhitched. In this business, a man had no right to marry, much less have kids. By its very nature, every day on the job he'd risk making a widow and orphans out of those he loved dearest.

Now, for the first time in two years, his mind took a different turn. Instead of conquering his demons, could he just... walk away from them?

Hand in his star. Get back to Nighthawk. Work his own place. Restart the life he had put on hold.

Tempting as it was, the answer was no.

He'd promised himself, as well as the town, he'd make Break Heart safe for decent people. He'd turn in his star when the mission was accomplished—or a better man for the job wanted the badge. He'd run the Deckoms out of town but, as the attack on the Steeles proved, not far enough. He couldn't claim success while they still lived in the county. Or even the state.

He'd always figured civilization itself

would take care of the Deckoms. With the mode of transportation moving from the river to the railroads, their source of business was dwindling. Eventually, they'd move on to easier pickings.

But Luke Steele's question—*Do you have any kids?*—forced Brady to reexamine the tactic of waiting for nature to take its course.

Eventually suddenly was too long.

A female voice echoed up from below and made him smile. Sounded like a schoolmarm lecturing a classroom of wayward children.

Right. His new employee. *Clerk*—no matter how many times Faith Steele insisted she was his deputy.

But definitely some kind of employee.

By the end of her first day, she'd had the office clean and neat as a pin. By the end of her second, she'd organized his paperwork. Faith Steele had accounted for herself, and he wasn't fool enough to deny it.

Today was her fifth day, and he didn't know how he ever ran the place without her. Though it would be nice if she quit giving him the side-eye for returning the Deckoms' firearms, including that Colt she took off Cole.

He splashed water on his face, shaved, and dressed while Faith's discourse below continued, though he couldn't make out the words. What a racket down there! She was sure giving the new prisoner an earful. In a world where the bad guys were mere nuisances, like their current guest, Faith would be a fine deputy.

When he came upon the Steele sisters being set upon by Frank Deckom and his boys, it had taken everything in him not to shoot Frank through the heart and keep firing until Cole, Jessop, and Red John, every one, were no more. In the interests of not starting a war between Break Heart and the Trading Post, he'd shot the coward's hat off instead.

He was glad he and Teddy and the others got there in time, but it still drove him crazy thinking what would have happened if they hadn't.

Orphaned and penniless, the Steeles' plight called on his sense of duty and gave him the chance to do the right thing, to prove to himself he could be of use. That he wasn't a poor excuse for a man. He'd failed Thalia. He'd spend the rest of his life making up for it.

He'd enjoyed having dinner with them and Mae Tagget the other night. They were fine young ladies who'd make welcome additions to Break Heart. The boy could use a father's guidance, like all boys, but Luke was a good kid and Brady figured he'd grow up a center shooter.

All the ladies were handsome in their way. Even Faith, gawky as she was, would be a looker after a few more years.

Charity was a corker. She had a wild streak and a rebellious nature.

Naomi was the dark horse. She was like many firstborn daughters, overworked, not enough fun in her life. When she smiled, you could see possibilities. Her kind of beauty didn't fade with youth, the loveliness that became more evident with time.

But it was Mrs. LeClair Brady kept returning to in his thoughts. She was the prettiest of them all. He'd noticed her first, and last, and longest. And kept on noticing every chance he got.

Belle. It fit her. She was more than a pretty picture though. He'd noticed how careful she was, how she measured her words, the gracefulness in her movements. The fact she checked the time whenever she passed the grandfather clock in the hotel lobby tickled him no end. The faraway worry in her eyes when she thought no one was looking intrigued him.

Belle Steele LeClair had a story she didn't tell, not even to her sisters. The more Brady saw her, the more he wanted her to tell him that story.

When Thalia was killed, he pulled away from women. He didn't deserve a woman's kindness when it was his carelessness that got her killed. If only he'd gone to Philadelphia to meet her and had traveled back to Break Heart with her. That would have been the right thing to do, the manly thing to do. He could have defended her. Protected her.

But he'd told himself he couldn't leave the ranch, not during roundup. He was needed bringing the herd down from the hills. As if Thalia was less precious than a few head of cattle.

When the need for a sheriff arose, he'd answered the call, thinking he'd somehow make up for his failure by protecting and defending others. The work couldn't bring Thalia back, but it had proved satisfying in its own right.

After a time, his self-loathing began to feel like self-indulgence, mere melodrama when compared to Doc Declan's grief-stricken self-condemnation. Doc had been there. Had actually felt the lives of those people slip through his hands. He was a physician, and still he couldn't save any of them. Doc's greater claim to unyielding self-flagellation had cured Brady of his own self-pity.

And now it seemed he might be cured of his antipathy toward romance.

For as surprising as it was to own it, *romantic* was how he felt about Belle LeClair.

He wanted to see her, be near her, whenever possible. To watch her work, listen to her talking with Charlotte or her sisters. He found himself wondering what he could do to make her life easier here in Break Heart. He wanted to woo her.

Not that he would. These inclinations would take no form beyond dangerous thoughts. Belle LeClair was off-limits. For reasons only heaven could understand, though that exquisite woman was not after all married, she wasn't free. She'd engaged herself to the pathetic excuse for a man now downstairs, locked in a cell.

Faith's words became clear as he reached the bottom of the stairs.

"*...a mocker, strong drink is raging, and whosoever is deceived thereby is not wise.*"

Yup. Sounded about right.

The door to the cells was open, and he called through while pouring himself a cup from the pot on the stove.

"Morning, McKinnon."

Faith's coffee wasn't as good as his own,

but it was head and shoulders above Charlotte's brew. Which, praise heaven, was no more, thanks to the Lilac's new cook.

Nothing topped Belle's coffee. Brady blew out a sigh. Or her biscuits. Or apple-walnut muffins. His stomach growled, urging him to get a move on. It was already late enough, and he didn't want to miss breakfast today.

"Mornin', Fontana." Faith's attempt at a western twang blended amusingly with her Minnesota accent.

"Sheriff, thank God!" The prisoner put in his two cents. "Let me out of here!"

The pathetic caterwauling had started last night, from the moment Chet McKinnon realized he was under arrest. The fact he was still bawling about it inclined Brady to let him stew in his own juices a spell.

"*Who hath woe? Who hath sorrow?*" Faith winked at Brady while he was at the stove. What the heck was she wearing?

"What did I do to deserve this Bible thumpin'?"

"Public drunkenness. Destruction of private property," Brady obliged. "Acting like a saphead in general."

"*Who hath contentions? Who hath babbling? Who hath wounds without cause?*"

"Aw, can't a guy have a little fun?"

McKinnon rattled the bars of his cell. The idiot. "I hadn't had a drink in a week."

"Who hath redness of eyes? They that tarry long at the wine!"

"Sweet Dee is plenty fried with you," Brady said. "I recommend, once you get out of here, you avoid her establishment for a spell."

Delilah was mad about a couple of things, McKinnon not being the most pressing. But he didn't need to know that.

The keys were in the desk, right where they should be. Brady took the ring back to the cells.

"I didn't do anything wrong." McKinnon moved away from the bars, as did Faith on her side, to give him room to unlock the cell.

"You fell on a table and busted it, dropped a full bottle of whiskey and shattered it, and then you insulted her favorite bartender."

Lily Rose had had her knife out, ready to have at it, when Brady grabbed her wrist and pulled her off McKinnon. The idiot didn't know how lucky he was.

"Impossible. You can't insult a painted cat."

Faith rolled her eyes. *"She girdeth her loins with strength, and strengtheneth her arms."* She went out to the front room and sat down to the paperwork on her desk. To her credit, she didn't let McKinnon rattle her.

Brady turned the key and the lock clicked... shut. "Just as I thought. I forgot to lock you in." He walked away.

"Hey, wait a minute."

At the door, Brady called over his shoulder. "I suggest you ponder what you want your reputation to be in this town—for the good of all concerned."

He shut the door on McKinnon's belly-aching and got to the subject truly baffling him. "You mind explaining that outfit?"

Faith was dressed like a deputy, all right. In a man's shirt, trousers, boots and belt. Her neckerchief was a pretty swath of cotton in a flower print, the only mark of femininity. A ribbon of black crepe was tied around her left arm. She hadn't given up mourning completely.

"We were going through Mae's clothes, and when I told her I envied her trousers, she offered to let me have some of her husband's things."

"I never thought of Mae Tagget as an influencer of fashion."

"I know Belle's glad to get out of that mourning dress and into something more practical for the kitchen." Faith sat down at the desk with a stack of forms that needed sorting. "But I couldn't convince her, or Charity either, to try pants."

"Praise heaven above for small favors. What about Naomi?"

He chuckled when she looked at him like he was crazy to suggest it, just what he was going for.

He wondered if the Steele sisters knew where their mourning clothes came from. Ophelia's wake would be long remembered in this town. Those dresses too, especially since Delilah's ladies had shucked the jackets while parading up Main Street. Lily Rose had worn her dress very well.

Lily Rose wasn't one of the fancy ladies. She was a bartender and ambitious and had worked hard to become Delilah's right-hand gal. When she spread a rumor of there being something between them, he'd done nothing to deny it. He had no care for his reputation then, and when other men thought the sheriff had staked a claim, she suffered less abuse from that quarter. He didn't mind offering her protection that way.

But they were friends and never meant to be more. Or so he'd believed until last Sunday after church, when she gave him a few odd, possessive   looks   that   made   him uncomfortable. Had he implied more to Lily Rose than he intended?

I miss you, Brady. Last night she'd fought like a tiger until she saw who it was that pulled her off McKinnon. She'd melted into his arms, all soft and full of promise. *Come see me later.*

She told him a lady has needs same as a man, despite what they say during the day, even so-called virtuous women. Maybe. But Thalia had never given any evidence of that being true. They'd kissed, of course, but he'd never felt the kind of desire from her as Lily Rose had shown him a few times in the past— or last night.

It's because of her, isn't it? she'd said. *Mrs. LeClair. People are talking, saying how much attention the sheriff pays the Lilac's new cook. The way I saw you looking at her after church, I'm thinking it's true. You've changed.*

That was the moment he realized Lily Rose was right. Belle LeClair had changed him. Even if she was off-limits, she'd reawakened him. Reminded him who he was. He *did* care about his reputation. He didn't want her to think he was seeing Lily Rose. Or anybody.

I'm sorry, Lily Rose. It's over.

He remembered choosing the supplies for

the Steeles' housewarming gift, how he'd paid special attention to what Belle might need or, better, enjoy. He'd been particularly gratified that Tagget's had a supply of honey in stock. Then when he and Mae got to the house, the front door was open. He heard Belle talking about marrying that lickspittle McKinnon. That alone had been consternating enough.

Then he saw her.

The gentle curve of her shoulders, the way that black gown hugged her waist and accented the swell of her hips, the delicate swoosh when she moved. The creamy skin of her arms.

He'd read the word *transported* but never thought he'd have call to use it. Not until then did he truly know what it meant. His guardian angel, if he had one, must be a trickster who'd brought Belle LeClair into his life to knock the sense back into him. It had worked.

But it was awfully hard, wanting to get his life straight for the one person he could never share it with. He sighed and picked up his hat from the stand.

"Heading over to the Lilac, Fontana?" Faith smiled.

"Reckon so." Was she mocking him? "As I do most days."

In point of fact, Brady had more to do at

the Lilac this morning than eat a late breakfast. Delilah Montgomery was on a raging tear and screaming for blood. Apparently, Charlotte and Teddy had stolen one of her girls.

Chapter 23

The kitchen doors swung open with a clatter, and Belle dished out the last of the scrambled eggs and ham as Roxanna bounced in happily from the dining room to collect the order.

"It's finally slowing down out there." The waitress deftly loaded three plates onto one arm and scooped up the fourth with her free hand. "No new orders for the moment."

Belle almost checked her watch, then stopped from reaching into her pocket. Even if it had been working, she didn't need to know the exact hour and minute. She was fine.

Everything was truly fine in her lovely new world.

She was doing work she enjoyed and was

good at with people she liked and who liked her. She felt secure and stable. At peace. All was as it should be. She was... content.

Different things brought joy to different people. With the exception of Naomi—who'd made a bad bargain, to Belle's mind—it seemed her sisters too were finding their way toward some kind of happiness.

Charity and Mae Tagget had hit it off right away. They were already talking of redesigning the layout of the general store to make it more efficient to find things and easier on Mae's back. Charity was revealing herself to be industrious and hardworking, and she'd never seemed happier.

Faith was having the time of her life at the sheriff's office. Belle could imagine her sister happily quoting scripture to ne'er-do-wells and trying to convince Brady to give her a deputy's star.

But the best news was Hannah. She seemed to be recovering from the ordeal on the river and the Deckoms' attack.

To be sure, Hannah dismissed Abigail Vanderhouten in the thoughtless way all young people dismissed their elders. But she was enthralled by Jane Stedman, who apparently had all the virtues and, at twenty-two, was old enough to admire while young enough to relate to. The seamstress was Hannah's new ideal, and all the better for it.

It had been a surprise to learn Jane and Belle were the same age. The seamstress seemed so much stronger, more worldly, more competent, more... complete, if still quite mysterious.

Last night all through supper it was *Jane made her own walking boots* and *Jane faces her seams this way* and *Jane showed me how to make a French knot!*

Charity had said then maybe Jane Stedman really was a witch and Hannah said maybe she was. No one cared. They all laughed happily, for Hannah was herself again and even blossoming. It was wonderful.

At the Lilac, Carmelita was a godsend. A hard worker, always cheerful—and as Trudy had predicted, a thoroughly entertaining storyteller. And though Belle would never fathom being happy as a waitress, Roxanna loved her new position.

In this moment, Belle could truly believe each person had their own guardian angel and their own path to happiness. The trick was understanding the road her angel was trying to guide her on and surrendering her own stubborn ideas about what was best. Was she supposed to marry Chet or work at the

Lilac?

The Lilac made her happy, and the thought of marrying Chet was... suffocating. Was that a guide? Or was she just being obstinate, trying to substitute her own will for God's? The dilemma was driving her crazy.

She didn't doubt Chet cared for her, though in the past she'd never seen him as a possible beau. He was Gregor McKinnon's boy. Daniel's little brother. But maybe he'd had a sort of crush on her all along. Now he wanted to build a good life and create a family together.

Maybe Chet McKinnon had survived the rapids and ended up with Belle in Break Heart for a reason.

"Everybody is still talking about how good the coffee is." Roxanna returned. She didn't mind in the least that Belle's cooking was enthusiastically preferred to hers. "And Mr. Grayson wants to know if there are any more muffins."

"Um..." Belle glanced at the counter where she'd set aside two apple-walnut muffins, wrapped in a tea towel. Yesterday Sheriff Fontana said how much he liked them. He hadn't been in yet today, so she'd kept those out for him.

"No, the muffins are all gone." Carmelita winked at Belle. "Tell Grayson to come again tomorrow."

"Will do!" Roxanna breezed out of the kitchen.

"I'm sure the sheriff will be in soon," Carmelita said as the door swung shut. "I heard he had a late night."

For being in town less than a week, the Lilac's second cook sure was a fount of gossip. Belle wanted to ask what she meant about the sheriff's late night, except she didn't want to show too much interest in Brady Fontana.

"We'd better get started on lunch. I need vegetables chopped for the stew."

"I'll get the carrots and more potatoes." Carmelita picked up a basket and headed for the root cellar down under the back stairs.

"We need more onions too!"

Belle washed her hands and dried them on the apron that covered her new frock. Mae Tagget was shorter and wider than Belle, but Hannah had made a few quick tucks and Belle had decided to wear it without letting down the hem. So what if her ankles showed? No one in the kitchen cared, and it was so much cooler and more comfortable.

Her next mission was to find a pair of shoes to fit. Too bad she couldn't make her own, like Jane Stedman! Her working hours at the Lilac were five thirty in the morning to two thirty in the afternoon, with Sundays off. It wasn't yet noon, and her feet were killing her.

All things considered, she had no real complaints. She couldn't stop pinching herself to be sure she wasn't dreaming. She'd never expected to feel optimistic again, but over the past several days she'd begun to really believe a contented life was possible.

She was free of Mrs. LeClair, and she had a wonderful job, kind employers, and a cozy house to live in with her own bedroom.

As long as she stayed there.

Chet was past the worst danger of his injuries, and he was making plans. He'd gone to Greeley, which he'd found out had a land office after all, to learn what parcels were available close to Break Heart so Belle could be near her sisters.

Before leaving, he'd asked her for an answer to his proposal, but she couldn't bring herself to give him one. When he pressed her, she told him fine, if he had to have the answer that day it would be no. He'd gone all cold on the outside and seething on the inside.

Not like Sheriff Fontana, whose little

outrages were over injustice or plain stupidity. No, Chet had been angry at Belle. For a fleeting second, she'd thought he might hit her. But the moment passed so quickly she wondered if she only imagined it.

"Keep frowning like that, you'll get a big fat line between your eyebrows." Carmelita came back with the vegetables, plenty of onions on top of the pile. "That's what *mi mami* used to say."

"She was right." Belle shook her head and grabbed a knife to help peel and chop. She'd fancied herself as a kind of Lady Bountiful, that she'd be Carmelita's teacher, but she'd been quickly disabused of that notion. Carmelita spoke of many dishes Belle had never heard of that sounded delicious. They were going to learn from each other.

"Who were you thinking of with such a sour face?"

"Was it that bad?" Belle laughed. She should just accept Chet and get on with things. Love would grow as they built a life together. And maybe he wouldn't mind if she kept working at the Lilac, at least until children came. Her wages would pay for stronger hands than hers to help on the farm.

"Not that fool Chet McKinnon, I hope," Carmelita went on. "I heard Sheriff Fontana clipped his horns good last night."

"That can't be right. Mr. McKinnon isn't in Break Heart. He has business in Greeley."

"I guess he came back. He got drunk as a skunk at Sweet Dee's last night and was bragging to everybody there on how his bride-to-be was the Lilac's pretty new cook."

"Oh no." So Doc wasn't the one spreading gossip.

"Oh *si*. And then when Lily Rose wouldn't go upstairs with him, he started tearing up the place. Sheriff Brady came and hauled him off to the calaboose."

Sheriff Brady. Charlotte and Roxanna called him that. Carmelita must have picked it up.

Wait. What?

"Chet's in jail?"

Carmelita shrugged, not subtly. "That's what I hear."

Apparently, the Break Heart gossip network rivaled that of Mrs. LeClair's circle in Boston.

The kitchen doors swung open again, only this time it wasn't Roxanna. Sheriff Fontana stood there, his hat between his hands. Respectful. Calm. But purposeful. There was nothing wasted about the man.

"Sheriff Fontana, hello."

He went cool and even more formal, if that was possible. *Darn.* They'd agreed to use their Christian names.

"I have something for you." Belle fetched the napkin from the counter, and when she turned around again, she almost bumped into him. He'd followed her and now took a step back, but he remained nearer than need be.

She set the napkin on the worktable. Their hands brushed against each other lightly as he reached for it, and she felt her face warm. He opened the little package with innocent anticipation. On seeing what was inside, he cracked one of his rare smiles and it felt like a reward.

"Let me get you a cup of coffee to go with that."

"I'd appreciate it." He took a quick bite and uttered a satisfied moan. "Delicious."

"I'm so glad, but I doubt you came into the kitchen for muffins and coffee."

"Don't be so sure about that. I did hope something along these lines would be included in this meeting."

"Is there something else you need?" She set the mug down.

He reached for the coffee and their hands brushed together. Tingles skittered up her arm and her cheeks burned, and he took a beat too long in answering.

It struck her then there could be a double meaning in her question. Her heart raced as she realized she *wanted* him to need something else. Something only she could give.

This was terrible!

She turned away—and caught Carmelita watching the whole thing with a big grin. The sly girl put on an innocent face and went back to chopping carrots.

Chapter 24

"Oh Brady, there you are." With Charlotte's arrival, the sheriff's attention shifted away from Belle. "Roxanna said you wanted to see me."

The moment had passed, but not its effect. Belle's sense of contentment flew away, replaced by the feeling something was missing. The emptiness she felt the day she moved into Mae Tagget's house returned. Emptiness, she knew in her heart, Chet McKinnon couldn't fill.

Not now. Not ever.

"I do." Brady answered Charlotte while looking at Carmelita. "It's about your new help in the kitchen. Delilah is having a fit. Says you poached one of her girls."

What?

"Nobody poached nobody!" Carmelita's eyes went wide. "I'm not going back to that *mujer*! She's the devil!"

"No one is going to make anybody do anything they don't want to. I take it you're Carmelita Ramon." Brady calmly sipped his coffee and finished his second muffin, giving Carmelita time to get hold of her nerves.

As if that girl would even try! She thrived on drama.

"Surely not," Belle said. "Mrs. Montgomery wanted to make Carmelita work"—she couldn't bring herself to say it— "somewhere other than the kitchen."

"That's not going to happen." Brady (*Brady!*) spoke so strongly it was impossible to doubt him. "But Delilah feels she's been taken advantage of."

"*She* taken advantage of!"

What kind of crazy town was this?

"I'm told expenses were incurred. A new dress. A broken lock and a busted door."

"That might be so." Carmelita chopped carrots furiously between waving the vegetable knife. "What was I supposed to do? Take off the dress and escape naked into the street?"

"No," Brady said drily. "That wouldn't

do."

"Oh dear." Charlotte's hand went to her throat. "What does Delilah want?"

"Ten dollars—for the dress, the damage to the door and lock, and for having to advertise for another girl."

"I'll never have ten spare dollars in all my life! It isn't fair!" Carmelita slammed the knife down on the worktable. "That lady told me I could work in the kitchen. She *gave* me this dress. Then after I put it on, she told me I had to pay her back... that way. She tricked me!"

"I believe you, Carmelita." Brady was gentle with her. This might be the way things were done in the West, to trick girls into sin, but he obviously wasn't going along with it. "Charlotte, what are Carmelita's wages?"

"Three dollars and twenty-five cents a week. She's going to run the night kitchen."

Oh. Good to know. Surely Belle would make as much. New shoes couldn't be too far away.

"All right," the sheriff said. "This is what we'll do. I'll pay Mrs. Montgomery her ten dollars out of the widows and orphans fund, and Mrs. Gensch will take fifty cents a week from your pay until the ten dollars is paid back. So for the next five months your wages will be two dollars and seventy-five cents."

"It isn't fair."

"I agree." Brady gave Carmelita a conspiratorial look. "But you did get a nice dress in the bargain, not to mention the satisfaction of breaking Mrs. Montgomery's door and escaping her nefarious designs."

Carmelita tried to fight it, but a begrudging smile escaped her.

"Will this be all right with you, Charlotte?"

"It will. Thank you, Brady." Charlotte looked at him hopefully. "I expect you'll arrange things with Delilah?"

"All in a day's work."

"Ah, I just thought of something." Carmelita broke out in a grin. "This means I'll have my job five months, at least!"

"There you go, seeing the bright side." Brady turned to Belle. "Thank you for the coffee and muffins, ma'am."

Ma'am? Belle followed him out to the lobby, almost to the front door. "Sheriff Fontana, could I talk to you?"

"Brady. I thought we settled that."

"We did, but you called me—oh, never mind. Yes. Brady."

"That's better." He didn't smile often, but when he did it was like a gift. This was merely a twinkle in his eye, but she liked it as much.

"And none of this *ma'am* stuff. You'll call me Belle?"

"Belle."

A sigh escaped her. She didn't like to ask, but she had to know. "Is it true Chet McKinnon is locked up in one of your jail cells?"

"I'm afraid so." A cloud replaced the twinkle in Brady's eyes. "He got a little rowdy up at Sweet Dee's last night and I brought him down to sleep it off, nothing worse than that. I'll let him go in a couple of hours. I doubt Delilah will press charges."

"Press charges..."

Had Brady heard Chet brag about their engagement? An engagement that didn't exist! That she knew now would never exist.

Belle would no more marry Chet McKinnon than Wesley LeClair. She blew out the breath she didn't know she was holding. It was a relief to have made up her mind.

"He shouldn't have acted like such a fool."

"I'm sure he feels the same by now. Your sister's been letting him know what the Lord thinks of his behavior."

She laughed. "Good."

Carmelita was right. Chet must have come

back early. What was he doing at Sweet Dee's anyway? It was embarrassing. She couldn't talk about it anymore.

"Things are different here than in Boston, that's for sure. Thank you for helping Carmelita."

"Poaching employees is considered a serious breach of civic etiquette in this town, what with every tradesman so short of labor."

"If I'd known that from the start, it would have saved me a lot of anxiety over finding work."

"Anyone would be lucky to have you."

They both smiled, suddenly shy of each other. Belle had the feeling they were being watched. Sure enough, Charlotte was at the front desk, pretending to examine the guest register. Belle took leave of Brady and thanked him again for Carmelita's sake.

"Say hello to Faith for me."

She turned away but didn't head for the kitchen. Brady's solution to Carmelita's problem had given her an idea. She fished Wade's watch out of her pocket and put it on the desk.

"Charlotte, would you lend me five dollars against my wages? This watch can be my collateral. It doesn't keep time—it was ruined in the river—but it's made of gold and silver and I'm sure it's worth more."

"I am sure it is. But dear girl, I need no collateral. Of course you can have five dollars against your wages—more if you like."

"Five will be enough. I need a better pair of shoes if I'm going to be on my feet all day. And keep the watch, just to humor me." Belle liked the idea of collateral. It made things tidy.

"If you say so. Come with me."

Charlotte led Belle to the office, unlocked the cashbox and took out the money in coins, then locked Wade's watch away for safekeeping.

Belle thought of the twenty dollars she had to repay Mrs. LeClair. Some would say she ought to sell Wade's watch, the only thing of real value she owned, but that felt like a sacrilege.

"Didn't we have some excitement today!" Charlotte headed back to the front desk. "It's a relief to have the matter settled. Between you and me and the fence post, Delilah has a dark side."

Obviously. Belle never would have guessed it when she'd first met the woman. All people had it inside them to go the wrong way, she supposed. That's why it was so important to love and support each other, give each other strength for when the test came.

She would have to be kind when she gave Chet the bad news. She suspected he had it in him to go the wrong way.

"It was good of the sheriff to help Carmelita like that," Belle said. "Isn't it wonderful there's a widows and orphans fund to help out with... emergencies?"

"My sweet, innocent girl." Charlotte burst out laughing. "There's no widows and orphans fund. The ten dollars will come out of his pocket. But don't worry about Brady Fontana. He's a very wealthy man."

Chapter 25

After work, Belle stopped at JOSEPH
WEISSENEGGER, SHOEMAKER, the shop next door
to Grayson's. She had her measurements
taken and ordered a sensible pair of low, six-
button walking boots. Charlotte's words still
rang in her mind.

He's a very wealthy man.

Not likely. Brady Fontana acted like no
rich man Belle ever knew.

Just look how he handled Carmelita's
situation, keeping in mind her needs and
resources when he came up with a plan to pay
Delilah Montgomery. The wealthy people of
Mrs. LeClair's circle barely noticed the
existence of those they considered the lower
orders, except as objects of their charitable

endeavors.

Even Evangeline, a good and decent person, was blithely unaware of life's realities and didn't understand why everybody couldn't have champagne and strawberry ice on a whim.

Brady Fontana wasn't like that at all. Obviously, Charlotte Gensch's idea of wealth was more modest than Belle's.

"These will be ready on Sunday." Mr. Weissenegger brought her out of her thoughts. "You can pick the pair up after church."

"Five days?"

"*Ach, nee!* They *could* be ready in five hours—if you don't mind them falling apart five hours after that." He laughed at his own joke. "The drying time between steps can't be rushed, my good woman."

It would have to do. Belle thanked him and moved on. She'd order another pair of shoes next month. Her wardrobe would never again attain the broad scope she'd enjoyed in Boston. On the other hand, her life in Break Heart wouldn't require so many clothes.

She'd be alone at the house for the next hour or so, but if Belle had her way, that wouldn't last—she intended to suggest they hire household help. With everyone but Luke bringing in wages, they could afford a housemaid at the least, and very likely a cook too. As much as she enjoyed her work, she wasn't about to be tied to an oven all the waking hours of every day.

Faith and Charity would probably agree, but she wasn't sure of Naomi, who was used to being in charge of all that. Pa had never brought in an income sufficient to provide so much as a chambermaid, and Naomi, more than Ma, had run an efficient, well-organized household, directing and supervising Belle, Charity, and Faith in the necessary arts.

Belle suspected Hannah's skill with needle and thread developed more from her desire to escape washing floors than an actual love of sewing.

This was the one subject where Belle bowed to Mrs. LeClair. After a lifetime being told servants were an extravagance and a vanity, she'd been shocked by her mother-in-law's sincere conviction that they were as necessary as food, clothing, and shelter to a civilized existence.

And then she'd promptly, and happily, converted.

The problem with domestic help would be finding it. As Brady had said, Break Heart was a labor-starved town—unlike Boston, where the constant inflow of immigrants provided ample workers and drove down wages. Here in the West, gold fever, and now silver fever too, made sweeter promises than the chance to wash dirty linens and change out chamber pots for two dollars a week and a stuffy room off a hot kitchen or a freezing top-floor garret.

The Boston house had crawled with servants. At first Belle had likened them to a colony of ants, always moving to an organized purpose. Of course, once she got to know the people, the metaphor foundered. Dottie and others in the kitchen even became her friends.

On the other hand, Belle came to see Finola as her enemy. Mrs. LeClair's spy. Maybe it had been wrong to lace that tea with laudanum on the night of her escape, but had Belle not done so, there would have been no escape.

She wondered what Dottie would think of her new position. She would write, as promised, but not yet. Not until she could repay the twenty dollars.

* * *

Brady left his meeting with Delilah Montgomery in a worse mood than going in.

She was a businesswoman, she'd told him, and it would be bad for business if word got out she let McKinnon off easy after he trashed her place and accosted her bartender. *Ask me again tomorrow.*

Brady wasn't getting rid of McKinnon today.

Delilah was right, of course. The fool had to face the consequences of his actions. But it meant more listening to that loudmouth blather on about marrying Belle.

Not just yet though. Brady wasn't ready to go back to the office, and with Faith Steele there, he didn't have to. Another point in her favor. He'd make the rounds through town, then stop by Calico Manor and let Belle know McKinnon wouldn't be free as soon as he'd thought.

Calico Manor. He smiled at the appellation the town had given Stan and Mae Tagget's place as soon as word got out the Steeles were moving in. He wasn't sure the ladies would like it. Luke surely wouldn't, poor kid!

"Sheriff Fontana!" Charlotte Gensch beckoned to him from the Lilac's veranda. "Brady, might I have a word?"

He crossed the street, and she led him back to her office where she opened the safe.

"I wondered if you might take a look at

this piece."

She handed him a familiar-looking gold jewelers case which contained a very fine B.W. Raymond. "Why do you have Mrs. LeClair's watch?"

"She left it with me as collateral for a loan—don't look at me like that, Brady Fontana. I told her I needed none, but she insisted. It's a beautiful piece, isn't it?"

"Excellent."

"But it was damaged in the rapids. Do you think you could fix it?"

"I'd be glad to try."

Charlotte wrapped the watch in a handkerchief. "Best she not know you have it though. Let it be a nice surprise."

"You mean you don't want Belle to think you've made known her private business." Brady smiled. "How much did she borrow?"

"Five dollars."

Brady blinked. A working B.W. Raymond mechanism sold for more than a hundred dollars, and that was before a jeweler added the case. Belle obviously had no idea of the piece's value—but that was wrong. To her, its value was sentimental. To her, this watch must be priceless.

"Let me pay."

"Stop that foolishness." Charlotte clucked

at him. "Brady Fontana, if you could, you'd solve every problem in the world but your own. The girl has her pride."

"You sound like Mrs. Tweed." But of course she was right. "Excellent advice."

He tucked the wrapped timepiece inside his jacket and didn't ask his friend what she thought his problem was.

"Thank you, Charlotte. You saved me from being an idiot."

Belle LeClair was a strong and clever woman. She'd lost her parents on the heels of losing her husband, and then she picked herself up and began again. On her own terms, she was making a new life in a new state, something Brady had set out to do himself once. He respected gumption and hard work more than just about anything in a person, male or female.

Another reason he couldn't understand why she'd marry a scapegrace like Chet McKinnon.

* * *

Belle reached home dreaming of a nice hot pot of the "Grey's tea" that had been among Brady Fontana's housewarming gifts. She kicked off her ill-fitting shoes, built a fire in the stove and put the kettle on, then took the shoes up to her room. She left her stockings on though. One couldn't be sure every single spider had been chased away.

Keenly aware of the emptiness in her pocket where Wade's watch should be, she collected the packet of his letters, still wrapped in oilcloth, and brought the whole bundle downstairs to the parlor, in her opinion the nicest room in the house.

The parlor occupied the corner of the house which faced the churchyard and the stands of birch and wild plum trees in full bloom beyond. She opened the windows to allow for a pleasant cross breeze and settled onto the sofa with her tea and letters and tucked her feet under her skirt.

Deadwood, DT, April 3, 1877

My darling bride,

Though we have been married many months now, I call you bride, not wife, with deep remorse for the disservice I may well have done you. Lately I've much considered how transient is this life on earth, and I regret having tied you, most unfairly, to my tenuous existence.

My darling Christabel, I have

been selfish. The moment I saw you I wanted you for myself alone. I couldn't bear the thought of another man capturing your heart while I was away in the Dakotas, and so I asked to make you mine without considering the full meaning of my request. I am ashamed. It was cruel and selfish to tie you to one who might very possibly be a dead man, the very definition of dishonorable behavior.

I don't regret taking this assignment. The cowards I've brought to justice were deplorable and brutal men, and when I've apprehended the last of them, the world will be a better place. But there is no man so dangerous as a coward, and I entertain no delusions of immortality. If I've made you a widow before I've had a chance to make you a wife, I pray that God will forgive me.

I must ask one more thing of you. If my demise comes before I see you again, I beg you wear mourning no longer than a month. If you must,

*forty days, which is how long our
Savior wandered the wilderness. It
would be vanity, I think, to wander
any longer.*

Belle laughed, even as a tear slipped down
her cheek. It happened every time she read
that paragraph. How fun it would have been
to watch Wade and Faith in a battle of
scripture quotes. Alas, as Naomi might say, it
would never be.

*Marry again, Belle. Quickly. You
deserve to be cherished, to be more
than the lovely bride I was honored to
make you. You deserve
companionship and mutual regard in
a partnership which adds to the
world's goodness—a lifetime of
friendship, care, and love. I pray to be
that partner, the man who earns the
honor of calling you wife, but if it will
not be, then I pray the angels above
guide a good and loving man to your
door—and that, when he arrives, you
invite him to cross the threshold.*

*I end this now, as I fear becoming
more maudlin with each sentence.
Take care, my dear Christabel. I
promise my next letter will reflect a*

more cheerful state of mind.

Your loving husband,
Wade LeClair

A next letter never came.

As a rule, Wade had written twice weekly, but not always, and when no second letter arrived that week, Belle hadn't worried. Early in the next week, the United States Attorney General, Mr. Charles Devens himself, appeared at Mrs. LeClair's door with the telegram that bore the terrible news.

A solid knock pulled Belle out of her reverie, and she went to answer the front door. Brady Fontana was the last person she would have expected, but there he stood on the porch, come to tell her he'd be keeping Chet at least one more night.

"I'm confident Delilah will drop the charges," he said, "but she refuses to consider it until he cools his heels another day or two."

"I see." Drat. He clearly had the wrong idea if he thought she was interested in when Chet would be let out of jail. She never should have asked about it.

"She can't let customers cause trouble without consequence."

"I don't disagree." Of course Belle was sorry Chet got himself into such a pickle, but she didn't excuse his behavior. She hoped Brady didn't think she would. "I was just having tea. Would you like to come in for a cup?"

An amused look passed over him, and she remembered she wasn't wearing shoes. Darn! But it was too late to do anything about it now. Anyhow, this was the West. Even Naomi said things were done differently here—though probably not so differently that it was acceptable to entertain a gentleman in one's stocking feet.

But she wasn't entertaining Brady Fontana. She had merely offered him a neighborly cup of tea. And he was a man of the law, someone—she reminded herself for the second time that day—whom she couldn't allow herself to care for in any dangerous way.

He was off-limits. Perfectly safe.

"I'd enjoy a cup of tea." He crossed the threshold and hung his hat in the vestibule. "It's usually Arbuckles' around here."

She showed him into the parlor. "I'll be right back."

She went to the kitchen to make a fresh pot, and when she returned, he was standing at the fireplace, examining the mantel clock. "I can set this if you'd like. It only wants winding."

"That would be very kind, thank you."

She set the tea things down on the table in front of the sofa and watched him work. His careful treatment of the clock's mechanisms, his movements precise and confident, made her feel warm inside.

"It seems you know what you're doing."

He laid his own watch on the mantel and referred to it to set the clock's time. "My grandfather was a watchmaker and a master clockmaker, and I was always fascinated by his work. In fact, I apprenticed with him for a while."

"Now I wish I had my pocket watch with me." She adjusted her position on the sofa so her dress's skirt covered her feet.

"Your watch." He looked at her strangely.

"It's with Charlotte Gensch at the moment. I..." She felt her face redden. She could hardly talk about loans and collateral with a near stranger. She felt so at ease with this man she'd forgotten they barely knew each other. "Did you complete your apprenticeship?"

"Sadly, no." He didn't press her about the watch, thank goodness. "In the midst of it, my life's course changed. My mother came into her inheritance, and my father decided our family was too fine for his son to be apprenticed to a watchmaker."

Ah, so Brady had come into money after childhood. That could explain why his head wasn't in the clouds. "How fine was that?"

"Fine enough to believe he should be the next congressman from Pennsylvania's first district."

"Goodness."

"Apparently, he was mistaken." Brady took a small tool from his pocket and used it to turn something inside the clock. "During a party meeting, a brawl broke out over vote buying and he was killed."

"Oh... That's terrible!"

"And pointless. Of all the candidates, my father had the least support among the electors."

From his dry tone, Belle sensed little love between father and son. Pa wasn't the sharpest knife in the drawer, but he'd always been loving and kind. Her heart went out to the stoical sheriff. "Did you return to your apprenticeship?"

"No." He smiled wistfully. "My grandfather was from the old country. He gave no second chances. Said I was a fool to leave him in the first place."

"That's... harsh."

"But he was right. Anyway, by then my mother's health was failing and the Philadelphia air did her no good, so I brought her out to Colorado to start a new life."

"The air here *is* wonderful," Belle agreed. "No factories."

"That's what I told Thalia—my fiancée. We met through my father's short-lived political career." He closed the clock and returned it to the mantel. "All set." The sadness in his smile made her change the subject for his sake. She poured the tea.

"I prefer coffee in the morning but tea later in the day. A habit I developed in Boston."

He came away from the fireplace. She expected him to take the chair opposite, but instead he sat down beside her on the sofa. She hadn't noticed earlier, but his usual overly vigilant demeanor was missing.

"I always enjoy the view from this room."

Ah, of course. This was his friend's house. He'd probably sat in that very place many times before.

Her unshod feet were terribly close to his booted ones.

"Do you take milk? And would you like sugar or honey?"

"Honey. Thank you."

She'd put some of the honey he'd given her in a lovely porcelain jam pot that was part of Mae's china. His eyes followed her movements as she made the tea. "I hope Chet doesn't give you and Faith too much trouble."

Ugh! As if saying Chet's name had broken a spell, Brady's vigilance returned.

"He'll take the free room and board. Your sister was getting ready to fetch him a meal from the Lilac when I left. But I'm not sure he appreciates her generosity with scripture."

Belle laughed and continued the ritual of pouring tea as if she were back in Mrs. LeClair's elegant drawing room. It was a pleasure to have use of Mae Tagget's pretty tea service. Again she felt Brady watching her movements—and she liked it.

"McKinnon finally told her to stop preaching at him, and she answered back with *hearing they hear not, neither do they understand*. Then she stomped off. As far as I know, she hasn't said a word to him since."

A woman can discern between a man who is slightly intrigued and one who's utterly entranced. Belle felt the fullness of Brady's interest as he followed the lift of the pot, the straining of the leaves, the stirring of the thick, amber sweetening.

"Faith and Pa used to play a game.

Dueling scripture." It was hard to keep her voice steady. "They'd carry on a conversation comprised of nothing but Bible quotes, taken out of context to mean something else entirely. They'd go back and forth until one couldn't come up with a response."

She couldn't stop herself. She handed him the cup slowly, gracefully, as in a delicate dance she was performing for him alone.

"That is something I would have liked to see." His smile brightened the room. Brightened her heart. He should smile more often.

"Faith isn't usually quite so fixated on scripture. I think it's her way of keeping Pa alive in her heart. She was the closest of us to him, and his loss hit her worst of all, I think."

"You all lost your parents, but none of your sisters lost a husband too."

"No."

But had she really lost a husband? Suddenly she understood what Wade meant about her being a bride to him but not a wife. They hadn't had time to become a true husband and wife to each other. She had never even poured tea for him.

"Wade and I were married only a few days when he left for the Dakotas. I'd lived with his mother nearly seven months when news came he'd been killed. I lost a bridegroom when he died, but not a husband, if that makes any sense at all."

"It does." Brady's voice was scratchy with emotion. He'd also lost someone far too soon.

"Wade's letters have been a great consolation." She set down her cup and indicated the correspondence on the table. "I was reading through them when you arrived. He had a premonition his end was near, and in his last letter he said I should mourn him no longer than forty days, then move on and live my life."

Brady put his cup down next to hers. "I'd say the man truly cared for you."

This was a mistake. She should have stepped out on the porch, not brought him into this private, intimate setting. Against her better judgment, she was drawn to Brady Fontana, and now she knew why. He was of the same mold as Wade LeClair. He cared for the troubles of his fellow beings and tried to make the world a better place. He paid attention. He was competent and brave. And under all that reserve, all that disdain for fools, he was kind.

"He did care for me. As I cared for him."

"And you always will, if I understand your character rightly."

What character? Belle couldn't even keep the promises she made to herself. She was falling hard for Brady Fontana. A sheriff. She *was* a hussy! She felt practically wanton. His nearness only made her more aware of her attraction to him.

"And you will always care for Thalia."

"I will."

He reached for his cup at the moment she reached for hers. Their hands touched, and this time he didn't pull away. He clasped her hand in his, his grip strong yet gentle, and she didn't withdraw it. He turned it over and gently traced the life line with a finger. She had to remember to breath, and when he raised her palm to his lips a small squeak of a moan escaped her.

"Belle." He pulled her close. His lips found hers and a fire born of loneliness and desire ignited inside her. Without thinking, she ran her fingers through the dark waves of his hair and deepened their kiss.

It was too sweet, too fierce... too *much*.

And she wanted more, more.

He pulled away, mortification written on his face. "I am so sorry. I had no right." He peeled her hand off his shoulder and stood. "I never meant to—I do apologize."

"Oh..." The sound came out weakly. She

was too devastated to say more.

He backed away as if she were a coiled rattlesnake, and she wanted to sink through the floor and die as he edged toward the door.

"I should go."

And he did.

Chapter 26

If he didn't get out of this cell soon, he was going to explode.

It'd drive any man itchy, being caged up and forced to listen to that rank, Bible-thumping Faith Steele. She'd had it in for him since the night she caught him under the stairs, watching Belle kiss that US Marshal who tricked her into marrying him.

Best day of his life was when he heard LeClair got what was coming to him.

But that Faith... He'd never forget how she laughed when he fell off the log right in front of Belle. It wasn't his fault! A knothole threw off his balance.

Faith Steele had no womanly kindness about her. And look at her, dressing like a man. Maybe there was no womanly anything there.

And it was unnatural, how she was a dead-to-rights shot. Her pa never should've let her enter the Independence Day shooting contest. She hit three times as many bottles as Chet and laughed at him then too. She was an abomination.

When he and Belle were finally hitched, that girl was going to be banished from his place, no question. When he was man of the house, lord and master of the domain, all those Steeles were going to show him the proper due respect.

Or maybe not. Maybe he'd just take Belle away from her sisters and their constant interfering altogether. No law said they had to settle near Break Heart. Or in Colorado, for that matter.

Last night he sure learned some things. That fella at the bar, Red John, had a lot to say about Break Heart in particular and Colorado in general. Said the territories was the place to be, where a man could still find opportunities.

The fella's family ran that trading post outside of town, the one they passed on the river with the painted cat and the huge old lady on the rock. Good thing Chet hadn't said what he was thinking—that old lady was Deckom's aunt they called Big Mama. Ha!

There was no love lost between Deckom's people and Fontana either. Big Mama used to have a cathouse right on Main Street in Break Heart until the sheriff ran the whole lot out of town on account of his highfalutin ideas about law and order and civilized society.

Why didn't Fontana go back East if that's how he felt? Why couldn't people leave good enough alone? *I suggest you ponder what you want your reputation to be in this town.* Pompous bull. This was supposed to be the West! The untamed country. If he wanted civilization, he'd go back to Minnesota.

Arizona Territory—Red John said that was the place. Enough silver to last a hundred lifetimes. Chet and Belle could start over in Tombstone. Easier than clawing a new farm from untouched land.

Aw, Belle! She was so fine, a real lady. She brought out the best in him. She wasn't going to like hearing about last night. If only he could remember what he said. Something about them getting hitched, but he couldn't remember what exactly or who he said it to.

That Brady Fontana better not go blabbing.

Belle was sweet on the sheriff, even if she

didn't know it. The other day, when Chet told her he was going to Greeley on business, he expected she'd be unhappy about it and anxious that he return soon.

She didn't even seem to care.

But then she'd asked what if his folks' and his brothers' bodies turned up while he was gone? He told her he expected Fontana would have 'em buried, same as her ma, and her face went all soft when he mentioned the sheriff's name.

She never looked at him that way.

But it didn't matter. She wasn't going to think so highly of Sheriff Do-Right once she heard about his lady love at Sweet Dee's.

And she *would* hear about Lily Rose. Chet had seen to that. He sure tarnished that halo Faith hung on her boss. When she brought supper in, Chet let slip what Deckom told him about the sheriff making time with that painted cat. Now that he thought about it, that was pretty smart of him. Being a woman—despite attempts to prove different—she'd lose no time spreading the news to her sister.

What was that noise? Was someone out in the main office?

"Let me out of here!"

He had to get out of Break Heart. His pa

made a mistake coming to Colorado. The do-gooders had already ruined the place.

Arizona, now. That's where Pa should have taken them. Still a territory. Still free. A man could make his mark there.

Aw, what was he thinking? He was stuck. Belle wasn't about to leave her sisters for somewhere like Arizona Territory. This place must seem bad enough after living so high in Boston. He'd never understand why she left that cushy life to come homestead.

But he was sure glad she did.

He loved her so much! Sometimes he couldn't breathe, just thinking about her. She was the most beautiful thing he'd ever seen in his life.

When she married LeClair, he thought he'd die from the pain of losing her. She never knew. The first time he truly and fully considered the subject of a man and a woman being together, he swore Belle Steele would one day be his. He'd only waited to make his feelings known until he was worthy of her. He never expected someone to sweep her off her feet behind his back, take her from him forever.

Now God had given them a second chance, and he wasn't going to ruin it. But he had to get out of this cell.

Fontana would let him out, just to please her. The sheriff tried to hide it, but he had a hankering for Belle. What man didn't? Chet had seen it in the man's face when he heard her name.

Thing was, Fontana had two problems. He was a do-gooder, and he was honorable. He'd let Chet out if he thought it was good for Belle.

"Fontana! Fontana, I hear you out there! Faith! When am I getting out of this place? I need to get to Greeley!"

Chapter 27

Belle finished putting away the tea things and went back to the parlor. She tried to distract herself with Wade's letters, but she couldn't stop thinking about Brady. The feel of him sitting here on the sofa wouldn't go away.

His intensity.

His warmth.

His kiss.

Being in his arms had been... overwhelming. Confusing. She'd lost herself in an embrace that felt, paradoxically, like just the right place to be. For the duration of that kiss, the world had made sense. She was safe. At home. Complete. She finally knew who she was.

And then he'd pulled away. Appalled by

her.

In the blink of an eye, she fell from surprised ecstasy to stunned despair. Humiliated.

She touched her lips, still tingling. Recalled his vital, male strength, the *wanting* urgency in his kiss, and the panicked *no!* that cried out inside her when he'd gone.

The front door opened.

"Hello!"

"We're home!"

Into the house spilled a cacophony of boisterous, happy chatter. Naomi and Luke wouldn't be home until later, since part of Naomi's job was to make the Overstreets' supper, but Faith, Hannah, and Charity bustled into the parlor.

"We three had a powwow." Hannah plopped down into the chair across from the sofa, her enthusiasm affording a glimpse of the child she was leaving behind. She was so much more mature than just a week ago. Life had forced her to grow up before her time. "You and Naomi have to cook for your jobs, so Charity and Faith and I are going to do the cooking at home."

"That's thoughtful." It wasn't the time to bring up the notion of hiring a cook. Belle couldn't think straight right now.

"Of course, we won't object if you *want* to cook on the odd occasion." Charity batted her eyes innocently.

"How about tomorrow?" Belle chucked. Thank heaven for her sisters! She already felt better. "When I get home I'll make a spice cake with orange frosting. There are still a few oranges in the provisions Sheriff Fontana brought us."

Ouch. She shouldn't have said his name.

"We'll have to do without Belle's cooking soon enough, now that she and Chet McKinnon are getting married." Faith sat down beside her and took her hand. "I should have asked for lessons when I had the chance."

"What do you mean? Who told you that?"

"Who do you think? The current guest of Hotel Fontana."

As Belle had feared. "But he had no right..."

I had no right. Brady's very words after they kissed.

"He's a horrible prisoner, I'll tell you that." Faith shuddered melodramatically. "You'll have to teach him some manners, Belle. He never shuts his yap. Fontana walked out of the office for an hour this afternoon—to get away from the caterwauling, I'm sure."

Oh dear. Brady had thought she was engaged to Chet when she kissed him. No wonder he was horrified!

"But I don't guess it helped," Faith continued. "He came back in a worse mood than when he left."

Oh no. No.

"The minute Fontana walked in the door Chet started carping to get out, using you as an excuse. Said he has to get to Greeley to file with the land office before someone else gets the parcel he wants. That you'll be upset to lose such a pretty piece of land."

"That's..." Belle shook her head in wonder. "I don't know anything about this. And Chet and I are *not* engaged."

"Well, he says different."

"You can't be surprised he'd stake his claim," Charity said. "To the land and to you. Remember that dandy on the train?"

Belle nodded. "I remember."

On the train from Minnesota, somewhere in the middle of Kansas, a fastidiously dressed character had approached her in the dining car while she was waiting for Naomi and Charity. *What's a pretty little calico like you doing eating all alone? No matter, sweet thing. I'll remedy that tragedy.*

Chet showed up and yanked the cad out of

the seat before his bottom could settle onto the cushion. *You're in my place.* He threatened to toss the man off the train while it was moving. Charity had thought the encounter hilarious.

"It was mortifying."

But now that Charity mentioned it, Chet acted—then and all along—like he had a rightful claim on Belle. Why, he treated her no better than Mrs. LeClair did!

"Chet's bellyaching didn't work. It just irritated Fontana more." Then Faith grinned brightly. "He told me to go talk to Mrs. Montgomery tomorrow about dropping the charges and letting Chet go."

Hannah's eyes went wide. "You get to go inside Sweet Dee's?"

"I suppose I do."

"Oh my." Hannah looked enraptured. "Do you need backup?"

"You can be backup after you turn eighteen." Faith chucked her chin. "But you'll never guess. I have a deputy's badge!"

"Let me see!" All Hannah's newfound maturity fell away. With a child's eagerness, she held the star Faith pulled out of her shirt pocket. In awe, she ran her fingers over the word DEPUTY emblazoned at its center.

"It's temporary. I only get to wear it to go

to Sweet Dee's." Faith couldn't stop smiling. "But it's a start."

"But why?" Belle said. "I mean, why you? I thought Sheriff Fontana was going to speak to Mrs. Montgomery himself."

"He had to leave town. Didn't say why. I'm officially in charge until he gets back day after tomorrow. Although I did have to promise I'd get Teddy Gensch to back me up if there's any real trouble."

"I think it's wonderful," Charity said. "My sister, a sheriff's deputy!"

"And *I* think it's mad." Everything about it went against the grain. Belle imagined the worst. "You're a clerk, not a deputy. What was Brady Fontana thinking?"

"If I were a man, no one would blink an eye."

"But you're not a man. He can't be in his right mind, leaving a nineteen-year-old girl alone to defend the town."

Faith sighed with hurt feeling. "Doesn't it matter what *I* want?"

That stopped Belle in her tracks. She'd once said those very words to her overbearing mother-in-law.

"You're right!" She wanted Faith to act against her nature—not for Faith's sake but for her own ease of mind. She was no better than Mrs. LeClair. "I'm sorry. Truly. I apologize."

"Apology accepted."

"Faith?" Hannah had silently watched from the oversized chair in the corner. Her legs were drawn up under her skirt, and she was hugging her knees. "What if the Deckoms find out the sheriff's gone?"

"They won't." Faith knelt before the chair and grabbed Hannah's hands. "He told me things are quiet in town right now, and he'll be back before anybody knows he's gone." Her smile turned sheepish. "And I'm to leave the sign out front directing people to Teddy Gensch."

"And you'll be with Jane Stedman most of the day," Charity said. "From what I hear, the Deckoms are afraid of her."

"That's true." Hannah relaxed and smiled. "I'm so glad Belle isn't going to marry Chet McKinnon."

"*O give thanks unto the Lord, for he is good.*"

I'm famished!" Charity rolled her eyes at Faith's quote. "Hannah, let's you and I go see what we can rustle up for dinner."

The two hurried off to the kitchen.

Movement outside caught Belle's attention. Beyond the churchyard, a gust of wind danced through the wild plum trees and their blossoms and leaves fluttered. *I always enjoy the view from this room.*

She could still feel Brady's kiss on her lips—and worse, a comforting afterglow of being enveloped in the strength of his arms.

She was so confused...

"Belle?" Faith had stayed behind in the parlor. "There was something else. I didn't want to say anything in front of the others, but after the sheriff left the jail today, Chet told me... He said when he was at Sweet Dee's last night he heard talk that Sheriff Fontana and Lily Rose were sweet on each other. I don't like to say anything, but I wouldn't want you to hear about it somewhere else."

Actual physical pain seared Belle's heart. "It doesn't matter." She wouldn't let it matter.

But it did!

"I think it does." Faith's kindness made Belle feel even worse.

"I told you before, I'm not interested in any lawman. I know you're happy, doing what you're doing, but I don't like that either. It terrifies me to think of losing you too."

"Someone's got to do it. Justice doesn't come by accident."

"Oh, Faith!" She was right, of course, but Belle couldn't bear to think of the dangers her sister could face. "What if the Deckoms come to town while Brady's gone?"

"Then I'll call on Teddy Gensch and we'll deal with it." Faith grinned. "I can always ask Jane Stedman to bring her drum."

"All right, I take your point. I'm being overly dramatic." Belle wasn't thinking straight. She'd let her emotions get to her. She huffed out a sigh. "I suppose whatever the sheriff had to do was important. I wonder where he went."

"He didn't say." Faith hesitated, then said, "Look, there's safety in numbers. If it would set your mind at ease, when I go to Sweet Dee's tomorrow, why don't you come with me?"

NEVER A LAWMAN

Chapter 28

Perched on a stool and obscured by shadows,
a bulky, ruddy-faced young man stopped
Belle and Faith at Sweet Dee's front door. He
was dressed in a dapper gray suit, and a long,
thick blond braid was draped over one
shoulder. Like a cliché, he ran his beady
cornflower-blue eyes over Belle
appreciatively before moving on to Faith.

"Everybody checks their guns at the door,
mister—uh... ma'am?"

He rose to his feet menacingly—then lost
the effect when it turned out he was several
inches shorter than Faith.

Belle turned away to hide her smile and
caught her breath. *Goodness!* The room before
her was not what she expected. She'd

prepared for tawdry faux elegance tricked up to separate trail-tired cowboys and lonely traveling salesmen from their hard-earned coins.

But no. This gentleman's bar and cardroom would satisfy the most fastidious expectations of—well, of Mrs. LeClair herself.

"No exceptions." The doorman eyed the Colt holstered at Faith's hip.

Faith chewed on her lower lip, and Belle agonized for her. She'd promised not to load the six-gun unless absolutely necessary and only wore it to boost her confidence. It would be downright embarrassing to turn over an unloaded pistol.

"Keep your firearm, Steele."

Lily Rose came out from behind the polished-oak bar. She wore a sky-blue muslin basque with capped sleeves over a navy overskirt and navy-and-white striped lower skirt, trimmed with fat bows of maroon satin running down one side. The bodice was cut low enough to hint at her feminine charms but not to allow a real view. This was a woman in command of herself as well as those around her. Belle understood why Brady admired her.

If Lily Rose knew he called Faith "Steele," the two must be on friendly terms at the very least. The thought made Belle irrationally jealous.

"Officers of the law are exempt from turning over their weapons, Cyril. You know that." She smiled at Faith. "This here is Sheriff Fontana's new deputy—and *this* is the Lilac's celebrated new cook."

Faith puffed up at being called a deputy, but Belle couldn't tell if Lily Rose was being gracious or silently laughing at them both.

With a dubious grunt, Cyril retreated to his perch.

"Howdy, ladies." Lily Rose beckoned them into the room. "Can I offer you a drink? On the house, of course."

It wasn't yet nine o'clock in the morning.

She chuckled and told someone to bring coffee for three.

Faith appeared duly impressed by the surroundings, and it struck Belle this might be the fanciest room her sister had ever been in. The bar's fixtures were all brass, the wall behind it covered with floor-to-ceiling mirrors. A small raised stage in the corner with the curtains open seemed alive with anticipation. Would there be a singer later? A play? Luxurious Turkish carpets covered the floor and muted their footsteps.

Some of the ladies on duty had been at

church. Today they were dressed more stylishly, their cheeks rouged and their lips painted. She wouldn't say there was any joy in their demeanor, but neither did they appear miserable or close to it. A sign on the wall read:

Anyone Who Hits a Dove
Will Be Banished Permanently

Couldn't argue with that.

Delilah Montgomery is like a dark mirror image of Abigail Vanderhouten. Despite the sign, Belle doubted the bawdy woman had the best interests of her "doves" at heart. Sweet Dee's was about profits. This establishment was an unapologetic moneymaking machine.

Lily Rose led her and Faith to a small table away from the customers where the coffee was delivered. "Brady said you'd be by to talk about letting that flannel mouth Chet McKinnon go."

He'd told her he was leaving town. She probably knew where he'd gone.

"That's right," Faith said. "Is Mrs. Montgomery available?"

"She never comes downstairs before noon. I can speak for her. But are you sure you don't want to keep that boy off the

• 324 •

streets as long as you can?"

"His constant blather makes the sheriff churlish," Faith said.

Lily Rose chuckled and gave Belle a look. "I don't know what any woman could see in Chet McKinnon."

"I'm not—"

Faith blurted out, "Are you and Fontana engaged?"

"Faith!" So *this* was her object in asking Belle to accompany her—not for moral support or safety in numbers, but to find out Lily Rose's relationship with Brady.

Maybe she was right. Maybe if Belle heard it with her own ears, she could banish Brady Fontana from her thoughts.

"Don't be silly!" Lily Rose outright laughed. "Can you see an upstanding citizen like Brady Fontana marrying a fallen woman like me? Besides, I'll never marry. I have a nice retirement accumulating at Emerson and West in Greeley, and I'm not about to let any man get his hands on it, no matter how upstanding he is."

The answer shouldn't give Belle such joy. But it did. She couldn't deny her feelings any longer.

What am I going to do?

"I apologize." Faith drank her coffee.

Even in this darkened room, her reddened cheeks showed. "Mr. McKinnon is of a different opinion."

"Mr. McKinnon holds several opinions that don't bear looking at twice." Lily Rose looked at Belle meaningfully. "I let the customers think Brady's sweet on me for my own reasons. When men believe the sheriff has laid claim on a girl, they leave the girl alone, if you know what I mean."

"Though I walk in the midst of trouble, thou wilt revive me: thou shalt stretch forth thine hand against the wrath of mine enemies, and thy right hand shall save me."

Lily Rose didn't bat an eye. "Exactly."

"It makes sense." Belle had to say something.

"I have a good thing going, and I'm not going to ruin it by giving it all to a man. In five years I'll have enough to retire. I'll buy a mansion in Denver and live like an heiress."

"And those men won't." Belle nodded at two rough-looking customers playing cards while one of the ladies served as dealer. Two others nursed whiskeys at the far end of the bar.

"It seems odd to be gambling and drinking in the morning when a man could be out doing something productive with his life," Faith said.

"I'd better give you what you want and get you out of here." Lily Rose chuckled again. "Such sentiments are bad for business."

* * *

"Belle? Can we talk?"

Chet stood inside the kitchen's swinging doors, hat in hand.

Frankly, Belle had expected him sooner. She and Faith left Sweet Dee's hours ago. The breakfast rush had already wound down, and the luncheon surge was nearly upon them.

He shifted from one foot to the other and grinned sheepishly. If he thought that hangdog look was going to win her over, he was mad. She wasn't going to forget him telling people they were engaged.

Standing at the griddle, she wiped her brow with her forearm. All morning she'd been miserable, pondering her feelings for Brady Fontana one minute and what she'd say to Chet McKinnon the next.

It was vain to deny her feelings for Brady anymore, but she was no closer to knowing what she was going to do about them.

With Chet, she was absolutely clear. She could never marry him.

It wasn't that she suddenly didn't like

him. She'd never liked him, even when he was a boy. Until today, she'd assumed there was something wrong with her. Her expectations were too high, or she was being a snob and she'd get over herself in time. But the truth was she didn't respect him. She still believed love could grow in a marriage over time, but not where there is no respect.

She thanked her lucky stars she figured all this out before she married him in one of her snap decisions!

"You look better than I would have thought."

If she sounded snippy, so be it. Let her tone convey her opinion of his public drunkenness, not to mention his spreading rumors and harassing Lily Rose. Come to think of it, why would he try to be with someone at Sweet Dee's if he wished to marry Belle?

Again, no respect.

"I got a room at the boardinghouse. Thought I better shave and put on a clean shirt before coming to see you."

Belle continued flipping hotcakes. Roxanna came in to pick up an order and stopped in her tracks. Carmelita had already stopped chopping onions to watch, and Sudsy stood in his doorway, his eyes never leaving

Chet.

The kitchen was strangely quiet, but for bacon and eggs sizzling on the stove.

"I'm awfully ashamed of my behavior at Sweet Dee's, Belle, and that's the honest truth."

Belle sighed. She had to get this over with sometime, and the quicker the better for them both. It might as well be now.

"Carmelita, would you take over here?" She wiped her hands on her apron. "I'll go fetch the eggs."

She told Chet to walk with her, and they went out back to the coop behind the hotel. Belle handed him the basket, and he walked beside her while she collected eggs.

"I was a darn fool, Belle, and that's the honest truth. One of the fellas at the bar got my goat. Said a real cowboy doesn't drink anything weaker than whiskey. I wasn't used to the stuff."

"What do you care what some stranger in a bar thinks? You're a farmer, not a cowboy— unless that's changed too. You said you were going to Greeley on business."

"I did go. My business went well too. I found a lawyer to handle my inheritance. He'll take care of selling the farm in Minnesota to my cousin. We'll have plenty to get us started improving our parcel. I found one, Belle. It's real pretty, and you can pick out where to put the house."

At the mention of money for the homestead, Belle thought of Pa selling all they owned only to have it end up at the bottom of the river and dragging him down with it. Life was so precarious. She *hated* how random it all was.

She wasn't cut out to be a homesteader. Maybe if she'd loved Chet—but no. Even then, she wouldn't look to that life with joy.

"I came to Colorado for the wrong reason." She said it to herself more than to Chet. "Running away from an old life, not toward a new one."

If there were no Mrs. LeClair or Wesley LeClair back in Boston, if that had been *Belle's* house on Bowdoin Street, she could have stayed there quite happily the rest of her life. Sure, the air was cleaner here, but she liked the modern niceties. She didn't want to depend on a kitchen garden outside her door subject to drought or flood or invasion by plagues of ravenous grasshoppers.

She wanted gas lighting and nights at the theater and the odd trip to New York. A lifestyle already established and on firm footing.

And yet... None of those delights compared to the freedom she felt in her spirit here in Break Heart. One day the modern conveniences would arrive, and then she'd have the best of both worlds.

But not with Chet, and not the way he wanted it.

She'd rather be a widow cook at the Lilac than a homesteader with anyone.

"It's the sweetest piece of land, just ten miles southeast of Break Heart," Chet was saying. "You'll be close to your sisters. Charity and Hannah and Luke can come live with us if you like."

Not Faith or Naomi?

"Stop. I can't. I can't marry you, Chet. I'm sorry."

His face fell. "But... you're out of mourning."

"At my husband's request." Belle chided herself for using Wade as an excuse, but she didn't want to argue and Chet would respect a man's authority more than her own wish. Another mark against him. "Trust me, it's better for you. I wasn't a good wife. I most assuredly wasn't a good daughter-in-law. I doubt I'll marry again at all."

When Charity said she never wanted to marry, it seemed the glib statement of someone young and foolish. She'd change her mind when she met the right man. But now Belle saw the appeal. She didn't have to be an heiress to be independent. She had employment and a place to live. She could make a life here in Break Heart, without a husband.

"I don't believe it. You're too pretty to stay single." Chet stepped closer. "You just married the wrong man."

"I don't think so." Belle pushed the basket of eggs against his chest. "But I'll never know."

"I can make you happy. I've wanted you from the start. It's our second chance."

That was the worst thing about people caring for you. They assumed they had the right to tell you what you thought. What you meant. What you wanted.

Although... Brady never did those things. Never corrected her. Never told her she was something she wasn't. Maybe he didn't care. The thought made her heart feel heavy.

But remembering his kiss, she knew that wasn't it. He cared. But he believed she was engaged to another man, and he respected her enough to honor that commitment.

"Please believe what I say. My mind is made up."

"I don't like it." Chet looked like he was going to get angry again, but then he stopped and seemed to give in. "But it's your decision." He stepped back and grinned wistfully. "You know what? Maybe I'll have Mrs. Vanderhouten find me a mail order bride."

"Why Chet, that's a wonderful idea."

What a relief! He took her refusal better than her most optimistic hopes—at least, he seemed to make an effort.

She started back to the kitchen and he followed with the eggs.

"There is one thing I'll regret." He walked along beside her. "Not being the lucky son of a gun who gets to eat your cooking every day. I was thinking it would be like home again, with Ma and Pa and my brothers. Remember the pot luck suppers we used to have at church?"

The poor man. How selfish she'd been! She remembered Chet had lost all his family.

"Tell you what." She stopped at the kitchen door and took the basket from him. "Why don't I make you fried chicken and a chocolate cake, one last time. Mrs. Gensch won't mind. You can pick them up tomorrow after three o'clock."

"I'll do that. And how about this? Let's

have a picnic at my parcel, and you can give me a woman's opinion on where I should put the house. Which view would be nicest."

"Oh, but—"

"Luke can chaperone. The boy'd like that." Chet smiled apologetically. "I promise not to renew my offer, if that's what you're worried about. I truly would value your opinion."

Belle had absolutely no interest in Chet's parcel, which only made her more certain she'd made the right decision. But she couldn't pull away just when they'd made friends. And if Chet could find a woman to love who would love him in return, it could be just the thing to turn him from the dark path she feared he was on. It would be petty to refuse her help.

"I'm sure Naomi can spare Luke. I'd be glad to help."

* * *

Like Chet figured, Delilah Montgomery was more bark than bite. At first she wouldn't let him past the front door, even when he showed his money. He had to go through the motions of an apology and promise to watch his p's and q's. She finally relented when he told her he'd just found out his whole family was buried in his absence while he was in Greeley and didn't he deserve a drink?

He'd actually come up to Sweet Dee's to soothe the humiliation of Belle's rejection, maybe find a little female commiseration. He'd said he wouldn't renew his offer, but that's exactly what he intended to do on their picnic.

Problem was, he had no idea what he was going to show her for a parcel. He never should have told Belle he'd already selected one. He'd looked at the land agent's plat map in Greeley, and there was a spot southeast of Break Heart available, but who knew what the real thing looked like? He'd just have to take his chances.

At least he was in luck for someone to talk to. Red John Deckom was at the bar, and Chet took the stool next to him.

"Hey there, Lily Rose. Bring me whiskey, darlin'."

She didn't glare at him, so that was something. Maybe he wasn't as bad the other night as Faith Steele liked to make out.

"What do you say, Red John? The world treating you right?"

"The world's an unfair place is what I say." Deckom slammed his glass down and motioned for a refill. "I finally saw the woman of my dreams and she ain't about to have me."

"That's going around." Chet pointed to his own empty glass. "Maybe some other fella already staked his claim."

Some other fella.

As the words came out of Chet's mouth, he stopped cold. Was that why Belle gave him the mitten? Because she'd fallen for someone else?

Thinking back, when he was locked in that cell, he'd heard Faith tease Fontana about going to the Lilac to sample Belle's cooking. And they'd talked a lot about the sheriff helping the girls move into their new house while Chet was in Greeley. Chet knew they were sweet on each other, but he didn't think either one had admitted it to themselves. He hadn't worried about it because Belle told him she'd never marry another lawman—but maybe Fontana had moved in on his girl anyway.

He wasn't having it! He wasn't losing Belle to another, not again. Tomorrow either she'd agree to be his, or she would be no man's.

Chapter 29

It didn't work. Brady had come to Nighthawk to get some perspective, to clear Belle LeClair out of his mind, but as he rode over the ranch or wandered through the too-big house, he found himself wondering...

What would she think of the place? Would she like his favorite spot in the east meadow where the old willow provided ample shade by the stream? Was the front porch wide enough? Did the library have the kind of books she enjoyed? Was the kitchen too small, not stocked well enough?

Yesterday morning, consulting with his foreman, it was clear he'd have to choose soon between his commitment to Break Heart and his obligation to Nighthawk. He had a good crew here, but the ranch would never be the success Brady envisioned until he came back to run it himself.

Decision made. He'd give up his star as soon as a man could be found who was willing and worthy of the office.

The balance of the day he'd spent riding over the ranch on Queenie, his sweet-tempered quarter horse. Every time his thoughts wandered, they wandered to Belle. He ate his supper alone with those thoughts. He'd stopped asking Mrs. Tweed to join him in the dining room. She insisted that sort of thing just wasn't done, and certainly not in any house run by her. *If you want company at your table, I suggest you get yourself a wife.* He'd pictured Belle sitting across from him.

He'd bought Nighthawk for the land and had remodeled the house to suit a family. Last night he'd noticed how large his bed was—and how lonely. But the one woman he could see himself having a family with was promised to another man.

The thought of McKinnon being on the loose made him restless. He decided to head back to town as soon as he finished with Belle's watch. He'd spent the past couple of hours in his study, taking it apart, cleaning the components, putting it back together. He was nearly finished.

Mrs. LeClair's watch, he reminded himself. Soon to be Mrs. McKinnon's. He growled at the thought.

He was happy to return the watch to good working order. He hadn't mentioned having it the other day in her parlor. It would be a surprise, as Charlotte wished. A present.

Wedding present.

How could he have lost control like that and kissed her? A moment of heaven that only made worse the hell of knowing she'd soon belong to another man. And *that* man. A lowlife, sad excuse who would never deserve her.

He'd known Belle little more than a week, and she'd utterly destroyed his resolve never to let another woman near his heart. In the past ten days, she'd been almost all he could think about. At odd hours, he'd find himself wondering what she was doing or how her day was going.

That first day at the river he'd noticed her beauty—what man wouldn't? But Belle's inner beauty was even more delightful. He loved the sweet smile that stole over her face when she watched a customer enjoy some dish she'd made.

And her thoughtfulness. She'd discovered

the path to Sudsy's heart: a steamed apple dumpling with hard sauce, like he used to have in Chicago before the fire that scarred him so badly. A little thing, but no one else had thought to ask. Charlotte's older brother was so damaged he rarely spoke to anyone but Roxanna, his daughter, or came out of the room where he washed the hotel's dishes and scrubbed the pots and pans. Yet Charlotte said he and Belle were already fast friends.

The whole world quieted and made sense when she was nearby. Being with her made Brady feel complete. But not satisfied. No, just thinking of Belle made him eager for more from life—with her.

With Thalia, things had never felt like this, so... *right*. He'd always suspected she'd somehow maneuvered him into proposing. But even when the doubts began to creep in, he'd done nothing to break off the engagement. He'd put himself in that position, and it was his duty to follow it through.

That's what he told himself. Looking back, that had been misplaced pride on his part.

If Belle had taught him anything, it was that he never loved Thalia. He'd had no idea what love was. Now he did know, and the woman he loved was going to marry someone else.

There was no getting away from reminders of her either. Her sister sat at the other desk in the office, and her place of employment stared him in the face every time he looked across the street at the Lilac Hotel.

So of course you had to go and kiss her, fool that you are.

"Goodness, my darling boy. That sigh had the weight of the world in it."

Mrs. Tweed came in, rolling a tea cart. He set the watch's time, then shut the case with a satisfactory click and came around from the desk to join his housekeeper.

His friend.

"I'd better get back to town," he told her. "It was wrong of me to leave Faith Steele holding the fort this long."

"I don't know. She seems a competent young woman. You say she doesn't object to tidying the office or organizing your paperwork?"

"Not a bit of it." He tended to slip into British idioms when he was around Hermione Tweed. She'd been his mother's lady's maid and had come over with her from England. When his mother passed, Mrs. Tweed stayed on and became his housekeeper—Nighthawk's majordomo, really.

Eladio was indeed a competent foreman, but if not for Mrs. Tweed, Brady couldn't leave the ranch so often as he did.

"And she's brave and a crack shot to top it off?"

"All true."

"So Faith Steele wishes to be a deputy, and you need a deputy. The only thing against her is her sex."

"True also, sadly."

"Bollocks. Your lack of vision disappoints me. This is the Wild West, my boy."

"Apparently, if Hermione Tweed will allow herself to say bollocks."

"What do Faith's sisters say?"

"I haven't spoken to them about it, frankly."

Mrs. Tweed looked at the watch. "It's lovely."

"Yes, she—it is."

She pursed her lips. "You know, Brady, life is for living."

"That's lovely too."

"Will you ever let Thalia rest in peace?"

"I honestly don't know."

"It was a terrible business, what happened. I've always believed Dr. Declan knows more than he's told about it."

"What do you mean?"

"Something in his eyes the day the Deckoms left Break Heart for good. I'd just come from a fitting with the modiste."

Brady smiled. *I'd just come from a fitting with the modiste.* Mrs. Tweed was the one person in the county who could say such a thing and not sound pretentious.

"I was driving the buggy, oblivious to anything being amiss, on my merry way up Main Street when the altercation between you and Frank Deckom came to a standstill.

"As I approached the Lilac Hotel, you were there in the middle of the street. I'd passed you by and had to stop and twist around on the bench to see you. You seemed so strange, so intense. I thought, *He looks as though he has murder in his mind.* And of course you did.

"There you two were, staring each other down, like gunslingers the newspapers describe in such purple prose. I thought, *This is it. This is the way it ends. I'm going to lose Brady too.*"

"I could have bested Frank Deckom."

"No doubt. But while you were shooting him, one of his gang would have shot you. And if you had survived, it would have ruined you. You were on such a dark path, my dear boy. Killing that man would have taken you all the way into the woods."

"I wonder. But I was saved by the drum," Brady said ruefully.

"Thank heaven for Jane Stedman's little drum trick. I was never one to praise superstition and ignorance, but on that day the tales of her being a witch saved lives. Of that I'm sure."

"What has any of this to do with Doc?"

"Ah. Yes. It was the most curious thing, and I've never forgotten it. As Jane Stedman played her drum, the whole town went quiet. I noticed the doctor at the sheriff's office, standing on the porch, seemingly in thrall to her. It wasn't fear so much as horror on his face. Why would an educated man like Dr. Declan be horrified by a would-be witch's trick?"

"Maybe she *is* a witch." Brady smiled. "After all, it worked."

"Yes, it did, didn't it? But I'd certainly like to know the whole story about that drum."

"If Jane Stedman hadn't cast her spell that day and I had killed Deckom, wouldn't that have been the better outcome?"

"At the time, Frank was more nuisance than threat. You were looking for revenge for Thalia, not justice for Break Heart."

"He's more threat now. The Deckom's live like outlaws."

Mrs. Tweed squeezed his arm. "You've done your penance, my darling boy—not that penance was ever necessary."

"Thalia would be alive today if not for me."

"You can't know that." Mrs. Tweed picked up Belle's watch and turned it over in her hand. "I have no idea why Thalia set off across dangerous country without a companion. She should have waited for you to come for her. We'll never know what was in her mind, but she was a selfish girl and never once thought of anyone but herself. There. I've said it."

"She didn't deserve to die for her selfishness."

"Of course not. But my dear boy, her selfishness was her undoing, not your lack of care. Don't ruin the rest of your life caught up in *if only*. Time to let it go."

"Can it be that easy?"

"Yes. Unearned guilt is as unseemly as false modesty. There comes a point when one is just being grandiose."

They both chuckled at that. "I wouldn't want to be grandiose."

"It's time you start living your life again.

Let yourself be happy."

The light moment passed. "I doubt that's going to happen." Chet McKinnon would have Brady's happiness.

Mrs. Tweed ran her thumb over the back of the watch. "I'd like to meet this Belle LeClair. Very much indeed."

"She's engaged to be married," Brady said. "To a newcomer, a homesteader from Minnesota, where she's from.

"I thought you said she was from Boston."

"It's a long story."

"It always is. But I doubt she'll marry this other man."

"What makes you so sure? You haven't met her. Or the other man."

"No. But I can tell from your tone you think this gentleman's character must be very bad. And you obviously approve highly of Mrs. LeClair; therefore, her character must be impeccable—in which case, she wouldn't show the bad judgment implied by marrying such a man."

"Your logic is pristine." Brady laughed. "And yet, Belle LeClair will marry Chet McKinnon."

"Did she tell you that?"

"He did."

"And you believed him. A man whose

character you doubt." She turned Belle's watch, examining both sides. "A gorgeous piece of workmanship."

"It is."

She handed it to Brady.

"I suggest you saddle Queenie and take this to her. Ask Belle if she and that man have chosen a date. And when she sets you straight, invite her here for a visit. I wish to meet the extraordinary creature who's managed to shine a warm light on that fortress of ice around your heart."

RACHEL BIRD

Chapter 30

Faith loaded the Colt and returned it to its holster, then laid the rig on her desk. She wasn't going against Fontana's wishes; she just wanted to get in some target practice back behind the office, nothing more. It wasn't like she intended to wear the loaded gun out on Main Street.

But first she poured a cup of Arbuckles' to have with the piece of chocolate cake from Belle. She took the cake and coffee out to the front porch bench and put her feet up on the rail to watch the people go by, not to mention let the town get used to the idea of a female deputy.

Criminy, the cake was delicious. She chuckled at Belle's ruse. Bringing the treat over from the hotel was obviously an excuse to find out whether Fontana had returned. More proof she had a hankering for the sheriff—not that Faith needed proof. Her suspicions were confirmed at Sweet Dee's yesterday by the smile Belle couldn't stifle when Lily Rose denied any claim on the man.

And Fontana! He was utterly tied up in knots over Belle. It would be comical if it wasn't so painful watching him battle his feelings while Chet McKinnon went on about marrying her.

Faith never did like that devious parsnip. She should have known he was lying. It would have saved the poor sheriff some grief. She couldn't wait to see the look on his face when he found out Belle wasn't engaged to anybody.

So Fontana wasn't bound to Lily Rose and Belle wasn't bound to the parsnip. All would be sunny in the garden once those two started reading the same page in the same book. Fontana was just the sort of man to make Belle happy. And Belle was just the sort of woman to show him the way and the light.

Not that Faith meant to blaspheme.

Where was he, anyway? It was almost three and he said he'd be back today. Not that she was worried. Break Heart had been as quiet as he predicted. Going up to Sweet Dee's was the only excitement she'd had as temporary deputy.

She'd been surprised to come away admiring—even liking—Lily Rose.

The bartender was about Naomi's age, and she ran Sweet Dee's for Delilah Montgomery just about the way Naomi had run the house for Ma. Lily Rose struck Faith as a no-nonsense businesswoman who cared about cleanliness, honesty, the safety of her "doves," and her own savings account. Not necessarily in that order.

Things certainly *were* done differently in the West!

But right was still right and wrong was still wrong. Surely a place like Sweet Dee's wasn't the best long-term answer to the shortage of females. Break Heart didn't need more tarts. It needed more brides.

Which led Faith to a newfound respect for Mrs. Vanderhouten. In this new light, Abigail's enthusiasm for her clients' happiness seemed more endearing than humorous.

Speak of the devil. The matchmaker emerged from the Lilac with Mae Tagget. Faith put her feet down and waved, and the two ladies crossed the street.

"We heard there was cake by the slice and came up for a piece," Mae said. "It's so nice having Charity at the store. Now I can step out from time to time."

"Mine was delivered personally." Faith showed her empty plate before setting it aside. Good thing Belle had made two cakes, one for the Lilac and one for that ridiculous picnic she'd agreed to go on with McKinnon.

Come to think of it, Chet should have come by already to collect her.

"Your sister is a revelation," Abigail said. "A miracle worker in the kitchen. And so beautiful! Oh, I *do* wish she'd avail herself of Vanderhouten Brides. I have the perfect suitor in mind for her. Rich, handsome—"

"You'd do well to find that rich, handsome suitor some other bride. I think Belle has found her kindred spirit."

Abigail raised an eyebrow. "You wouldn't mean our sheriff by any chance?"

"Really?" Mae's eyes went wide.

"Matter of fact, I do," Faith said. "I didn't think anybody else noticed."

"Granted, Brady Fontana is a hard case," Abigail said. "But I've seen the way he looks at her. If anybody can soften him, it's your sister."

"Belle is something of a hard case too.

Neither one can admit their feelings to themselves, let alone to each other."

"Give them time," Mae said. "They've only known each other ten days."

"That's true." Faith blinked. "It feels like we've been in Break Heart for ages."

"That's because you belong here." Mae nodded like she was dispensing the wisdom of the ages. "When you find your true home, it's as if you've lived there all your life."

True home? Faith wasn't sure about that. They hadn't heard back from Uncle James yet, but it wouldn't matter what he advised. She couldn't return to Minnesota. And yet...

All this—the sheriff's office, the house on Church Lane, wearing trousers—felt like playing a game to her. A waystation, not her destination. She had no clue what that might be. That was her problem—she didn't know anything anymore.

Mae and Abigail moved on. She ought to feel disloyal, gossiping about Belle like that. But she didn't! Belle had been quick to fall in love before. With a little push, maybe she would again. That an expert like Abigail Vanderhouten saw the same possibility told Faith she was on the right track.

She'd always been a keen observer. She'd learned from the example of her parents how to recognize when two people couldn't get enough of each other. Like Fontana and Belle.

Fontana wanted Belle as much as Wade LeClair ever had, and more than that dirty dog Chet McKinnon did now. But unlike those men, Brady Fontana placed Belle's wishes above his own desires. Faith was rooting for him.

If only Belle would get over her ridiculous objection to law enforcement, she and Fontana could make each other deliriously happy.

A rickety old one-horse wagon rolled up to the Lilac, driven by dirty dog himself, with Luke riding in the back.

"Hey, Faith!" Her brother jumped out.

"Howdy." McKinnon touched his hat and gave her a smile that *almost* wasn't a smirk. "Mighty fine day for a picnic, wouldn't you say?"

He didn't fool her, acting all nice like that. Chet had always hated her, and they both knew it. He disappeared inside the hotel, and Luke came over to talk.

"Where's your treasure?" He never left the house without his pouch.

"Belle told me to leave it behind. She was afraid it might get lost."

Afraid McKinnon would finagle it away,

more like.

"I don't know how she can stand that blowhard," Faith said. "I was going to tear my hair out if we had to keep him any longer."

"Yeah." Luke sighed. "I wish we were going with Sheriff Fontana instead."

Chet and Belle came out of the hotel, and Faith walked over to the wagon with Luke. Chet stowed Belle's picnic basket, then handed her up to the driver's bench as Luke jumped into the back.

"You want to join us, Faith?" Chet said sweetly, as if butter wouldn't melt in his mouth. "I'll bet there's plenty to eat."

"I don't shirk my obligations." She had a bad feeling about Belle going off with that man, Luke's presence notwithstanding. But she couldn't leave her post, even if the town was lazier than an old dog on a hot day.

Chet smirked, facing away from Belle. "You're a real go-getter."

"We'll see you at home later." Belle looked uneasy as Chet turned the wagon around. Like she too thought the picnic was a mistake but didn't know how to get out of it. "Don't wait supper."

"Be careful!" Faith watched the wagon rolled away, then returned to the porch. She put her feet up on the rail again and adjusted her Stetson.

The hat was a gift from Fontana. *If you're going to dress like that, you'd best not wear a bonnet.* She was mighty proud of it. She knew it set him back a pretty penny and took it as a sign that, deep down in his heart, he knew she'd make a good deputy.

Rushed footsteps sounded on the boardwalk. Faith bolted to an upright position, disoriented. Had she fallen asleep? Lily Rose traipsed up the porch steps, and she wasn't smiling.

"Is Brady back? Is he inside?"

"No, but anytime now." Faith perked up. This could be a chance to see some action. "What is it?"

"Something rotten is going on with the Deckoms, and that Chet McKinnon is involved."

"What do you mean?"

"Last night he came in to Sweet Dee's. Red John was there, and those two really tied one on."

"I knew it! I knew Chet was putting on that choirboy act for Belle." *Wait a minute.* "But the Deckoms aren't allowed in Break Heart."

Lily Rose shrugged. "Delilah has no objection to taking their money. Brady turns a blind eye so long as they sneak in the back way, don't cause trouble, and never ride through the town proper. Don't raise your eyebrows, all indignant! It's a practical arrangement that keeps the peace."

"You didn't come down here in a snit just to tell me that."

"No. Red John drank so much whiskey he was afraid he'd fall of his horse on the way back to the Trading Post, so he stayed the night. He woke up a while ago, and when Lucinda brought his breakfast, he complained it wasn't to his liking. She told him either get himself a wife to cook for him or go home and have some of the Trading Post's god-awful swill.

"He told her funny she should say that because Big Mama's kitchen was about to have the best food in the county, and not only that, he was about to get himself a wife. Lucinda said that may be true about the wife but she doubted about the food because the Lilac Hotel had the best in the county. Then Red John said the Lilac was about to lose their pretty new cook."

"That's... crazy talk." A chill ran up Faith's spine. It dawned on her she had no idea where Chet had taken Belle and Lucas.

"I went to ask Red John what the heck he

was talking about, but he was already gone. He told Lucinda he was going to Tagget's on his way out of town—to get his bride."

"Criminy."

Faith went into the office and strapped on the loaded Colt. This could be an emergency—and if it was, there was no time to find Teddy Gensch. She put Fontana's sign in the window and locked the front door.

"You don't have to come," she told Lily Rose. "It might be dangerous."

"I'm no delicate flower. I've faced down brutes worse than Red John Deckom." Lily Rose pulled a sweet little Derringer out of her skirt pocket. "Besides, I want to know what the Deckoms are up to."

They rushed down to Tagget's, but it was empty of customers. The only thing passing for excitement was Mae and Charity up at the counter, sorting mail.

"You came at the right time," Mae said to Lily Rose. "There's a passel of letters here for Sweet Dee's."

The little bell at the front door rang as the door opened and Hannah and Jane Stedman came in. "Did anything come for Mrs. V?" Hannah said. "We saw the mail coach go by."

"A letter from Morning Star Ranch would

make her day." Jane and Hannah grinned at each other. Faith didn't get the joke.

"Nothing for Break Heart Brides." Charity was staring at an envelope.

Hannah frowned. "It's not—"

"But look at this," Charity said. "Here's a letter from Minnesota to the Steele sisters, care of Naomi Steele, Break Heart, Colorado." She started to tear the envelope open.

"What are you doing?" Faith said. "It's addressed to Naomi."

"It only says in care of her. Which I don't understand, since I'm the one who wrote Uncle James. Anyway, it's addressed to us all." Charity's face softened as she began to read. "It's from our cousin Persie:

"Dear Cousin Charity—"

Charity gave Faith a "see?" look, as if to justify opening the letter.

> *"Papa was so upset by your terrible news I told him I would write you. We are all so very sorry for your loss. Aunt Laura was a good and kind lady, and Uncle Jared was a wonderful man. We will miss them both terribly.*
>
> *Though Papa was against your*

*family moving to Colorado, Connie
and I thought it was awfully brave.
Between you and me, we were
terribly envious of your going off on
such a tremendously exciting
adventure.*

*But now Papa says you must of
course come home and live with us
and that the Lord sends no burden we
cannot bear.*

*Have you met any handsome
cowboys? Do write and let us know
which train you will be on.*

*With all the love and condolences
in the world, your cousin,*

Persistence Steele

*PS: Connie sends her love and
condolences too.*

*PPS: A Mrs. Sophronia LeClair
has written to Papa, asking if he
knows the whereabouts of Cousin
Belle. From the tone of the letter,
you'd think she ran away from
Boston like a thief in the night."*

Charity looked up and blinked.
"Golly," said Hannah.

Lily Rose uttered a short laugh. "Well, isn't Mrs. LeClair a dark horse?"

"There she is, my strawberry tart!" A man's crusty voice boomed and Red John burst into the room behind the counter. "You better not have a knife on you this time. Ha!"

Charity cried out in surprise as he grabbed her around the waist and pulled her close. He must have come in through the back storeroom. She tried to twist out of his grip, while Mae kicked at his shins and tried to stomp on his feet. Faith drew the Colt, but the sound of another six-gun cocking made everybody freeze.

Red John had a pistol aimed at Charity's temple. "Best you holster that cannon, Faith Steele. I'm not as slow as my cousin, you see."

Faith knew she could take him. But if he got a shot off, there was no knowing what, or who, it might hit. Reluctantly, she put the Colt away.

"Get out." Red John jerked his head at Mae, indicating she should move from behind the counter to stand with the others.

"You fool!" Lily Rose sounded like a disgusted schoolmarm. "What do you think you're doing?"

Faith's heart pounded. What would Fontana do?

"Let's all just take a deep breath and calm down," she said. "Hannah, you go sit down on the floor, there by the counter." That would at least put her little sister out of the line of any errant shots. "Mr. Deckom, answer Lily Rose. What do you think you're doing?"

"Don't worry. I mean no harm." Red John grinned at Charity. "I've come for my bride."

Chapter 31

It was almost four o'clock when Brady got back to Break Heart. He felt light. Optimistic. Like the man he hadn't been in a very long time.

Mrs. Tweed had to be right—Belle couldn't possibly have accepted a man like Chet McKinnon. He must have lied. He was low enough.

What a fool Brady'd been to believe him.

Mrs. Tweed was also right about something else. Belle had captured his heart. It was time to let the past go. *Life is for living.* If there was even a chance Belle cared for him, he was going to grab it. He'd court her like there was no tomorrow.

Starting today.

He pictured their kiss for the thousandth time and smiled inside. There was definitely a chance. There was every chance in the world.

Passing by Tagget's, movement inside the store caught his attention. Chuckling, he shook his head. Looked like Jane Stedman's geese were having another gaggle. But he'd barely moved on when an uneasy feeling came over him. Something about that scene wasn't right.

He tied Queenie to the hitching post two stores up, walked back to Mae's and peered through the window. He immediately pulled back. Red John Deckom was inside Tagget's behind the counter, holding fast to Charity Steele with one hand and waving a six-gun with the other.

Praying Deckom hadn't seen him, Brady headed for the back of the store. Deckom's Appaloosa was there, tied to a post. Brady drew his pistol and moved in through the delivery entrance. Barely breathing, he crept through the storeroom, gun in hand.

He could hear Deckom ranting to an unwilling audience, the words becoming clearer as Brady neared the front of the store.

"I'll be a good husband to you, Charity, I promise. You just swear you'll be a good wife to me, and nobody here has to get hurt."

The varmint was drunk. Or being a lunatic. Likely both.

Through a doorframe with no door on the hinge, Brady scanned the area behind the counter. Red John's back was to him, not three feet away. A quick look told him Belle wasn't there. In addition to Charity, he saw Mae, Jane Stedman, Hannah, Faith, and Lily Rose, all frozen in place, all eyes following Red John's waving gun.

Brady waited, and when Red John seemed to momentarily tire of his own voice and lowered his weapon, Brady stepped in, pressed his Colt to the back of the man's head, and cocked the trigger.

"You mind telling me what's going on here, Red John?"

* * *

The farther they drove from Break Heart, the more uncomfortable Belle felt. *This was a mistake.* She was always making mistakes, but this was a really big one.

"Shouldn't we be there by now?"

Chet didn't answer.

"Why do we keep heading south? I thought you said your land was east of Break Heart."

"Woman, do you ever shut your yap?"

"What?" His tone of contempt shocked her more than the actual words.

Chet grabbed her wrist. "Just be quiet, and you'll be fine."

Belle tried to pull away, but he wouldn't let go. "You're hurting me."

"Leave her alone!" Luke jabbed his pocketknife at Chet.

"What in tarnation?" Chet reached for his ear, and when he took his hand away, there as blood on it. "You little devil. You'll die for that!"

Chet pulled out a pistol and cocked it.

"Chet, stop! Stop it, Chet. What's the matter with you?"

"This is your fault, Belle." Chet kept the gun trained on Luke. "You led me on, then jilted me. You don't get to be happy in your little town after that. I won't have it, do you hear?"

"Fine. I'm sorry. I'll go with you." She'd say anything to get him to take that gun off Luke. "Anywhere you want. Only don't hurt Luke. He's just a child!"

Chet hesitated, then closed the hammer. "You're lucky you're kin, kid." He waved Luke off. "Now go on. Get out."

"What? No! He'll get lost out here. Or... or bit by a snake, or—"

"Shut your caterwauling woman or I swear to God I will shoot him where he stands and leave him for the carrion crows!"

Belle bit her bottom lip and choked back tears of rage. She looked at Luke helplessly.

"Now, go on. Git," Chet told her brother. "Oh don't cry. Follow the path back to town. You'll be fine. You'll make it back, if you do make it back, by dark. Or close enough to it. By then it'll all be over."

His laugh made Belle's skin crawl. What would be over?

"It's all right, Luke. Do as he says."

"No, I—"

"Do it, Luke." She gave him a pleading look. Maybe he could run fast enough. Maybe he'd be able to get help, maybe not. But at least he would be out of Chet McKinnon's sights.

Chet clucked at the horse and the wagon started moving again.

Belle stole a look at him. How had she missed his true nature? Looking back, the signs were always there. Quickness to anger. Selfishness. But worse than that, his cruelty. She had no doubt he would have killed Luke, just out of spite.

After a few minutes, she couldn't bear not knowing. "Where are we going?"

Chet faced ahead, and she almost gave up on getting an answer, when he said, "At first I thought, if I can't have her, no man will. But then I heard about the bounty Big Mama pays for the real pretty ones, and I thought..." He looked straight into her eyes with pure hatred, and for the first time Belle was afraid. "I thought if I can't have you, then every man will. Though I just might go first."

Belle had asked Lily Rose about Carmelita's claim that Mrs. Montgomery tried to trick her into working upstairs. They'd learned it could be worse, that some madams paid for girls and kept them locked up until they were ruined and then wouldn't try to escape.

"Not the Trading Post, Chet. You wouldn't do that."

"You'll fetch a prime bounty too. Red John says Big Mama will pay seventy-five dollars."

"You'll never get away with this. Sheriff Fontana will kill you."

"I'll be long gone, darlin'." Chet smirked. "Red John said Frank'd probably throw in another twenty to be first to have you."

"Then *you* wouldn't be first." It was folly to talk back, but she was so furious she couldn't resist.

Chet cocked his arm back to hit her, but the horse lurched to the side, demanding his attention. Belle took the chance and jumped.

She hit the ground on her feet, her full weight on her blisters. *I hope I live long enough to wear a nice pair of shoes again.*

At the thought's absurdity, she burst out laughing.

"Where do you think you're going, girlie?" Chet immediately caught up to her.

"*Girlie*? Listen to yourself. You're becoming a monster."

He dragged her to the wagon, scooped her off her feet, and threw her into the back. The sheer strength of the man was terrifying. He climbed into the wagon and straddled her.

"I told you to shut up."

She saw the butt of the pistol coming toward her just before the pain blasted against the side of her head and the world went black.

* * *

Queenie nickered at Brady as he passed by in the street, hauling Red John up to the jail.

"Hold up there, Sheriff! Slow down!"

"Walk faster." He had to get this idiot locked up before someone got killed.

"I'm so sorry, Fontana." Faith trained her gun on the prisoner as they moved. "I couldn't take him out."

"Now, darlin', why would you want to do something like that?"

There was no accounting for some. Red John appeared truly bewildered, with no idea how recklessly he'd acted. No thought for anything but his own crude, half-understood desires. How did such a man live with himself?

"I didn't trust myself to draw fast enough," Steele went on. "I was afraid of bystanders being hurt, and I... I didn't know what to do."

"Your firearm's loaded, is it?" He gave her a teasing wink. "Correct move, my opinion. You were right to load your weapon, and you were right not to fire it. Nobody ended up dead. I call that a win."

"So what are we fightin' over?" Deckom tried to shrug.

Brady dragged him up the porch steps, through the office, and tossed him into a cell.

"Wait a minute! I didn't do nothing!"

"*The wise person fears and turns away from evil, but a fool is reckless and overconfident.*"

"I was just having a little fun."

Brady locked the cell door. He just wanted

to get out of there and go see Belle. She must have gone home and luckily missed the whole thing.

Something made him stop. "Tell me, Red John. What on God's green earth made you think you could waltz into town and just take Charity Steele away with you?"

"If Frank can have a bride, why can't I?"

The blood in Brady's veins ran cold, every nerve on edge as he gritted out, "What are you talking about?"

"That McKinnon fella is on his way to the Trading Post, right now as we speak, with the beautiful Belle LeClair. If Frank can have her, why can't I have my pretty Charity?"

"Frank—"

"That's not right, Fontana. He's lying," Steele said. "They've taken a picnic to see Chet's land. My brother's with them."

Deckom barked out a laugh and slapped his leg. "That piker never staked no claim on no land. I don't know nothin' about no boy, but McKinnon's taking Belle to the Trading Post. Then he's taking off for the Arizona Territory."

"That makes no sense." Brady fought the sickening feeling Red John was telling the truth. "Why would he take her to Frank when he wants her for himself?"

"Decided she's too much trouble. Might as well make something off her."

"Make something."

"The bounty." Red John looked at him like he was naïve fool. "Happens all the time."

The Deckoms had been at their game so long, the man had no sense of shame, no thought of concealing their dirty business.

"People bring in girls that can't earn their keep. Big Mama pays top dollar for a looker like Belle LeClair. Especially since she can cook—hey!"

Brady's fist shot out at Deckom's face, but the man stepped back, ironically protected by the cell bars. "You're telling me he's going to *sell* Belle LeClair to Big Mama?"

Red John was a fool, but Brady had underestimated Chet McKinnon. The man was a monster.

The ammunition was stored exactly where it was supposed to be. He set a box of fifty rounds on the desk and told Steele, "While I load these belts, you go across the street and ask Charlotte to send over some supper for Red John later. We may be late getting back. Teddy has a spare key."

"I'm coming with you?"

"Just don't get yourself killed. You say you can ride? Let's hope you and Deckom's

Appaloosa make friends fast."

Steele was gone and back in minutes. They strapped on their guns and went for the horses. As she led the Appaloosa gelding around from the back of Tagget's, Jane Stedman came rushing out of Abigail's with all the other ladies not far behind.

"Sheriff Fontana! Take this with you."

She handed Brady her drum.

"Thanks, Jane, but I'm going to need more than a magic trick to—"

"Take it!" She slammed the instrument against his chest. "You show that to Big Mama and trade it for Hannah's sister. Show her the rose. Tell her to ask Frank Deckom how it got there."

Chapter 32

The width and definition of the path along the river both surprised and disturbed Brady, and for the same reason. It could only have been created by a goodly volume of traffic between Break Heart and the Trading Post.

It didn't bode well for the town's future if so many felt the need for what Big Mama was selling. He made a note to encourage Abigail in her side business. Break Heart needed more brides.

He spotted Luke struggling toward them before Steele did. The boy looked like he'd reached the end of his strength. But why was he alone?

Not a good sign.

"Is that your brother?" he said, more to

warn Steele than hear her answer.

"Luke!" She urged the Appaloosa forward. Already, horse and rider were on good terms.

"Faith! Sheriff Fontana!" the boy cried out. "It's Chet. He has Belle! I don't know where they went."

"It's going to be fine, son," Brady said. "We know where they're headed, but there's no time to lose. Can you wait for us here, even if it gets dark? I know it'll be scary, but you'll have to be brave. Sit on that rock, and don't move from it. Then we'll know where you are."

Luke climbed onto the boulder near the edge of the path and pulled out a carved object that looked like Teddy Gensch's handiwork. "If it gets dark, I'll blow my whistle."

"Good man."

Steele leaned down to kiss her brother's cheek. She handed him her John B. "It's just a loan," she said, "but you're so sunburned I want to cry."

They rode on, with Luke calling out, "Get him, Faith!" at their backs.

A few minutes later, they passed Break Heart Bend. The rapids had decreased in force dramatically. If the Steeles had waited another week to make their journey, they might have avoided tragedy altogether. And Brady might never have met Belle LeClair.

Steele grew quiet, and he didn't intrude on her thoughts.

Another quarter mile and the Trading Post came into view, a ramshackle collection of huts, cabins, and lean-tos gathered around one large, two-story building. Its expansive porch and four white columns bespoke a project begun with better hopes than it ended.

A wagon was stopped in front of the porch, where Chet McKinnon was pulling Belle out of the back. Brady's stomach turned as McKinnon her on her feet and guided her unsteadily toward Frank Deckom, coming out from the main building.

Deckom took hold of Belle and handed something to McKinnon, likely his thirty pieces of silver.

"Belle!" Brady couldn't help yelling as she tried to break free of Deckom.

McKinnon had heard the shout. He bolted for a horse already saddled and waiting, then high-tailed it out of there. He wasn't worth chasing after. Belle was all Brady cared about now.

Deckom was so caught up in her he didn't realize he had company. Brady pulled his rifle from the scabbard and aimed, with the sense of having been here before.

"Stand where you are, Frank Deckom."

"Huh?" Frank kept hold of Belle with one hand and drew his six-gun, but a woman's clear voice stopped everything.

"I don't think so."

The click of a breech block being sealed punctuated Big Mama's sentence.

Brady hadn't noticed her standing on the porch. She stepped out of the shadows, her rifle trained on him, but her attention on Steele, who *had* seen Big Mama and had her Colt trained on the huge woman.

"*Tsk-tsk*. My Cole says such nice things about you, Faith Steele. Cole! You get out here now!" Big Mama's gaze was as cold as the north wind.

Cole appeared on the porch, stripped to the waist and grinning at Steele like a lovestruck loon. He was the one who'd attacked Steele that day at the river. She'd taken his gun from him, so of course he thought he was in love.

Even a Deckom couldn't be that stupid.

But then, Red John thought he'd marry Charity, so all bets were off.

"Hey there, Faith. You're looking mighty fine." Cole looked at Steele all cow-eyed.

"That's my cousin's horse you're riding."

"He's in no need of her at the moment." Faith didn't flinch. Cool as you like, she never took her eyes of Big Mama, awaiting Brady's instructions.

He sighed inwardly. There was no way he could refuse to make her his full-fledged deputy now—if they got out of this thing alive.

They were in a standoff. His rifle was trained on Frank. Frank's pistol was on Faith. Faith's Colt was aimed at Big Mama. And Big Mama had Brady in her sights.

"That's a fine-looking weapon you have there, Big Mama. A Sharps carbine, if I'm not mistaken?"

"All thirty-six inches." The woman lumbered off the porch. "I always said you had a good eye, Brady Fontana. This here was my husband's John Brown." She stopped beside Belle. "They say there's more moral power in one Sharps carbine than in a hundred Bibles."

"You spout abolitionist platitudes two minutes after you purchase a woman?" He kept his eyes on Big Mama. If he looked at Belle, there'd be no accounting for his actions.

There were too many loaded guns aimed

at people he cared for.

"No buying. That's a bounty. After she works it off, she's free to go."

"Now you know that's not going to happen, Big Mama. Let's end this peaceful-like."

"Or not."

"Nobody has to get killed today."

"Feels like someone does."

Big Mama could be right. Things did look headed sideways. He stole a glance at Belle. She gave him a shaky but brave smile, and his heart felt like it would pound out of his chest. She must be terrified.

He might as well try Jane Stedman's trick.

"Tell you what. Let's make a trade."

"Trade? For this *very* prime piece of calico?" Big Mama played with a lock of Belle's hair. It glimmered like spun gold in the sunlight. "What have you got I could want more than this moneymaker?"

A flicker of triumph flitted across the avaricious old woman's face. She suspected Brady had more wealth than she could dream of, and she could tell he wanted Belle LeClair safe more than all the gold in the world.

"This." He lowered the Winchester into its scabbard and slid off Queenie to the ground. He took a few steps toward Big Mama and showed his empty hands, then retrieved the drum from where it was tucked into his belt.

"Jane Stedman's drum?" Big Mama let out a belly laugh. "Brady Fontana, I'm not the idiot my son is. And I don't mean poor Bobby. You think a magic trick is going to work on *me*?"

"Honestly? No. I don't think you're one for magic, Big Mama. The thing is, Jane Stedman told me this drum can tell a secret if the right person listens. A secret that someone's been keeping from you."

He twisted the drum to make the beads hit the skins, and the oddest thing happened.

Frank paled. "Don't listen to him, Big Mama." He was sweating. Badly.

Maybe Jane Stedman wasn't so crazy after all.

Brady moved closer. "She said to look at the rose."

The woman's eyebrows shot up. She leaned forward, lowering the rifle slightly.

"I said don't listen to him, Big Mama!" Frank growled. "That crazy woman's put a spell on Fontana now."

"You hush now, boy." Harsh words from a rough, ruthless soul.

Brady stopped twisting the drum. The

beads fell, and he aimed the rose toward Big Mama.

The woman let out a cry of anguish so forlorn Brady almost felt sorry for her.

Almost.

"Jane Stedman says to ask Frank how the rose got there," Brady said. "Does that mean anything to you?"

By the rage that flowed from the woman with the violence of a volcano, Brady figured it did.

She turned her ire on Frank. "You told me Bobby fell off the mountain."

"It wasn't my fault, Big Mama!" Funny how bullies quiver like jelly when they have nowhere to go. "It was that crazy Jane Stedman! She went loco. I just wanted Bobby to have some fun."

Two shots rang out. Or maybe it was only the one, echoing back off the river. Frank Deckom, shot point-blank by his own mother, fell dead to the ground.

Quicker than lightning, Belle scooped up Frank's gun and aimed it at the woman crying over her son's body.

"Slick move," Faith said.

"I learned it from my sister." Belle smiled, but she was wobbly on her feet.

"Frank!" Sobs racked Big Mama. She

ignored Belle. "Oh, Frank. See what you made me do?"

Belle cocked the pistol.

Every instinct in Brady's being told him to go to her, to protect her.

Although, just at the moment, she apparently had all in hand.

"We're finished here, right?" Belle's voice shook with barely controlled rage of her own.

It took all Brady's strength to stand where he was, but going to her now would deprive her of the pleasure of chastising her tormenter.

When she got no answer, she pushed the pistol against big woman's temple. "Right?"

Big Mama blinked. "What about my money?"

"Chet McKinnon has it." Belle took a step back. "I suggest you look to him for satisfaction on that point."

Brady couldn't help smiling inside, for all the tenseness of the situation.

Big Mama hesitated, then at last nodded in defeat. She looked down at Frank's body. "We're through."

Belle backed away, as triumphant and fierce as Joan of Arc. At last, she came to Brady.

That's when he saw the bruised cut at her

temple. A raised swell was turning purple, and a thin trickle of blood ran to her cheek, damage too severe to have come about by accident.

"Belle." He crushed her to his chest, and she hugged him furiously in return. His lips to her ear, spoken low, for themselves alone. "My love."

But then she went limp in his embrace, and when he lifted her chin, her eyes rolled back in her head. "Belle!"

Brady scooped her up into his arms, fear racing with his heart. For a split second, he considered putting her in the wagon, but dismissed it. He wouldn't trust Belle's life to a horse he didn't know.

He'd never been so strong. Belle was out cold, a dead weight, but somehow he got her onto Queenie, secured between his arms. Faith mounted the Appaloosa, and they headed out.

The problem of the Trading Post would wait for another day.

Luke saw them coming and blew his whistle. It helped, for the afternoon light had begun to change. Brady checked his pocket watch. A little before six, yet a few hours of enough light to ride by.

From standing on the boulder, the boy

climbed onto the back of the Appaloosa. That's when he noticed Belle's condition. "Is she..."

"She's just hurt." Faith meant to reassure her brother, but her expression told Brady she was as worried as he was.

"I'm splitting off, taking Belle to my ranch," Brady said. "It's half the distance to town from here. Ride like the devil for Break Heart. Stable Deckom's horse and tell them to hitch Doc's wagon. Then find Doc and tell him to get to Nighthawk."

"What about Red John?"

"Let him cool his heels in his cell. No telling how the Deckoms are going to react to losing Frank. If I know Big Mama, she'll find a way to blame anybody but herself for his death."

"But she shot him."

"Logic isn't Big Mama's strong point."

"You mean she'll blame you."

"Me, or Belle, or the town. But without Red John's help, I don't think Jessop can interest Cole in doing much damage." Brady winked at Faith. "He's a lover, not a fighter."

"Oh please." She rolled her eyes.

His chest tightened, and it hit him that he cared for her like a little sister. And he cared for Luke too. *We could be family to each other.*

The life he'd always wanted was suddenly so close—right here in his arms—and yet so far away. He kissed the top of Belle's head and murmured, "You're going to be all right."

Then he urged Queenie on to Nighthawk.

Chapter 33

Momentarily banished from the guest bedroom, Brady paced the hallway and nearly ran over a housemaid bearing a tray loaded with clean towels and a pitcher of water. He hated feeling he was of no use. At least he could open the door for the maid.

"We're not ready for you!" Mrs. Tweed's stern warning cut him off before he could see anything.

With an apologetic shrug, the housemaid slipped into the room. He closed the door and resumed wearing out the carpet. How badly was Belle hurt? Where was Doc?

What an idiot he'd been, holding back his feelings for Belle. He'd fought even *having* feelings, let alone sharing them. Worse than ridiculous, it had been cowardly. Destructive.

How many lives had been ruined—or lost—because he couldn't face the truth? If only he'd told Thalia how he truly felt about her, she would have broken off their engagement. She never would have left Philadelphia. She'd be alive today. She died, never knowing he didn't love her.

And now Belle might die, never knowing he did.

I do. I love her.

The bedroom door cracked open and Mrs. Tweed poked her head out. "You can come in now." She spoke so gently his heart sank. It must be bad.

Belle looked like a sleeping angel. The grime of battle had been washed away, and she was dressed in a pale blue nightgown, her golden hair sprawled over the pillow. Her eyes jerked behind closed lids, as if she was having a bad dream. Brady sat down and clasped her hand.

"I couldn't protect her."

"Oh pish. From bad dreams? No," Mrs. Tweed said. "But you saved her from the fate McKinnon had in mind."

"There's that." He shuddered at the thought of Belle stepping one foot inside that evil place. Someday soon, he was going to have to raze the Trading Post and run the Deckoms out of the county for good.

And then he'd turn in his star.

"She is lovely, Brady," Mrs. Tweed said. "Like a princess in a fairy tale."

If only, like Sleeping Beauty, a kiss could make those lovely eyes flutter open! He pressed the back of Belle's hand to his lips. She showed no sign of awareness he was there.

"That she won't wake worries me more than anything." Had Steele made it back to town? Had she found Doc?

"This isn't what I meant when I complained of the guest rooms being empty." Mrs. Tweed smiled weakly. "Sorry. Bad joke."

The mantel clock chimed the quarter hour. It was already past seven. Tomorrow would be the first of June and the days were longer, but still the light would fade in the next hour or so. "Doc should be here by now."

"He's the only physician in Break Heart. He may have been called away to some other—"

"Where is my patient?" Declan burst in, hair disheveled, suit crumpled, medical bag in hand. Brady and Mrs. Tweed hastened out of the way to allow him room. "I'll need water that's been boiled at least five minutes."

"What's in the pitcher has been." Mrs. Tweed switched from the consoling mother figure to the efficient majordomo. "We'll bring more."

With a nod, she sent the housemaid to it while Doc opened his kit, brought out clean bandages, and lined up several impressive-looking vials on the bedside table.

Belle whimpered as he touched her temple, and Brady had to still his anger at her feeling any kind of pain.

"Someone's been here before me." Doc nodded approvingly at the cut, still swollen but clean. "It's good work, Mrs. Tweed. Don't be insulted if I go over it again, just for my own ease of mind."

"Not at all, Doctor."

"Can you tell how she got that wound, Doc?" It no longer bled, but Brady thought it looked redder and more swollen than before. He knew the signs of a looming infection. "She had it when we got to her."

"It's the result of blunt-force trauma inflicted by something hard having an irregular surface. I've seen the like before, when a man had been pistol whipped."

"McKinnon." Brady uttered a low growl. He didn't try to suppress his animal rage—he relished it. When he and McKinnon next met,

Brady doubted that man would survive the occasion.

Belle whimpered and fidgeted against the blankets.

"She's been restless like this all the while," Mrs. Tweed said. "But she hasn't regained consciousness or said anything intelligible."

"You'd make a fine nurse, ma'am."

Doc managed to get a few drops of laudanum past Belle's lips, and she calmed. He checked her pupils and her pulse and finally blew out a relieved breath.

"Doc?" Brady needed more than a sigh. He needed to *know* she would recover.

"With any luck, she'll sleep a few hours. I want someone with her at all times. There's so much we don't know about head trauma, about... everything."

"Will she live?"

"Most likely she sustained a concussion. There may be internal swelling in her brain, preventing her from attaining consciousness. She needs restful sleep, but I fear giving her too much laudanum, which can depress the lungs."

Brady grabbed Doc by the lapels of his very crumpled, very fashionable jacket with more force than he'd intended. "Will she live?"

Doc spoke kindly, gently, which filled Brady with far more dread than anger would have. "It's as frustrating to say as it is to hear, Brady, but it's still true. At this point, time and observation are all we have to work with."

"What can I do?"

"Let her rest. Let her hear the voice of someone who cares for her—but don't go bringing in all her sisters. I'm sure they care, but there's too many of them and she'll sense their distress. She needs peace and quiet."

An idea occurred to Brady. A crazy idea. Intrusive. Shocking. In fact, it would be just plain wrong to do it. But it was all he had.

"I'll be back soon."

He raced to the stables and saddled Queenie himself. "I need you one more time, girl. Then you can pasture for a week and have apples and carrots every day."

The light was fading, but Queenie knew the way to Break Heart in the dark. He could be back in an hour. He reached Calico Manor, hoping Steele would be there.

She *might* trust him enough for what he had in mind.

Chapter 34

Brady found Steele not at home but at the Lilac Café, sitting with Abigail Vanderhouten and enjoying a piece of chocolate cake.

"How is Mrs. LeClair?" Abigail saw him first.

"Is she hurt seriously?" Charlotte had followed him from the front desk.

"Bumped her head. Doc says she just needs rest." He didn't want to alarm Steele, but he let Charlotte know Belle wouldn't be in for a few days. "That cake looks mighty fine."

"It's the last piece." Steele slid the plate over in front of the empty chair next to Abigail and smiled. "I'm as bad as Charity. Belle set this aside for you earlier today. Suppose you ought to finish it."

"I could do."

He ignored the ladies' knowing smiles, but it did please him to know Belle had thought of him. He was in a hurry to get back and made quick work of the cake, letting out moans of pleasure at the first bite, the second, the third and last.

Abigail said, "Whoever lands Belle LeClair for a bride is going to be one lucky man."

Belle would be an exquisite bride, Brady thought. But more than that, she would be a wonderful wife. *His* wife, if he had anything to say about it.

Roxanna brought out a bowl of lamb stew with bread and butter for Abigail and put down a basket in front of Steele.

"What can I get you, Sheriff?" Roxanna picked up the empty plate in front of Brady. "Lamb stew's good tonight. Or Carmelita made a batch of chicken enchiladas to die for."

"Not tonight." He got up from the table. Everything was taking too much time. "But tell her I look forward to trying them soon."

Steele stood up too and grabbed the basket. "I was just fetching supper for the prisoner," she said. "Evening, Abigail."

"Good evening, Faith."

Brady tipped his hat to Abigail, took the

basket from Steele, and followed her out the door. She was conscientious as well as outlandish and brave. It was a shame to object to her as a deputy on the basis of her sex when she performed all the duties so exceptionally well.

And she didn't mind cleaning. Or take offense when he insisted his coffee tasted better than hers. Which it did.

But she *was* a woman. Sooner or later Faith Steele would marry and start a family. She'd be certifiably insane to want to carry on here then. Law enforcement was mostly long stretches of dullness spiced with occasional danger, but the danger was real. No married woman—or married man, for that matter— had any business taking on such work. Belle LeClair had been right to object to her husband's profession.

He'd better make use of Steele while he could and be grateful she was willing to serve. But first to the task at hand. He waited until she came out from the cells after giving Red John his supper.

"I need to ask a favor."

Her eyes narrowed as he made his odd request, but she gave him no argument.

"I can get them for you." She nodded her assent. "Or do you want to come to the house?"

"I have one more errand before I head back. Can you bring them to the Modiste?"

"Sure thing, Fontana. It won't take twenty minutes."

Of course she could.

"Steele, wait. I have something for you." He took the deputy's star from his desk and pinned it on her shirt. "You are now Break Heart's official deputy sheriff—if you want the job, that is."

From the way she jumped up and down and squealed with delight, he figured she did.

"What's going on out there?" Red John yelled.

"Eat your supper and be quiet if you want dessert," Steele yelled back.

She took off running for Calico Manor, so excited to tell everybody about the badge Brady wondered if she'd remember the rest.

Meanwhile, he unhitched Queenie and walked her down to Abigail's. When he was finished, he'd be ready to head back to Nighthawk and Belle.

As he pushed open the door to the showroom, Jane Stedman uttered a little cry.

"You scared me, Sheriff. I was just locking up."

Abigail lived in the rooms upstairs, and

Jane slept in the back of the store. Brady had never really spoken with her except to exchange pleasantries, but he was always acutely aware they were due for a conversation.

"I came to tell you I did what you suggested. I showed Big Mama your drum. I'm afraid she kept it."

Jane nodded. "But she let Hannah's sister go."

"She did. And after she took a good look at that drum, she shot Frank."

Jane grew still. Brady waited.

"Is he dead?" her voice was very small.

"He is."

A fierce kind of joy played over Jane's features, then as quickly faded. "Good."

Still he waited. Jane Stedman was a mystery, but she was no witch. She was a human being, and there was some empathy in her. She cared about Hannah Steele.

But she was no more forthcoming.

"What happened to Thalia?" he blurted out.

She hesitated, and he sensed the gears grinding in her brain. Would she answer? *Could* she?

Jane Stedman and Doc Declan were the last two people to speak with Thalia. Jane had shared the journey by coach with her from Philadelphia. Brady had no idea what Doc knew. As much as the man liked a good gossip, whenever the subject of Thalia came up he grew maudlin and turned to brandy and laudanum.

Jane was worse. Like granite. So unyielding you'd think she'd never met Thalia.

"Take pity on me," Brady pleaded.

"She thought I was a lady, like herself," Jane said at last. "Because of my fine clothes, you see. We boarded the same stagecoach in Philadelphia, bound for Colorado. She talked a lot, like people do when they're nervous. I've always been a listener, so we fit well together.

"She was the only person who ever treated me like an equal. She told me she was going to Colorado to marry a very rich man, but she wasn't sure she wanted to go through with it. Oh, she liked him well enough, but she wasn't sure she could bear leaving her social circle in Philadelphia.

"She was going to take a look at his ranch and see if it was grand enough to make up for the loss of civilization. If not, she'd end the engagement with no one the worse for it. She seemed to me a sensible person, but quite unfeeling.

"She didn't love you, Sheriff. I can't... say more, but you deserve to know that much."

Somewhere a dog barked, and he noticed the shop door was still open a crack. Queenie nickered as footsteps sounded on the boardwalk. He recognized Steele's galumph.

"Thank you, Jane. I'm much obliged."

Brady stepped out of the shop and inhaled the cool evening air. *She didn't love you...* This must be how prisoners feel when their time ends and the cell door finally swings opens.

Free.

It was indeed Steele coming up the boardwalk with the package he'd asked for. There was another favor to ask. Assignment, really, now that she was official.

"Can you stay at the jail tonight? Keep an eye on Red John and get his breakfast in the morning. Use the guest bedroom upstairs. It's small, but serviceable."

"Sure thing, Fontana."

"We won't keep him long. I just want to be sure things are quiet at the Trading Post."

"No problem."

"Good man."

He frowned to himself. That wasn't quite right—*good man*—but she didn't seem to mind.

They'd work out the nomenclature as they went along. Maybe soon he'd be able to call her sister.

He tucked the package safely inside Queenie's saddlebag and rode for Nighthawk.

Chapter 35

"Thank Providence we found her. We'll keep her with us now. We'll keep her safe."

"Yes, Mrs. LeClair."

Something quite like terror gripped Belle when she realized she was back in Boston, on Bowdoin Street, in her mother-in-law's gloomy parlor.

She was clothed in mourning again. Her black satin day slippers felt like heaven.

"You're awake." Mrs. LeClair smiled, too sweetly. "You lost your veil, but no matter. Finola and I have another for you."

This is a mistake. Belle struggled to her feet and ran—but somehow Mrs. LeClair and Finola beat her to the door. They raised up a long black veil and came at her, throwing it over her head. It reached her knees, but it was made of lace, and she could see.

"We'll be so happy, Belle." Wesley was there, standing beside her. "I'll make you a good husband, so long as you promise to be a good wife to me."

But it wasn't Wesley. It was Chet—no, that wasn't right. It was Frank Deckom!

"Now we'll have a little class around this place." Mrs. LeClair opened her mouth, but Big Mama's voice came out. "You'll take good care of my Frank, and we'll get Charity for Red John and that Faith for Cole."

Finola laughed and laughed. "You should have had a baby. Then none of this would have happened."

"Let me go!" Belle pushed Wesley/Chet/Frank off her and ran from the room into a hallway that seemed to go on for miles and miles both ways. Should she go left or right?

"Take this, Madam Belle! You'll need it." Dottie appeared in front of her, holding up a twenty-dollar bank note from the First National Bank of Boston.

"Come to me, Belle." That voice! It was low, warm, strong—safe.

"Wade?"

"Come to me."

She ran toward Wade's voice, but the door at the end of the hall opened up on another world, above a rushing river.

"Jump, Belle," Wade said. "It's a leap of faith."

She jumped and fell and fell and fell until she landed on a raft. She was back on the river, at Break Heart Bend, but she was alone. She should take off her veil so it wouldn't drown her if she fell into the water.

"You won't drown, Belle. You're going home."

"Why didn't *you* come home, Wade? I waited."

"You did."

"I missed you."

"I know."

"But you were gone. I could only find you in your letters. You disappeared from everywhere else."

"Which is as it should be."

The water was rushing faster than it ever did. She didn't want to die. Where was Wade?

"Sometimes I feel a great kinship with Odysseus, a man adrift on an ocean, who only longs to be at home again."

Belle's whole body relaxed on hearing the familiar words from one of Wade's letters.

"I used to prefer the *Iliad,* you know, but

now I find the *Odyssey* more satisfying."

Wade's words, but no longer his voice. Still, the river slowed and the sense of impending doom eased.

"The stories of Achilles and Hector and the foolish battles of prideful men are for the young who know nothing. Like Odysseus, I've grown older and weary of war."

She knew him then. It was Wade's letter, but it was Brady Fontana's voice.

"I long for the pleasures of home."

"Home."

"Yes, home. Belle? Are you here?"

Was she? Where was here?

"Come home to me, Belle." His hand closed around hers, warm and strong. She wasn't on the river. She was lying in a comfortable bed, with soft pillows and thick blankets. "Come back to me my darling."

She opened her eyes.

Chapter 36

Faith came downstairs at 8:42 a.m. She knew the precise time because Sheriff Fontana kept several clocks here, including one on a shelf in the tiny second bedroom of the living quarters above the jail, where she'd slept last night—though *slept* might be too strong a word.

She reached the landing and heard Red John scramble to his feet back in the cells.

"Good morning, Madam Deputy. Finally, you're up!" he called out cheerfully. "I hope you slept as well as I did."

"You didn't sleep at all." She was already spoiled, living at Mae Tagget's place. It was so lovely being lulled to sleep by the song of night birds accompanied by the rush of the wind in the trees. All last night she'd been kept awake by noises spilling out from the saloon next door punctuated by Red John's caterwauling spilling out from the cells. "You were still making a racket at three in the morning."

"Naw, I slept like a baby. This surely is the cleanest cot I've had in a while."

"Ew." She checked the stove and made a mental note to warn Doc. On his next self-imposed lockup, he'd best check for fleas.

"So, Madam Deputy, what's for breakfast, do you think?"

That man was an awfully happy prisoner. It was disconcerting.

Ugh, no coffee. Faith got the fire going and put a pot on, chuckling at herself. She really was spoiled! Until this moment, she'd never given a thought to it, but all her life someone else had been up earlier to boil the first water of the day.

"I hope there's more of those muffins I had with last night's supper."

Too happy.

But then, Red John was blissfully ignorant of yesterday's events at the Trading Post. He didn't know his cousin was dead—and that his aunt had done the killing.

Faith couldn't even think what scripture

to throw at him. To cajole or to comfort? He was a disgusting lout, and she'd never forget the Deckoms attacking her family at the river or his ridiculous attempt to kidnap Charity only yesterday.

But now there'd been a death in Red John's family.

It was confusing to feel pity for someone who truly did not deserve it.

For the grace of God that bringeth salvation hath appeared to all men...

Then the grace of God was stupid—no. She couldn't think like that.

The coffee started to boil over. She removed the pot from the flame, filled two mugs, and took one back to the cells.

"It's my lucky day," Red John accepted the coffee with a big grin. "What a pretty picture to wake up to—though you got nothin' on Charity, no offense. You should put a dress on, you know. Where's your boss? Did he catch that rat, McKinnon? How long am I going to be in here?"

"*That* rat? You *do* remember yesterday you were the one waving a gun around at Tagget's? You could have killed somebody, including my sister."

"Oh."

That wiped the smile from his face.

For one second.

"But I didn't mean anything by it. That Charity's got spirit. And she's a real looker." He made a face like he was thinking and scratched his head, then moved to his belly. Faith would definitely tell Doc about the fleas. "My Colt wasn't even loaded, I don't think."

She frowned and went back out to the main office, leaving the door to the cells open in case she wanted to yell at him. She opened the weapons locker and checked his six-gun. *Huh.* Unloaded. *Idiot.*

What she *should* do was go out and have a look around town. Big Mama had agreed everything was over, but she might think differently now the dust was settled. The Deckom matriarch didn't strike Faith as especially rational.

Or trustworthy.

She downed her coffee and checked her Colt. She strapped on the holster and pinned on her DEPUTY star. She didn't even try to stop grinning.

Belle. What she really wanted to do was high-tail it out to Fontana's ranch and see her sister.

Two problems. One, Doc had forbidden Belle visitors until she was stable, and two, Faith had no idea where Nighthawk was. But she was dreadfully worried. She'd held out hope Belle's injury was as light as Fontana implied, but when he asked for Wade LeClair's letters, thinking it would comfort Belle to have them with her, that's when she knew. Belle must be in bad shape.

But she was stuck. Nothing to do now but wait.

"I'll be back in a while," she hollered at the prisoner. "Be good and I'll bring you a muffin."

She locked the office and headed for Sweet Dee's. The town was quiet, as unaware as Red John of yesterday's trouble with the Deckoms—though of course word of his shenanigans at Tagget's had spread like wildfire.

And that she and the sheriff had raced out of town as soon as they had him locked up.

And that she'd returned to Break Heart in a state and interrupted Doc having his dinner at the Lilac, demanding he leave at once to attend to her injured sister.

Who was at Nighthawk.

There was nothing about the Trading Post in the story. Apparently she and Fontana were the only people who knew of Chet McKinnon's scheme, apart from Red John, safely locked up, and one other soul.

Which was why Faith now headed toward Sweet Dee's, to ask Lily Rose to keep quiet for the time being in the interests of not starting a war between the town and the Trading Post.

No point riling anybody up, Fontana had said, *until there was something to get riled up about.*

It was worth a try, and Lily Rose would probably agree since Fontana had made the request and she was partial to him. But Faith felt sure the time would soon come when being quiet wouldn't be a good enough strategy to deal with the Deckoms.

"Take ye heed, watch and pray," she muttered as she walked, *"for ye know not when the time is."*

Chapter 37

Belle woke in a lovely fairyland. At least, a western version of fairyland. Her bed was wonderfully comfortable, with luxurious sheets of linen. Open windows framed by roses and wisteria let in songs of morning birds with the fresh warm air of early summer.

Brady had been here. Or had she dreamed it?

Wade's watch lay on the bedside table. That was no dream—it was ticking. Beside it sat the packet of his letters. She tried to sit up, but her head hurt like the dickens.

"Let me help you, love." A prim-looking woman on the other side of middle age rushed to Belle. She propped the pillows and helped her to a sitting position. "I'm Mrs. Tweed. The housekeeper at Nighthawk."

"Nighthawk?"

"Brady Fontana's ranch." She poured a cup of something hot and brought it to Belle on a bed tray. "This is chamomile tea. And here are scones and butter and strawberry jam if you think you can take a bite."

"I'm starving." Belle tried the tea first. "Oh, this is wonderful. What happened?"

"As near as Dr. Declan can tell, you took a blow."

Belle nodded, remembering Chet hitting her with the gun. She touched her cheek and wondered if it was broken. "Is Doc here?"

"He is. He finally went to get some sleep."

"And Brady—Sheriff Fontana?"

"All through the night he refused to leave your side. I threatened to regale him with stories of my sainted father if he didn't go put something in his stomach. I'm sure he'll be back momentarily."

"This nightgown is lovely."

"Yes. It was meant for Brady's mother, part of a season's order from New York. But she fell ill, and when the clothes arrived after her death, I hadn't the heart to dispose of such beautiful things. So I put them away, thinking one day they might be put to use."

"What is all this?"

Brady filled the doorframe. He looked terrible. His hair was a mess, and he had a two-day growth of beard—which was actually quite attractive.

Belle took it back. He looked wonderful.

"I'm gone ten minutes and come back to find you sitting up, fresh as a daisy, chatting away as if nothing had happened."

"I don't feel fresh as a daisy, I promise you."

"Well, you look... beautiful." He sat in the chair beside the bed, and a memory of him being there through the night flashed in her mind. She glanced again at Wade's things on the bedside table. What portion of her strange dreams had been real?

"I see you've met Mrs. Tweed. She runs this place. Her accent couldn't have escaped you." If Brady noticed Belle's confusion, he said nothing. "She was my mother's lady's maid in England, and when dear Mama married a brutal American and crossed the pond to be with him, Mrs. Tweed wasn't about to let her go alone into those barbarian lands."

"You joke." The woman smiled at him with the fondness of a loving aunt. "But you're not far from the mark."

"Mrs. Tweed is the very model of propriety. But she loves me more than anyone living in the world."

"Excepting your sister."

"I think not."

Mrs. Tweed hmphed, but she seemed to enjoy being accused of loving Brady more than any other living soul.

Belle's heart hitched. Who did Brady love more than any other living soul? *She* wanted that honor. Because the reverse was true.

She loved him. Goodness! She loved him more than any other soul.

Living or not.

"The point is, Mrs. Tweed loves me. So despite her being a very proper British woman, she'll indulge my very improper request she leave us alone for ten minutes."

Mrs. Tweed blinked.

Mrs. Tweed blinked again.

Then Mrs. Tweed said, "She will indeed." And she was gone.

Brady moved the tea things from the bed and took Belle's hand in his. It felt so right.

"Just now with Mrs. Tweed, *you* sounded like a British gentleman."

"I see. And you know what a British gentleman sounds like?"

"Quite. In Mrs. LeClair's circle in Boston, I

heard plenty of them."

He chuckled and turned her hand over and kissed her palm tenderly, as he had that day on the sofa. It seemed ages ago.

"I want to tell you about Thalia," he said softly. "About my engagement. I learned something about my fiancée just last night, and over the past hours I've been reevaluating our relationship.

"I cared for her, but I didn't love her as you did Mr. LeClair. We'd been thrown together by our fathers. Mr. Merrick wanted a rich husband for his daughter, which he figured I would be one day, and my father wanted the political connections Merrick offered.

"I am ashamed to think of my behavior then. I was caught up in the wonder of it all. The power of money, of political influence. One man's ability to influence the direction of an entire city, or the state or, for that matter, the country. It was intoxicating.

"I knew my father would never be elected to anything. No one liked him. But I thought maybe I could be. Some men catch gold fever. I caught my father's fever for politics. I wanted the power. Thalia wanted it too. She saw me as her ride to greater things. To be a society hostess in Washington, DC was her heart's desire.

"Then my father was killed and my mother wished to go west for her health. Thalia wasn't happy about it. She was from a progressive family, very keen on women's education, and she told me she wanted to finish her studies at the university. I had no objection. By then the scales had fallen from my eyes, and I was glad to have time apart.

"I think her plan was to let me down softly, break our engagement after I'd settled in Colorado, but one day my sister inadvertently revealed to her just how much I stood to inherit, believing I wouldn't have kept such information from my intended wife.

"My mother's fortune was made in the mills of Manchester, England, and then invested in railroads. It was quite extensive, and Thalia found she could love me quite well.

"Please don't think she was a bad person or only after my money. We liked each other well enough, and until yesterday I believed we could have made a successful marriage— though after I came to Colorado, I no longer wanted a political life."

"Being sheriff is political, I'd think."

Brady smiled. "You're right about that.

But it's a little different. I don't want power over other people. I do want to make the world a better place, but I think now the best way is to add to the world's goodness myself.

"I never loved Thalia. I didn't know what love was until I met you. Belle, I love you." He kissed her fingers and pressed her hand to his cheek. "I was never so afraid of anything in my life as when Frank Deckom aimed his gun at you. The thought of this world without you is unbearable to me."

Belle's heart was so full she couldn't speak, but she squeezed his hand.

He looked at her hopefully.

"If you need more time, I understand. This is sudden, I know. But I do love you. Could you consider doing me the great honor of becoming my wife?"

He was the embodiment of the two things she'd believed she didn't want: a man of the law, and a man of wealth. But what could she do? She loved him.

He'd already shown the error of one objection. All rich people weren't the same. Brady Fontana was a level-headed man who saw his wealth as a resource, not a weapon. He would never use it to control or abuse her.

As for his being a lawman... How could she object to him pursuing what he wanted when she wished to do the same? It would be wrong to benefit from his bravery and goodness, then deny the people of Break Heart the same.

"I agreed to marry my first husband only hours after meeting him," she said. "In comparison, ours has been a drawn-out and well-considered courtship."

"Then you..."

"I do love you, Brady Fontana. Nothing could make me happier than to be your wife."

"Oh Belle." He leaned in and wrapped his arms around her, pulling her to him for a kiss that warmed her better than any blanket.

The door pushed open and Mrs. Tweed stepped in. "Oh don't mind me," she said cheerfully. "I'm only here to ensure your virtue."

Chapter 38

"Train's on time." Belle absently checked her watch. At fifteen past eleven on Friday morning, the whistle could be heard all the way across town here at Calico Manor.

She smiled. By now, they all knew the nickname for Mae Tagget's house. Poor Luke was not amused.

Today the place really earned the name—it was packed with ladies, all come to help Belle get ready to marry the sheriff. It was but two weeks since Belle accepted Brady's proposal.

Neither of them were interested in a long engagement.

"The train's generally on time in summer." Jane Stedman looked up from the floor where she sat cross-legged, completing last-minute touches to Belle's wedding dress. "Come the snows, Break Heart quiets down for the winter—little one, would you bring me the blue thread?"

Only Jane Stedman could get away with calling Hannah that. Belle was glad her little sister had found a mentor. Jane was an odd sort, but she'd taken to Hannah like a champion. Belle might be alive today because of it.

"The Lord works in mysterious ways, as Faith might say."

"No. I wouldn't." Faith frowned at her. "But Parson Hood might."

"As long as the trains run, it seems the people keep pouring in," Charity said. "It makes Mae happy to have so much business."

"I wish a schoolteacher would pour in," Naomi said. "Sally and the demon are in sore need of an education, and I haven't the qualifications or the patience to give it to them."

Naomi was clearly unhappy in her job. She wouldn't leave Mr. Overstreet in the lurch, but she was definitely thinking to make a change. Brady had told Belle none of her sisters need work another day if they didn't want to, that he'd be delighted if everybody came to live at Nighthawk. Belle had relayed the offer.

And was unsurprised when it was politely refused.

Even Uncle James's most recent letter had been powerless to move the Steeles from their new lives. He'd excoriated their desire for independence and as their eldest male relative demanded they return to Minnesota at once—all but Belle, who was to be commended for getting married again, which was a woman's proper state.

They all had a good laugh over that one.

Faith had put it best. "I won't do this all my days, but for now, I like my life. I don't want to give it up."

Neither did Belle. She planned to stay at the Lilac until a child came, if she and Brady were so blessed. Carmelita was ready to take over anytime. The fact was, she'd worked in her uncle's hotel kitchen in Santa Fe since she was nine years old, and she could have run the Lilac Café as well or better than Belle from the day she escaped from Sweet Dee's.

Belle wondered what Mrs. LeClair would say about her marriage. She hadn't yet written to tell her the news. She was waiting until the vows were spoken, the ring was on her finger, and no man had the power to put her and Brady asunder. No woman either.

Through the parlor windows, she watched the people arrive at the Little Church. They'd been coming for half an hour, at least. Everybody wanted to see their sheriff get married. Parson Hood's sister had objected to decorating the pews with ribbons and flowers, deeming it unseemly, but she'd been delighted when Brady asked her to play the organ for the ceremony.

Charlotte, Carmelita, and Roxanna had dolled up the Lilac Café, which would be closed to the public today. Brady had reserved it for the reception and arranged for musicians for dancing too.

Belle tried not to let his spending spree stir up her anxieties about money. She told herself it was just momentary, that he'd settle down as soon as they were married. She nearly fainted, however, when he presented her wedding gift—a brand new carriage with a matched pair of palomino ponies. *To match your golden hair.*

Butterflies invaded Belle's stomach, and under her breath she whispered, "There he is."

Brady had just driven up to the church in the new carriage. Someone—she suspected Hannah—had tied little pink bows in the palominos' manes. Brady had told her he didn't want his bride walking to the reception in her new shoes. It was either the carriage, even for such a short distance, or he threatened to carry her from the church.

"What are you doing?" Charity pulled her away from the window, aghast. "It's bad luck—"

"For the groom to see his bride in her gown before the ceremony," Naomi said happily. "I never heard anything against a bride stealing a glimpse of her groom."

"Well, they've all gone in," Belle said. "Now I just have to wait for Luke to come back out again."

Her brother was to give her away. He'd come for her as soon as Parson Hood told him all was ready.

"Just think," Faith said. "In half an hour, you'll be Mrs. Brady Fontana."

"Will your name be Christabel Fontana or Christabel Steele Fontana?" Hannah asked.

"Christabel Regina Steele LeClair Fontana," Belle said. "I don't want to forget any of my names. But Mrs. Fontana does sound very fine."

"Are you ready, little one?" Jane looked at Hannah.

Together they carefully lifted Belle's veil,

a magnificent length of delicate white Brussels lace that had belonged to Brady's mother. They fitted it over her hair, which Mrs. Tweed had swept up into a glorious mass of golden curls, then spread the gossamer material over the pale blue gown the two had spent the past week making, to the detriment of all their other projects.

Abigail Vanderhouten had given Belle silk stockings and several other lovely unmentionables as a wedding present. *The present is for your husband too—I can say that, since you've already been married.*

Yes, Belle had been married. But she'd spent only four days in her first husband's presence. They'd been intimate only twice, and she didn't have high confidence she'd made him happy in that area. In every way that mattered, this would be far closer to a first marriage than a second.

"There," Jane said and stepped away. Faith and Charity had brought down the cheval mirror and Belle examined herself in it.

"Oh!"

"Oh is right!" Faith said. "You're beautiful, Belle. Vain to deny it."

"Preston Morgan will never know what he missed," Abigail said, shaking her head wistfully. "But I'm so happy for dear Brady. His scary side has evaporated. Well... mostly."

"Here comes Luke." Naomi kissed Belle's cheek, then turned to the others. "Time to go!"

The ladies filed out of the house and paraded across the yard to the Little Church of Break Heart Bend.

Luke wore a suitcoat that had belonged to Brady that Hannah had cut down to fit. He stuck his arm out jauntily. "What about it?"

Delightful. He must have practiced that for the past two weeks. Grinning, bursting with happiness, Belle let the veil down over her face.

"Let's go."

When they got to the front door, Luke leaned in and gave Hortensia Hood a thumbs-up. She launched into a rousing performance of a hymn Belle didn't know, but with such gusto that she decided it was perfect.

It was hard to walk to her bridegroom in a dignified manner. She wanted to run to him, say I do, and kiss him right there in front of God and everybody.

The music ended and Parson Hood launched into the ceremony. He got nearly every word right.

Belle and Brady couldn't stopped

grinning at each other. He looked pretty silly, and she was glad she had the cover of the veil, thin as it was. The preacher got to the part about if anybody knows why these two can't marry. It was almost over. In another minute, Belle would be Mrs. Brady Fontana.

"I do! I know!" A woman's shrill voice rang out from the last pew. "This ceremony must cease! I object!"

It can't be... Belle turned, hoping against hope it *wouldn't* be. Her world came crashing down around her.

"Mrs. LeClair!"

Chapter 39

Why be astonished? Of course that woman had the tenacity to discover her whereabouts—and then the audacity to travel across the country to impose her will.

But Belle's initial despair faded when she noticed something strange. Had Mrs. LeClair shrunk?

She pulled back her veil for a better look at her formidable nemesis marching up the aisle, Wesley tagging behind. Mrs. LeClair's head didn't reach his shoulders.

"You're so... small."

"I've come to take you home, Belle."

"Now wait just one minute." Brady put on his reasonable face. "I don't—"

"Wesley forgives you and is willing to

take you back." Mrs. LeClair ignored Brady, ignored Parson Hood, ignored the two aisles of people gaping at her. "I've never said a word about the money you stole—"

A collective gasp filled the church. The twenty dollars!

"—and I never will if you come home with me now."

To her shame, Belle had done nothing to repay the debt. She hadn't even begun to save. She looked at Brady. What must he think of her?

But what did twenty dollars matter to Mrs. LeClair? The woman was rich. It was all so unfair! Belle wanted to cry out like Carmelita had that first day in the kitchen.

"Why do you care? And why do you want me to marry Wesley? You don't even like me."

Mrs. LeClair stepped back as if she'd been struck. "That's not true!"

Belle waved off her protest. "I never resented the locked door, you know. Not really. I knew everything I needed to about Wade through his letters. You couldn't take that from me."

Wesley turned bright red.

"But how can you hate me so much for marrying one son, and still want me to marry the other? Wade's death should have freed us from each other."

"Why would I want that?" Mrs. LeClair looked genuinely hurt. "You're the daughter I never had." Either she was a very good actress, or Belle had misunderstood her terribly.

Brady looked at Wesley. "Maybe you could escort your mother outside." He turned to Mrs. LeClair and put on his stern look. "Ma'am, I'm going to have to ask you not to upside my bride."

It rolled right off her.

"Bride, fiddlesticks! I hear you're a man of the law. You wouldn't want to marry a thief, would you, Sheriff?"

"First you call me daughter, then you call me thief!"

"I highly doubt Mrs. LeClair is a thief."

"I'm Mrs. LeClair."

"I mean my Mrs. LeClair."

Somewhere in the pews, Hannah laughed.

Mrs. LeClair—the real one—looked triumphant. "Tell him, Belle."

"It's true," Belle admitted. Better to own it than let the blame be shifted to poor Dottie or some other innocent bystander. "I took twenty dollars from the household cashbox for traveling money to get away from Boston and come west with my family."

"I'm your family," Mrs. LeClair said. "Wesley is your family."

"You aren't. Family is about love, not... possession."

"Then you leave me no choice. I always knew you were too common for my son. Either of them. You are a thief, Belle Steele, and I want you arrested. Sheriff, arrest this criminal."

Belle wanted to sink into the floorboards and disappear. You could hear a pin drop. She felt as though she was a villain in a melodrama.

"Now hold on." Brady was having none of it. "Mrs. LeClair, I understand you're quite a wealthy woman."

She nodded half-heartedly and mumbled something.

"So let's agree twenty dollars is more symbolic to you than anything you really care about." He pulled a twenty-dollar gold piece from his waistcoat. "But if not, I'd be glad to give you this in repayment."

Mrs. LeClair hesitated and looked at the coin, but she got control of herself and scoffed.

"That's what I thought." Brady looked at Wesley. "Your brother was a wealthy man too, I take it?"

Wesley cleared his throat self-consciously. "All the LeClairs are comfortable." His face was still red. To his credit, he wasn't happy about his mother's scheme.

"I suppose Wade left a will."

An anguished cry escaped Mrs. LeClair.

Brady looked at Belle. "Well?"

She shook her head. "Wade never told me anything about his will."

"Yes," Wesley said. "He did."

"Shut your mouth!" Mrs. LeClair hissed.

"No, Mother. I won't. I'm tired of shutting up and doing as I'm told." He looked at Belle. "Wade explained his will in his last letter to you, one you never received. He left everything to you."

"I don't understand."

"Mother intercepted the letter. When she realized what it meant, she kept it from you."

"Wesley, you ungrateful—"

"She read all his letters to you and resealed them. The ones you didn't see first, anyway."

Mrs. LeClair pointed at Belle. "But she's still a thief."

"That is open to debate, ma'am." Brady asked Wesley, "Would part of *everything* be the house on Bowdoin Street?"

A slow smile came over Wesley's face. "It would, as a matter of fact."

"No!" Mrs. LeClair cried.

Brady went on. "Belle, you said you took the money from the household account?"

"Yes."

The bridegroom faded and Brady became Sheriff Fontana, his steely gaze fixed on Mrs. LeClair. "Then in the eyes of the law, if Wade LeClair left that house to Belle, she is guilty merely of availing herself to what is already hers."

Mrs. LeClair paled and leaned against Wesley.

"On the other hand, tampering with the US mail is a federal offense."

Mrs. LeClair glared. "You have no proof. You'll never find any letters."

Letters, plural? The nerve of that woman.

"You terrible, terrible person!" Belle said. "I believe you'll find Wade's letter, or letters, in his study at the house. She's the only one with the key, the only one who goes in there."

Belle did what she should have done the first day she entered the house on Bowdoin Street. She faced her once-formidable mother-in-law and stood her ground.

"What was your plan? You couldn't

counter Wade's wishes by keeping them secret. If he left a will, the lawyers will contact me eventually."

"But if you were married to Wesley by then, it wouldn't matter. As your husband, it would all belong to him. The house, the holdings, the money—everything would stay in the family. You're nothing! You're no one! You were married to him for months. He was my son for twenty-nine years."

Mrs. LeClair broke down sobbing, and Belle blew out a sigh. The woman had a point. The irony of it was Belle didn't care about the money. She never had.

"There's nothing we can do about it at the moment." She put her arms around the pathetic little creature.

The embrace alarmed them both, and they immediately broke it off and stepped away from each other.

Belle lowered her veil. "Right now I'm going to marry Mr. Fontana, and then let's all go up to the Lilac Café, have a nice glass of champagne, and take stock. Things will surely look better after that."

RACHEL BIRD

Chapter 40

The reception was still going strong, already declared as good as Ophelia's wake. It seemed the whole town was here. Belle handed Wesley his third piece of wedding cake, according to her sources, and sat down with him to watch the dancing.

The café tables had been cleared away from the center of the room and the refreshments were displayed on a long table in the private dining room.

"I'll miss your cakes." Wesley reddened. "And your lovely self too, of course."

"Of course."

"*Ach, nee!* Mrs. LeClair—I mean Mrs. Fontana." Mr. Weissenegger stopped on his way to the refreshment table. "May I be bold to say you are a lovely bride. And how are your slippers holding up with all the dancing?"

"Thank you, Mr. Weissenegger, and very well. They're the most comfortable shoes I've ever danced in. Truly worth waiting for."

He beamed and moved on. Wesley leaned closer, nodding at the dance floor. "Your husband and my mother make a very strange-looking couple."

Belle almost spilled her champagne. "Indeed."

Brady and Mrs. LeClair were engaged in a lively reel, but his height and her lack of it made for some awkward swings and allemandes.

"I'm surprised she let him talk her into dancing, still being in mourning."

"That's because none of her friends will ever know. She wouldn't be caught dead tripping the light fantastic back in town," Wesley said.

"But when among the heathens...?"

"Exactly."

Belle laughed. "Seeing her laugh is so strange. It's almost... endearing."

"Now you've gone too far." Wesley smiled and finished his cake.

"Let's be serious for a moment. Do you

find my proposal satisfactory?"

Belle's first inclination had been to renounce whatever Wade left her in his will, but on the drive to the Lilac from the church, she realized that would be disrespecting his wishes. So she'd decided against the snap decision.

She would be patient, talk to Wade's lawyer, talk things through with Brady, and come to a decision in the proper time—like waiting for a pair of Mr. Weissenegger's shoes.

However, on one thing she was clear. As far as she was concerned, Mrs. LeClair could live in the Bowdoin Street house for the rest of her life.

"More than satisfactory," Wesley said. "I find it generous and kind. You see, to my mother, that house represents everything she's achieved in her life. I believe it would kill her, literally, to have to leave it."

"Let's not test that theory."

"You're better to her than she deserves."

"Once, I would have agreed," Belle said. "But now I think not. I could have been a better daughter-in-law. I was always so worried she was trying to control me that I never really got to know her. I doubt I ever offered her a kind word or thought. Everyone deserves that. With the exception, perhaps, of Finola Burke."

As they chuckled over the comically villainous lady's maid, the tune ended and Brady and Mrs. LeClair joined them.

"Wesley, dear, do fetch me a glass of champagne, will you? That's a good boy."

Wesley offered his mother his chair and shared a smile with Belle. "I'll take your words to heart, Mrs. Fontana. Everyone deserves kindness."

Brady gave her that twinkle she adored and crooked his elbow much like Luke had earlier. "What about it?"

One more time, Belle got up to dance with her husband.

Mrs. Tweed and the household staff and ranch hands wouldn't leave the reception until the stars were out and the moon was high, but when the afternoon light began to bend, Belle and Brady said goodbye to their guests. They would catch the train east tomorrow to begin their honeymoon, but tonight they'd stay at Nighthawk and discover more of each other's finer qualities.

Brady handed her into the carriage then passed her the reins when he climbed in beside her. She raised a questioning eyebrow. He'd driven to the hotel from the church.

"They're your pair." He reached under the bench and brought out a box containing a pair of pale blue kid gloves, the same color as her dress. "They need to get used to your touch."

"Yes, they do." She eagerly pulled on the gloves and took the reins.

She was so... happy. The diminishment she'd been expecting was yet to settle in. She felt as free as she had before she said *I do.* As in charge of her own life as she was of this carriage.

She urged the ponies onward, down Main Street, past Tagget's and the Modiste, past Mr. Weissenegger's shop and Grayson's, and finally past the Little Church of Break Heart Bend, with Calico Manor across the lane and up the little hill.

She could never go back to Boston or Minnesota. She loved it here.

On to Nighthawk!

"What's this?" Brady said. "My bride frowns? Nothing should be amiss on your wedding day."

"This doesn't feel like a happy ending," she told him. "There's too much to do. Too much to look forward to."

"A happy beginning, then." He scooted closer and kissed her cheek. "I like that."

They rode quietly, listening to the sounds of the open country, the occasional raptor's scream, the breeze in the trees.

After a while, Brady said, "It was magnanimous of you to allow Mrs. LeClair to stay in the house."

"It's her home, and I have no intention of living in Boston again. And I'd rather she were happy with me than not—although I don't know how she'll take my stealing one of her servants."

"She already knows you're a thief."

"Hey!"

"You stole my heart, didn't you?"

"Ha-ha-ha."

"Is it someone in particular you intend to poach?"

"A wonderful cook, as a matter of fact." Dottie might not wish to leave Boston for the West, but it wouldn't hurt to ask. "Carmelita will need help when I leave the Lilac."

"Leave?" It was Brady's turn to frown. "Don't get me wrong. I don't like the idea of you working so hard every day—but I thought *you* liked it."

"Oh, I do. But eventually..." Belle felt her face go red.

"What?"

He honestly didn't know what she was

talking about.

She felt suddenly shy. In a small voice, she said, "Eventually, when we start a family..."

"I see." The goofiest grin spread over Brady's face, and his eyes crinkled at the edges. Belle didn't think it was possible to love him more, but at that moment she fell further than ever.

"Anyway, Dottie is too good a cook to remain an assistant all her life. I think she'll see coming to Break Heart as a real opportunity."

"You're quite the Lady Bountiful." Brady smiled. "I believe I'll enjoy being married to a magnanimous wealthy woman."

Apparently, it was true. Belle was now indeed very rich. She wasn't sure how she felt about that. After all the harsh thoughts she'd had about wealthy people, she was secretly embarrassed.

"I will enjoy being on an equal level with my friend Evangeline. She was always uncomfortable having too much when I had so little. Now she won't feel she has to hold back."

"Hold back?"

"She's an extravagant person, to say the least."

"Let's go to New York then, after Boston, and pay her a visit," Brady said.

"Oh, I would love that."

They had planned to go to Philadelphia so Belle could meet Brady's sister. During the reception, they'd added Boston to their itinerary to deal with the legalities of Wade's will. They could tack a week or two in New York onto the journey.

"And if I ever get the Deckoms straightened out and turn in my star," Brady continued, "we might take a tour of England one day. See the land of my mother's birth."

"The Tower of London, Big Ben," Belle said. "The Crystal Palace."

"Precisely."

"I'm sure it will all sound simply wonderful when I'm not so exhausted." At the moment, she just wanted some peace and quiet with the man she loved.

This wonderful man belonged to her utterly, as she belonged to him. A lifetime lay ahead in which to love each other. No matter how much time heaven granted them, it wouldn't be enough, but she meant to thoroughly enjoy every moment.

She pulled the carriage up to the front door, and one of the ranch hands came around to take it on to the stables. Brady jumped out first and handed her down. His touch was as gentle as it was strong, and she felt more than loved. She felt cherished. Safe and sheltered, while at the same time, paradoxically, she felt free.

All her life, Belle had believed that loving a man meant letting him take from her whatever he wanted while she set aside her own dreams and desires in favor of his. But Brady delighted in her without consuming her, and she reveled in his delight.

This was why she felt no diminishment.

She hadn't come to their marriage as a sacrifice, but as a gift. A gift she would give him every day, so long as they both should live.

As he opened the door, his stomach rumbled, and he patted his belly. "I danced so much at the reception I forgot to eat."

"You're hungry."

Her lawman stopped at the threshold, pulled her into his embrace, and kissed her a good long while. When he pulled away, his eyes twinkled.

"Ravenous."

"Let's go in." She laughed and went ahead, pulling him over the threshold, her heart full to bursting. "I'll make you something wonderful."

RACHEL BIRD

~ The End ~
Never A Lawman

RACHEL BIRD

BEASTIE PRESS U.S.A.

Made in the USA
Columbia, SC
26 December 2021

52769739R00271